CROSS ROADS

OTHER TITLES BY DEVNEY PERRY

Calamity Montana Series

The Bribe

The Bluff

The Brazen

The Bully

The Brawl

The Brood

Jamison Valley Series

The Coppersmith Farmhouse

The Clover Chapel

The Lucky Heart

The Outpost

The Bitterroot Inn

The Candle Palace

Maysen Jar Series

The Birthday List

Letters to Molly

The Dandelion Diary

Lark Cove Series

Tattered

CROSS ROADS

DEVNEY PERRY

Text copyright © 2024 Devney Perry
All rights reserved.

Published by Montlake, Seattle

www.apub.com

Amazon, the Amazon logo, and Montlake are trademarks of Amazon.com, Inc., or its affiliates.

ISBN-13: 9781662518782 (paperback)
ISBN-13: 9781662518799 (digital)

Cover design by Sarah Hansen, Okay Creations
Cover image: © isciuceodor, © Teemu Tretjakov, © Oksana_Schmidt, © SpicyTruffel, © Angyalosi Beata / Shutterstock

Printed in the United States of America

CROSS ROADS

Chapter 1
INDYA

"You've reached Grant Keller. Please leave a message, and I'll return your call as soon as possible. Thank you."

The beep following Dad's voice echoed through my car's speakers.

"Hi, Daddy. Just wanted to let you know I made it." Well . . . almost.

The hum of tires on pavement had been my stoic companion for the past four days. From Texas to Montana, the miles in my rearview mirror were endless, with only twenty to go.

Except I wasn't ready yet.

I needed more miles.

"I love you," I added before ending the call.

The GPS route on the console chimed, signaling the turn off the highway was approaching. The directions were unnecessary. I'd keyed them in only out of habit.

I hadn't been on this road for years, but I knew the way. And once I hit gravel, service would be spotty, at best.

Dad loved that about Montana. How one minute, you'd be fully connected to the world. The next, this place would decide for you that it was time to put the devices away. Like Montana knew you weren't paying attention to its beauty because you were too focused on a screen.

And it was beautiful. Breathtakingly so.

Fields of green streaked past my windows. They rolled to foothills covered in towering trees. Beyond them were indigo mountains capped in snow.

My stomach climbed into my throat as I crested a hill and a sign came into view.

Crazy Mountain Cattle Resort

Both the letters and the arrow beneath were faded and nearly impossible to read from a distance. The white paint had chipped and flaked away from too many hot summers and cold winters.

What if I turned around? Big Timber was forty-five minutes from the ranch. The small town had more bars than stoplights, but there was a nice hotel. I could book a room and stay far away from Haven property.

Or I could keep going. What if I drove and drove and drove?

It would be so easy to breeze past the turnoff. I could stay on this highway and find out what town came next. In all my years of visiting Montana, I'd never passed that sign. This had always been the final destination.

And this trip could be no different.

I forced my foot off the gas pedal and to the brake.

My nerves spiked as I slowed to turn. The moment my wheels hit gravel, my stomach dropped.

I'd thought a lot about what I was going to do, to say, over the thousands of miles I'd traveled this week. Every idea, each planned speech, flittered out of my brain and floated away like the dust rising in my wake, disappearing on the wind.

Was this a fool's errand? Had I let Dad's love for this ranch cloud my judgment? The chances of the Havens accepting me into their lives were slim to none.

Especially West.

Just thinking his name made my heart twist. Did he hate me for this? *Probably.*

Every vacation to Montana came rushing back, replaying on loop. Campfires and s'mores when I was eight. Wildflower picking when I was nine. Paper airplanes at eleven. A broken heart at twenty-three.

What the hell was I doing here?

This was a job for Dad, not me. For every bit of my anxiety, he'd feel twice the excitement. It was June. He loved Montana in June and always said it was impossible to beat. He said the Crazy Mountains in summer—with their proud, jagged peaks—called to his soul.

He should be here. He was the right person for this job. Instead, I was dodging potholes on this miserable road.

"Good God," I muttered, my teeth clattering in my skull as I rolled over a stretch of vicious washboard.

When was the last time they'd had the road graded? I slowed my Land Rover Defender to a crawl, veering side to side to find a smooth stretch. There wasn't one, so I fisted the wheel and pressed onward.

To the mountains.

To the ranch.

The road wove past groves of trees. It followed the incline of the land, up and down over hills and into coulees, until it reached the Haven River.

From there, the drive followed the path of the clear, cold water. The river was too shallow for floating anything but an inner tube, but it was perfect for fly-fishing.

I made a mental note to check the ranch's website for a listing of activities. I couldn't remember seeing fishing on the list—maybe they'd stopped offering it to visitors.

An archway that spanned the road marked the point when I crossed onto Haven land. The logs of the archway looked as weathered as the sign on the highway. At some point in the past four years, the brown had flecked away to show gray beneath.

Those logs looked as tired as I felt. They'd need to be restained. It went on my to-do list along with a call to county services to have the gravel graded.

On both sides of the road, black cattle grazed in the fields. The fences keeping them company were made of straight and tight barbed wire with green steel posts.

The fences were pristine—no surprise. West had always made his priorities clear when it came to the resort.

He'd kick a guest out of their bed if one of his cows needed a room.

The Defender rattled as I rolled over a cattle guard, the marker that separated ranch from resort.

The first log cabin I passed looked lonely. Empty. The grass around its porch was overgrown, and like the archway, the paint was in need of a refresh. The second cabin looked much the same.

Updates to both went on my list. A list that seemed to grow with every turn of my tires. Maybe it was just those two cabins. Maybe everything else was in better shape.

My hopes sank when I reached the third cabin and it was arguably worse than the others. One of the gutters had fallen down and was hanging like a limp noodle from the roof. The flower beds were overrun with tall thistles.

Those three cabins were the oldest and smallest on the ranch. They'd always been slightly outdated. But they were the first impression, and if I were a paying guest, I'd be contemplating a short-notice cancellation.

It hadn't always been like this, right? Had my memory failed me? Usually by this point on a vacation, Dad would be vibrating with excitement to finally be here. Mom and I would be just as elated.

Had our excitement clouded reality? Had it made everything seem better? Brighter?

There was no eagerness today. Dread weighed like a hundred thousand bricks in my gut.

My sigh of relief filled the cab as I passed the next cabin. It was set apart from the initial three, and there were no visible issues in sight. There was even a hanging basket of purple and pink petunias on the porch.

Next came the largest of the private cabins. Other than a cursory glance, I didn't let myself study its condition. Not yet.

I wasn't ready to face that cabin yet.

So I kept my eyes locked on the lodge and its red tin roof. Nerves swarmed in my belly like wasps, stinging and buzzing as I pulled into the gravel lot.

The lodge looked deserted. There were only two other vehicles parked outside. As I opened my door, nothing but the singsong of birds and rustle of leaves greeted me. No laughter. No conversation.

Where were all the guests?

I spun in a slow circle, taking it all in. Maybe it was run down. Maybe it was quiet. But the bones were the same, and with them came a flood of memories. Dull memories that zapped my energy. Sharp memories that slashed and shredded.

I pressed my palm to my sternum, rubbing the ache away.

I couldn't do this. I couldn't stay here. Live here. What was I thinking?

Temporary. This was only temporary. I'd made my choice. I'd made this deal.

There was no going back.

So I headed for the lodge, my heels clipping on the dirt as I crossed the parking lot. The breeze tugged at my blouse and slacks. It lifted a blonde curl that wouldn't stay trapped in the knot I'd fashioned this morning.

The lodge's porch had five steps. My legs felt heavier as I climbed. How many times had I raced up these stairs? How many times had I rushed inside the lobby, smiling and laughing and ecstatic to just . . . be here.

It took all my strength to get past that top stair.

The moment I went inside, everything would change. There'd be no undoing this.

Except I couldn't turn back, and I couldn't go home.

There was no home.

So I steeled my spine and walked to the door, adding more items to my list.

The porch needed to be swept and power washed. There should be chairs out here, a place for people to sit and take in the view. Rocking chairs would be best, in red, like the roof. The double doors might look nice painted red too.

Maybe I'd make that the signature color.

Deep red, like blood.

Because the Crazy Mountain Cattle Resort would get my blood. It would get my sweat.

I'd already given it too many tears.

Above the door was a sign with the resort's name tooled into the wood.

Crazy Mountain Cattle Resort

Oh, God. That was a horrible name. How had I not realized it before? It sounded like a resort for cattle. A place to bring your cow for a weekend of pampering.

I had a better name in mind. Changing it would cause a massive fight. The first of many, no doubt. I'd probably piss someone off within the hour.

The door creaked, its hinges in desperate need of oil, as I pulled the handle. The overpowering scent of vanilla greeted me as I stepped inside the lobby.

No one was stationed at the reception desk, so I rang the silver bell. As it dinged, I leaned toward the candle burning next to a rack of brochures and snuffed it out.

Effective immediately, no more cheap candles.

The lobby felt smaller than I remembered. Had it always been this old? Didn't it used to be . . . shinier? Brighter?

Maybe it wasn't actually that dull. Maybe it was simply my attitude.

My positive, cheery attitude had taken a major hit over the past four years.

Well, at least the lobby had a rustic charm. But it needed more light. The wood paneling was dark, and the only light came from an antler chandelier overhead. Its bulbs were too small and too yellow for the space.

Where was the receptionist? I dinged the bell again.

"Coming!" The shout came from a faraway hall. It took a full minute before a young woman emerged. Her face was framed with a blunt black bob. "Hello. How can I help you?"

I returned her smile, reading the name tag pinned to her navy polo. "Hi, Deb. I'm Indya Keller."

"Welcome to Crazy Mountain Cattle."

Crazy. Mountain. Cattle.

I cringed. The name definitely had to go.

Deb riffled through the papers behind the counter, probably searching for something with my name on it. Did she have a computer or iPad? Was everything done on paper? When she came up empty, confusion clouded her blue eyes. "Um . . . do you have a reservation?"

"No, I don't. I'm looking for Curtis."

"Oh." Her frame relaxed. "I just saw him in the kitchen. I'll go track him down and let him know you're here. Miss . . ."

"Keller. Indya Keller."

"Right. Sorry." She gave me an exaggerated frown. "I'm bad with names. Be right back."

I sagged against the counter and pinched the bridge of my nose as she scurried off. Then I checked my watch. Four thirty. Still early. And the real misery hadn't even begun.

It was 4:39 before Deb returned, cheeks flushed and breathless. "Curtis is on his way. Sorry. He snuck out, so I had to chase him to the barn."

"No problem. While we wait, could I please get a room?"

"Oh. Uh . . ." She blinked, then opened a drawer and pulled out a laptop. There it was. "Yes, of course. Here at the lodge? Or would you like a private cabin?"

"The lodge. Please." Later, I'd commandeer a cabin. But there were discussions to be had first.

Deb had just finished taking my information when a throat cleared.

Curtis walked into the lobby with dirty boots, dingy jeans, and a faded green button-down shirt with pearl snaps. His hair was more salt than pepper, and the fine lines on his face had turned to heavy wrinkles. He looked thin. Tired. He was limping. Why was he limping?

The past four years had been hard on Curtis. I could relate. It might not show on my face like it did his, but he wasn't the only person who was worn down.

"Hello, Curtis."

"Indya." His eyes softened for a split second, like he was seeing an old friend. Then he must have remembered why I was here, and that gentleness disappeared. His lips pursed, and he jerked his chin toward the hall. "We'll go meet in an office. Deb, get Miss Keller a room. Comp it."

"Already on it." She gave him a mock salute, then went to work, her nails clicking on the keyboard as she typed.

He shouldn't be comping rooms, even for me. But I kept my mouth shut and followed him as he walked to the hall. With a limp.

It had been ages since I'd been in this part of the lodge. With every open doorway we passed, I peeked inside. A bathroom that needed to be cleaned. A tiny office coated in dust. A storage room in complete disarray.

My task list kept expanding, and with it, a headache bloomed.

Curtis walked into the office at the end of the hallway—the corner office—and flipped on a light. The air was stale. Dust motes caught the light that streamed through the glass. The room wasn't big, but its windows gave the illusion of space. The panes framed lush green meadows and the forests beyond.

"Have a seat." He waved a hand to the walnut desk. "Boys are on their way. I'll grab a couple more chairs. Can I get you anything to drink?"

"No, thank you." I offered him a kind smile.

It went unreturned as he stepped out.

My heart climbed into my throat as I walked to the executive chair that was pushed neatly into the desk. The leather was cold and stiff as I sat. The lumbar was too pronounced, and the armrests were a rough plastic. Either this was a brand-new chair for the office, or it had been a long time since someone had taken this seat.

Given the reason I was here, probably the latter.

It didn't feel right to be behind this desk. It didn't feel right to be in this room.

It didn't feel right to be in Montana.

Curtis returned to the office with three folding chairs tucked under his arms. He snapped them open and practically slammed them on the floor, each landing with a hard bang that made me flinch.

Three chairs. For three Havens.

On the wrong side of the desk.

"I'll, uh . . ." He dragged a hand through his hair, making it stand on end. Then he left the room without finishing his sentence.

The awkwardness was expected. It was only going to get worse.

My insides knotted as I waited, my gaze glued to the dusty desk. If I looked around, I'd probably find more items for my list, and it was already too long.

Dad should be here to do this, not me. He'd know what to say to defuse the tension. He'd know how to soften this blow.

Curtis returned with four water bottles. He set them on the desk, snagging one for himself, then took the farthest folding chair from the door.

"Thank you." I took a water, then twisted off its lid and took a sip.

He wouldn't look at me. He stared at his own bottle. He inspected his scuffed boots. He faced the window, his eyes unfocused as he stared into the distance.

Silence stretched between us as uncomfortable as my seat.

"The boys don't know about this." Curtis's announcement was no more than a murmur, but he might as well have screamed it in my ear.

"W-what?"

"I didn't know how to tell them."

My jaw dropped. "So you just . . . didn't?"

He shook his head.

Oh, hell. Seriously? How could he have kept this a secret? Was this my punishment for trying to do the right thing? Having to watch as he delivered the bad news? Or was he expecting me to tell them?

My temples throbbed with every question. This headache would be a migraine before the day was done.

"You will tell them." I steeled my spine and splayed my fingers on the desk.

My desk.

This was my desk.

I wasn't a guest. I wasn't a spectator. I was here on business.

I was here to do what Dad had taught me to do.

From this moment on, I was in charge. And I was going to make Curtis tell his children that I was now the owner of the Crazy Mountain Cattle Resort.

"I'll tell them." Curtis nodded.

As the color drained from his face, my heart twisted.

He'd had over a month to tell them. Any other situation, and I wouldn't feel an ounce of pity. He'd made his bed.

But this was Curtis. This was the man who'd helped me on my first horse. The man who'd befriended my father. The man who'd always made sure my family had an escape.

If he couldn't do it, if he couldn't tell West and Jax, then I'd do it for him.

Footsteps sounded in the hallway.

I sat up straighter as my pulse raced. *Breathe. In and out.*

Four days on the road, prepping myself for this, and I still wasn't ready. I wasn't ready to face him.

"Dad?" Jax called.

Phew. The air rushed from my lungs. The relief would be short lived, but I'd take every millisecond I could get.

"In here." Curtis kept his gaze trained out the window.

Jax breezed into the office, drawing up short when he spotted me behind the desk. "Hi. Sorry. Thought Dad was alone."

"Hi." I stood and held out my hand. "Indya Keller."

"Nice to meet you, ma'am." He studied my face as he returned the shake. "Or have we met?"

"We have." I nodded. "But it was a long time ago."

The last time I had seen Jax, he was a teenager, finishing his senior year of high school. Had he gone to college? Or had he been here for the past four years?

He'd filled out his broad frame and lost the softness of youth. Dark-blond whiskers covered his jaw. His smile was easy. Charming. Not something he shared with his brother.

West's smiles were always charming but never came easy.

Jax took the seat beside his father, kicking an ankle up over his knee. His posture was relaxed, but his eyes narrowed, no doubt wondering what I was doing on the wrong side of the desk. "What's this about?"

"We'll wait for West," Curtis said.

Jax hummed and snatched a water, gulping half the bottle in the time it took for another pair of footsteps to echo in the hallway.

My shoulders drew toward my ears, but I forced them down. I donned the impassive expression I'd mastered lately. The expression Blaine hated. Ironic, because our marriage was the reason I'd learned it in the first place.

But despite the neutral facade, my heart drummed faster and faster. Then it stopped. The moment West appeared, everything stopped.

The world faded to a blur, and I forgot how to breathe.

God, he looked good. As rugged and handsome as the day I'd vowed never to visit this ranch again. His dark hair was a mess. There was a slight ring around it, like he'd been wearing a hat for hours today and he'd used his fingers to comb it out. His chiseled jaw was covered in thick, dark stubble.

11

His broad frame filled the doorway. The top two buttons on his chambray shirt were undone, the skin beneath tan and sweaty. There was a pair of leather gloves tucked in the back pocket of his faded Wranglers.

"What's—" The moment he spotted me behind the desk, he came to an abrupt halt outside the door. "Indya?"

Once upon a time, I'd lived to hear that deep, gravelly voice. "Hi, West."

His hazel eyes roamed my face, taking in every detail. Then they dropped to my hands on the desk. To the finger that used to wear a diamond ring.

"Have a seat," Curtis said.

West's gaze shifted to his father. Whatever he saw made his frame lock and his jaw clench. "Think I'll stand."

Of course he would.

There was no more obstinate, stubborn man on this planet than West Haven.

Curtis sighed, like he'd expected that reaction from his oldest son. He nodded, then swallowed hard, but didn't speak.

Would he tell them? Or was he just going to sit there and stare at me?

The sound of my pounding heart was so loud, I was sure the men could hear it too.

Curtis kept his attention fixed on me like we were playing a game. Who would crack first? He wasn't going to tell them, was he? Coward. He was going to make me do it.

"Dad?" Jax asked. "What's—"

"I sold the ranch."

The breath I'd been holding rushed from my lungs. The temperature in the room plummeted as Curtis's statement settled deep.

"What the fuck?" Jax exploded out of his chair, the backs of his knees sending it skidding across the floor. "You sold the ranch?"

Waves of icy fury rolled off West's body, but he didn't move. He fixed his stare on me, pinning me to this horrible chair.

Curtis dropped his chin and managed a nod. The shame seemed to weigh so heavily on his shoulders I feared that flimsy chair would collapse.

"To you?" Jax pointed to my nose. "He sold it to you?"

"Yes," I answered, still holding West's gaze.

"What does this mean?" Jax asked. "Do we have to move? Are we out of jobs? What about our homes? What *the fuck* is going on?"

His questions filled the room while I stared at his brother.

When I was younger, West's stare would have made me nervous and jittery. But then I'd learned it was simply his way.

West stared when he wasn't sure what to say.

So I stared back, taking in that face.

Even angry and confused, he was gorgeous. And oh, how I'd loved him once.

I'd loved West Haven so much I couldn't see straight. So much I would have given up anything and everything to be at his side.

What a stupid little girl I'd been.

"West." Jax smacked him on the arm. "Say something."

He wouldn't. West would walk away without a word. He'd stay quiet to ensure he didn't say the wrong thing. The mean thing.

And as expected, one moment I was staring into blazing hazel eyes.

The next, I was staring at his back while West turned and disappeared.

"Fuck," Jax clipped, chasing out of the office on his brother's heels.

I waited until the hallway was quiet. "You should have told them."

"Guess I figured it would be better this way. You could be here to make sure I didn't share too much."

Was that a threat? "We have a deal, Curtis." A deal that required he keep his damn mouth shut.

"I'm well aware of the deal, Indya," he snarled. He shoved to his feet and left the room.

The silence returned slowly, like a feather floating to the ground. I waited for it to fall, for my heart to stop hammering, then finally surveyed the office.

There were no bookshelves. No photographs. No paperwork or laptop. Nothing personal except for a lone painting across from the desk.

The watercolor was of a horse's face. Its tangled mane was draped over an eye. The brown, gold, and rust colors were blended to perfection.

I stared at the horse as I took out my phone and called Dad.

"You've reached Grant Keller. Please leave a message, and I'll return your call as soon as possible. Thank you."

"Well, Daddy. That went . . . it went. I'll tell you about it later." I ended the call and set my phone on the desk.

This was wrong. This was all wrong.

I never should have come back to Montana.

"What the hell am I doing here?" I whispered.

The horse didn't have an answer.

Chapter 2
INDYA

Age Eight

"Crazy Mountain Cattle Resort." I read from the brochure on the cabin's dining room table. "That's a cool name, huh, Daddy?"

He hummed from where he was lying on the couch. His eyes were closed, his head resting against two brown throw pillows.

"Indya, your dad is going to rest until dinner." Mom took the brochure from my hands and tucked a lock of curly hair behind my ear. "Why don't you go outside and explore? I saw a swing set over by the lodge."

"I don't want to go outside." I sighed. "Do I have to?"

"No. You can either go outside or go to your room and read."

"Mom," I moaned. "The books I brought are boring."

"Then go outside."

I almost rolled my eyes. Almost. But Mom got mad when I rolled my eyes. "Are there other kids here?"

"Maybe." She shrugged. "There's only one way to find out."

By going outside.

"Fine." I trudged toward the door.

"Indya," Dad called, and when I turned, he had a finger pressed to his cheek.

I ran to the couch and gave him a smooch.

"Thanks, pumpkin." He cracked his eyes. "Just let me take a quick nap; then we'll go to the campfire dinner. Grown-ups get steak, but kids get hot dogs. Maybe you can sneak one for me."

"Okay." I smiled, studying his face for a moment.

He looked the same as normal. He was still the tallest dad at my school. He was still the strongest person I knew. But he was tired a lot lately. He took naps all the time.

Mom was always shuffling me to my room so he could rest. And when they thought I wasn't listening, I heard them say *cancer*.

I knew about cancer.

Mrs. Davy was supposed to be my teacher in first grade, but she was gone that whole year for cancer. Sometimes our principal would come to our classroom and show us pictures. Mrs. Davy didn't have hair anymore.

Was Dad going to lose his hair?

Mom said I was her mini except for my hair. It was the same as Dad's. Curly and blond and wild. Well, mine was wild. I had a lot of hair.

I hoped Daddy didn't lose his.

"Out you go, honey," Mom said.

I huffed and climbed off the couch, then shuffled to the door.

"I love you," Dad said.

"I love you too." I waved at Mom, then went outside and hopped down the cabin's porch stairs.

We were in the Beartooth Chalet. It was the biggest cabin at the resort. That's what the lady had said when we'd checked in today. There were four bedrooms and a loft.

I had picked the loft to sleep in even though it had the smallest bed.

We had a kitchen that Mom said we weren't going to use because she didn't go on vacations to cook.

Sometimes she was really confusing, because she didn't cook at home either. Our chef made our meals. Did she even know how to cook?

I skipped along the stone path that led from our cabin to the lodge, twirling as a yellow butterfly flittered past me. I loved butterflies. We had them in our garden at home. Mom had asked the gardener to plant flowers for butterflies and ladybugs.

Were the butterflies in Montana the same butterflies we had in Texas? Could a butterfly go that far? How long would it even take?

I was spinning, watching the butterfly, when the toe of my shoe caught on a stone. I yelped and crashed to my hands and knees.

"Ouch." I shoved up to my feet, then checked my hands first. My palms were scratched—but no blood.

Until I looked at my knee. Red pooled from a scrape, and a tiny flap of skin was hanging loose.

Owie, owie, owie. I sucked in a sharp breath, waiting for the sting to pass. If I went inside, Mom would pour that fizzy stuff—hydro something—on it that stung ten times worse than the actual cut.

"Owie." I squeezed my eyes shut.

"Are you okay?" A boy came jogging over from the lodge.

"Yeah." I nodded.

"You're bleeding."

"It doesn't hurt." Not that bad.

"Need a Band-Aid?" he asked.

I shook my head. "My mom has a lot. She says I'm clumsy."

"Oh." He looked me up and down, his eyes narrowing. "Are you going to cry?"

Not while he was watching me. I jutted up my chin. "No."

"Girls cry. Especially when they get hurt."

"Not me." Sometimes I cried. But the sting was already fading, and he seemed like a boy who wouldn't play with me if he thought I was a crybaby.

"Cool." He nodded. "What's your name?"

"Indya."

"India?" He gave me a funny look. "Like the country?"

"Kinda. I-n-d-*y*-a. It's spelled with a *y*. What's your name?"

"West."

That was a cool name. Not as cool as mine, but pretty cool. "I've never heard of the name West before."

"I've never heard of Indya before. Where are you from?"

"Texas. Where are you from?"

"I live here."

"Like on this ranch?"

"Yep. With my dad and mom and baby brother and grandpa and grandma."

This seemed like a fun place to live. "How old are you?"

"Ten."

"I'm eight. Want to play on the swing set with me?"

"Not really."

"Oh." My shoulders sagged.

"Want to see my horse?"

"Okay." I nodded wildly and chased after West to the barn, the scrape on my knee forgotten.

His horse's name was Chief. We climbed over a fence and walked out to him in a field. West had a handful of grain in his pocket, and Chief ate it from his palm.

Mom got mad when she couldn't find me on the swing set and made me promise to tell her before I went anywhere with West again. Before dinner, she poured that fizzy stuff on my knee, even though the bleeding had stopped. The medicine made it hurt way worse than it had in the first place.

Dad helped me cook my hot dog at the big campfire they built that night. And he took a lot of naps.

Mom always made me go outside, which was okay. Sometimes I had to play on the swing set by myself. But other times, West was there, and he'd let me go with him to pet his horse.

Montana was a pretty fun place to go on vacation.

Chapter 3
WEST

This wasn't happening. This wasn't real.

I stalked away from the office, lengthening my strides until I was nearly jogging. I needed to get the fuck out of this building so I could think. So I could breathe. So I couldn't smell Indya's sweet rose perfume.

"Hey, West. Could I—"

"Later." I raised a hand, cutting off Deb's question as I breezed past the front desk.

She probably wanted to know if I was going to give her those two weeks in July off so she could travel with her boyfriend to different rodeos around the state.

Since I was pissed off at her boyfriend, I wasn't really inclined to say yes at the moment.

Casey had agreed to work for us this summer and take guests fishing. We'd been short a guide for the second summer in a row, and I couldn't take off time to go fishing. But instead of showing up to work, Casey had called in sick the past three weekends so he could go team roping. Which meant I'd had to stop offering fishing to guests. Again.

My irritation with the boyfriend aside, Deb didn't have any vacation time left. She'd already gotten an extra week. And we couldn't afford to have her gone for two weeks during our busiest season.

Who else would sit at the desk? Jax? Dad? Me? The three of us were already stretched thin.

Grandma was already taking the early-morning shifts. But being on her feet all day wouldn't be good for her hip. Besides that, it just created extra work for me. She didn't like the computer system, so before dawn, I'd come to the lodge and brew her a pot of coffee. Then I'd print out every reservation on paper so she could have it when guests came in.

She preferred to have everything done the way she'd done it for years. In the days when she and Grandpa had built this lodge. When they'd created the Crazy Mountain Cattle Resort.

Did my grandparents know that Dad had sold their ranch? That he'd taken what they'd gifted him and cast it aside?

Fucking hell. This was a nightmare. This wasn't real.

He sold the ranch?

My stomach roiled as I shoved through the lodge's front door so hard it slammed against the wall, the hinges creaking as they rebounded.

This wasn't real.

"West," Jax called, running to catch up as I hurried down the porch stairs.

"Not now." I kept walking, dragging a hand through my hair as I headed for my truck.

It was a nice day. Clear blue sky. Fresh, crisp air. Warm yellow sunlight. Why were the worst days of my life always on nice days?

"West," he called again as his hand clamped down on my shoulder.

"Not now, Jax." I shrugged off his grip and continued toward my truck.

"You're just going to walk away? Let this happen?"

I spun around to face him. "What the hell do you want me to do? I can't even . . . I don't even know what is happening right now."

"Neither do I." He threw his hands in the air. "You have to stay. You have to fix it."

Fix it? I'd been trying to fix it for years.

"Please," Jax begged.

Fuck. "Later. I promise."

Dad emerged from the lodge, scanning the parking lot. When he spotted us, he took the porch steps, wincing with each one. That limp wasn't getting any better, but the stubborn bastard refused to go to the doctor. He'd hurt his hip, and maybe his knee, when he'd gotten bucked off a horse two weeks ago.

The horse was a young black gelding that needed time and patience. It needed daily rides and lessons on how to be a great horse. Not a good horse, a great horse.

My horse.

The last horse that had truly been mine was Chief. When he'd died, it had left a void. A hole I hadn't been ready to fill. So for the past ten years, I'd ridden whichever horse was available. But as the horses we used for guests got older, slower, it was time to start training new horses.

And it was time for me to have my own horse.

I'd bought five and chosen the tallest for myself. The other four, Jax and I had been riding hard, taking on trail rides with guests, and training on the daily routine.

But that gelding wasn't going to be a trail horse, and there weren't enough hours in every day. His training hadn't taken priority.

Apparently, that wasn't good enough for Dad, because two weeks ago, I'd come home from a long day moving cattle, and he'd been limping. He'd taken my horse for a ride and had a wreck.

If he just would have waited—if he just would have talked to me . . .

About the horse.

About the ranch.

About Indya.

Indya.

Why? What was she doing here? Four years and not a word. Then this? Goddamn it. I couldn't breathe. My head was swimming. My heart felt like it had just been ripped into pieces.

I needed to get the fuck out of here.

Dad held up a hand before I could escape. "Stop right there, son."

Thirty-one years old, and I still didn't argue with that tone. "Not in a mood to talk, Dad."

"Tough." He stopped beside Jax, planting his hands on his hips. "I'm sorry. I know this was a shock. There's more to say. I should have explained, but . . . I did what I thought was best."

"By selling the ranch?" This wasn't real.

Except it was real, wasn't it?

"How could you?"

"We're in trouble, West."

"I know we're in fucking trouble," I barked. "This wasn't the answer."

"It was the answer. The only answer. You'll have to trust me on that."

"Trust?" Did he even know the meaning of that word? "Fuck you."

He flinched.

Jax too.

"We're not just sinking. We're drowning."

"We?"

This had never been *we*. It was always him.

His decision. His choice.

His ranch.

"Me." His voice cracked. "We're—I'm—*broke*."

Broke? More like broken.

We were broken.

It should have hurt more. It should have taken me by surprise. But deep down, we'd been riding hard down this road for years.

"What do you mean, we're broke?" Jax asked.

"There's no money." Dad's eyes were watery. "We owe more to the bank than we can hope to pay."

"So you just sold everything?" Jax asked. "You didn't even talk to us."

"Look, if I had another choice, I would have made it."

"Alone," I said. "You would have made that decision alone. Like always."

He'd sold the ranch.

This was real. This was fucking real.

Unreal.

Not only had he ripped it away from our family, but he'd done it alone. He'd talked to her alone. He'd poured salt on the gaping, bleeding gash in my heart.

"How long?" I asked. "How long have you been planning this in secret?"

Dad dropped his gaze to the dirt. "A month."

"What?" Jax erupted, tossing both hands in the air. "You sold it a month ago?"

"No. Contract was signed last week. But we've been . . . negotiating."

Negotiating. With Indya Keller.

No, not Keller. Hamilton. Indya Hamilton was her married name. Though she hadn't been wearing that massive, gaudy diamond on her finger today. Why? Where was *Blaine*?

Was he a part of this too? The idea of that son of a bitch owning the ground beneath my feet made my blood boil. This was Haven land. Even before Grandpa and Grandma had started the resort, this ranch had been in our family for generations.

"This is our legacy."

Was our legacy.

And now it belonged to her.

How had we gotten here? How had it all fallen apart so epically? I couldn't catch my breath. Someone had knocked the wind from my lungs, and I couldn't fill them up.

"You really sold it to her?" Jax asked.

Dad nodded. "I did."

"But . . . you didn't talk to us." The lilt of a question hung on Jax's statement.

Once upon a time, Dad's autocratic tendencies had taken me by surprise too. It used to baffle me that he wouldn't consult with his children over decisions that impacted *their* lives.

But I'd learned over the years that Dad didn't ask, because he didn't want our input.

Jax hadn't experienced that enough, mostly because he was still young.

My brother had spent the past four years away at college in Bozeman. He'd been fairly removed from ranch and resort business.

But he'd come home last month, proudly waving that bachelor's degree, and declared he was ready to help with the business.

Dad hadn't had the heart to tell him the truth about the business. Neither had I.

I'd known for years we were in trouble. It was getting harder and harder to make those bank payments. My proposed solution was to put some land up for sale.

Just not all the land.

Did he really sell *all* the land?

"It's not ideal," Dad said. "But at least we know Indya. She's been here. Her family has spent time here. She knows the resort. And the Kellers are good people."

Except she wasn't a Keller, not anymore.

"Better her than have some developer buy it and break it apart," Dad said.

"How do you know she won't?" I asked.

"She gave me her word. I believe she'll keep it."

Maybe. Maybe not. "Is it in the contract?"

Dad shook his head.

"Oh, hell." Jax rubbed both hands over his face. "We're fucked. Absolutely fucked."

I wanted to argue. To tell him we'd figure it out. That we'd be okay. But I didn't make promises to my brother I couldn't keep.

"Trust me." Dad's eyes searched mine. "Please."

"I can't."

Dad opened his mouth but closed it with an audible click. Maybe he had more to say, but I wasn't going to listen. I'd heard enough. So he turned on a heel and stalked toward the barn. Hopefully he'd choose a horse other than my gelding if he went for a ride.

"What do we do?" Jax asked.

"I don't know."

He shifted to stare at the shiny black SUV with Texas plates. Indya's, no doubt.

"We have to trust him. And work for her?" Jax scoffed. "I'm not fucking working for her. She can kiss my ass."

"Don't—"

"Don't what?"

Don't talk about her that way. "Don't overreact. Until we learn more."

Jax didn't know about my history with Indya. Neither did Dad—at least not all of it.

No one knew. It had been easier that way.

Easier when she came to Montana for a week in the summer, then went back to her rich life in Texas.

She was here. For how long?

I hated that I still hoped for more than a week.

Without another word, I went to my truck and ripped open its door to climb inside. The engine roared to life as I turned the key. Then I slammed my foot on the gas, peeling out of the gravel lot in a cloud of dust as I raced down the road.

What I needed was a long, hard ride, but Dad had beaten me to it, so a drive would have to do.

The truck bounced and shimmied on the road. It was on my list of things to do to call the county to come out and have the gravel graded. It was riddled with washboarding and potholes. But every time I remembered, it was long after five, and their offices were closed.

Before I reached the main archway and entrance to the ranch, I hit the brakes, skidding as I slowed to turn onto the two-track road that wound through a pasture. I followed the trodden grass path as it wove through a grove of trees and onward toward the mountains in the distance.

Another half mile, and I'd be out of cell phone service. With any luck, I'd get a flat. At this point, I'd rather be stranded out here with nothing but my truck than anywhere near that lodge.

Was Indya planning to stay? What exactly did she think would happen now that she owned it? Were we out of jobs? Homes?

My head was still spinning. The pressure in my chest was crippling. My pulse boomed so loudly in my ears I couldn't think.

I slammed my fist on the wheel at the same time I took my foot off the gas and let the truck coast to a stop. The moment it was stopped, I flew out the door, needing some air.

Five steps into the meadow's tall grass, I dropped to my knees. Then I dragged in a shaky inhale, holding it until my lungs burned.

This was my land. This was my home.

Why would Indya do this? Revenge?

Did she really hate me that much?

Indya knew what this ranch meant to me. To my family. It was as much a part of my body as my bones.

An eagle screamed as it soared over the trees.

Screaming seemed like a damn good idea.

So I buried my face in my hands.

And roared, "Fuck!"

I closed my eyes, breathing until the sound faded.

My fault. This was my fault.

As much as I wanted to blame this on Dad, if I was being honest with myself, our financial problems had started with Courtney. And that was on me. I'd brought her to this ranch.

My hand went to the ground, my fingers digging up a clump of dirt to turn over in my palm.

This was Haven land. My land.

There had to be a way to undo this sale. There had to be a way to fix this.

I took a few minutes to breathe, to let my anger and shock fade. Then I stood, brushing the dirt from my hand on my jeans, and walked to my truck. I made the return drive to the ranch at a slower pace, giving myself time to think.

How much money did I need to come up with? What was the price tag he'd given Indya?

There was a neighbor's place outside Big Timber with similar acreage that had sold two years ago for ten million dollars.

Too many zeros.

We're broke.

I didn't have millions of dollars. Could I borrow it?

The summer season was always when we brought in money. Then we'd sell this year's calves in the fall. We were running lean on expenses. I had already cut back on resort staff and was doing as much as possible myself.

It wasn't enough.

Why did Indya even want this place? What was she doing here?

There was only one way to find out.

Her SUV was still in the lot when I pulled up to the lodge. I parked beside it and headed inside.

The lobby was empty. Where the fuck was Deb? Why was it so hard for her to stay at the desk? I didn't bother with the bell. I just riffled through the paperwork until I found Indya's name.

Room 208. I took the stairs two at a time and rounded the landing, then marched for the end of the hall. With my fist raised to knock, I drew in a calming breath—it didn't work—and pounded on the doorframe.

It was a little too loud, a little too violent. Three doors down, another door whipped open, and our head housekeeper, Tara, poked her head into the hallway.

"Everything okay, West?"

"Fine," I lied.

"Okay," she drawled, then disappeared into the room again.

A muffled yelp came from inside Indya's room before she opened the door, rubbing her elbow.

"Funny bone?" I asked.

27

"Yeah. I tripped on my suitcase."

For a moment, the familiarity of it chased away all the other bull-shit. This was us.

Indya, having injured herself, because there wasn't a soul on earth with as much clumsy running through their veins.

And me, always a few seconds too late and never quite fast enough to catch her before she fell.

"Hi, West."

"Hey, Indy."

A lock of her curly blonde hair had escaped her bun, and she tucked it behind her ear. It wouldn't stay. Her hair never stayed put, but she fought it anyway. Her caramel eyes were harder than they had been four years ago. Their light had dimmed, and she looked . . . tired. And yet every time she came to the ranch, she was more beautiful.

She was dressed in a pair of black slacks. The sleeveless gray blouse she wore had a high collar and was molded to her torso, accentuating the curves of her breasts. The scent of roses wafted from the room, and with it came memories of dark nights and stolen kisses.

The window was open, and a gust knocked that curl loose again, freeing it to skim her temple.

Once upon a time, I would have tugged the pins out of her hair. I would have buried my hands in those curls and locked us in this room for a week.

But that was before she'd stolen my legacy.

"How much for the ranch?" I crossed my arms over my chest.

Indya sighed. "It's not for sale."

Fuck. "How. Much?" If I could just get her to name a price, then I'd figure out a way to make it happen. Somehow, I'd find a way.

"West." Her voice gentled. "I'm not selling it. And if I was . . ."

I couldn't afford it.

If she named a price, it would be astronomical. It would be more money than I'd see in my lifetime.

Dad was rich now that he'd sold the ranch.

But I wasn't. Not even close.

Humiliation burned a hot trail through my insides, but I wasn't here to save my pride. I was here to save my family's land. "I'll work my whole life to pay you back. You can't take this from us."

"That's not what I'm doing."

"The hell it isn't." My voice bounced off the walls.

She held up a hand. "I know it came as a shock today, but—"

"A shock," I deadpanned. "Yeah, it was a shock. I walk into the lodge because Dad calls me to say we need to have an urgent meeting, and there you are after four years, sitting behind my desk. You took my chair before anyone had the decency to tell me it was no longer mine."

"West—"

"This is my home. This is my livelihood. Don't you dare fucking take it from me."

The color drained from her face. "It's already done."

No. There had to be a way out of this. There had to be a way to take it back.

Maybe my only option was to drive her away.

I hated myself for what I was about to say, but it wasn't the first time I'd hurt her. It wasn't the first time I'd told myself it was for her own good.

"You don't belong here, Indya."

She flinched, her gaze dropping to an invisible spot on the floor. "I know."

"Sell it back to me. Please." I wasn't above begging, not for this.

Indya raised her chin. There was nothing but steely determination etched across that beautiful face. "Tomorrow morning. Eight o'clock. *My* office. I expect you, your father, and your brother to be there. Then we can discuss who exactly belongs on *my* ranch."

She stepped back, almost tripping over her bare feet. But she caught herself in time to grip the door.

And slam it in my face.

She slammed it so hard that Tara, smart woman, knew better than to poke her head into the hallway again.

Chapter 4
INDYA

Age Nine

Dad swung my hand between us as we walked the stone path from the Beartooth Chalet to the lodge. "What should we do this week? Horseback riding? Fishing? Hiking?"

I shrugged. "I like all that stuff. Whatever you want."

"Then we'll do all of it." He smiled down at me. "And we'll drag your mother away from her book and make her come along too."

I giggled. "Good luck, Daddy."

He chuckled, glancing over his shoulder. "Wait. Where'd she go?"

"I don't know. Can I go play?" We had just gotten here, but I wanted to see if West was around. Maybe we could go visit Chief again.

"Indya, don't run off." Mom flew out of the cabin's front door carrying two bottles. Bug spray. And sunscreen. "Let's not have a repeat of last year."

The sunburn and the mosquito bites hadn't bothered me *that* much, but she wouldn't let me go play until I was covered.

"Plug your nose," Dad said, motioning for me to run back.

With my eyes squeezed shut, my fingers plugging my nose, and my breath held, I stood on the porch as Mom doused me head to toe.

"There." She smiled and brushed a lock of hair off my forehead. "Be right back."

As she returned the cans to the cabin, I jogged back to Dad. "Done. Blech."

He laughed and drew in a deep breath, then held the air in his lungs. "Feels good to be here, doesn't it, pumpkin?"

"Yeah." He said the Montana air was his favorite. I think it was my favorite too. We'd been here for only an hour, and I already dreaded next Friday, when we had to leave.

This trip was Dad's carrot. That's what he'd been calling it.

He'd drawn me a picture of a man riding a donkey and holding a fishing pole with a carrot on the line in front of the animal's nose. It was how the man got the donkey to walk. The animal wanted the carrot, and when they made it to their destination, it would be his reward.

Dad drew me pictures a lot when he had to explain hard stuff.

He'd drawn me a lot of pictures this year, so I knew what cancer meant.

This trip was his carrot for getting through surgery and his treatments. Chemo. It was supposed to be medicine, but sometimes he called it poison. I wasn't exactly sure why. If I asked, Dad would probably draw another picture, and I was sick of cancer pictures.

"Howdy." West's dad—what was his name?—rounded the back side of the lodge, tugging off a cowboy hat and tucking it under his arm as he extended a hand to Dad. "Good to see you, Grant."

"Happy to be here, Curtis."

Oh, yeah. Curtis.

"How are you feeling?" he asked.

"Good." Dad nodded. "It's been a rough year, but it's nice to have it behind me."

"Glad it's behind you too." Curtis clapped Dad on the shoulder. "Whatever you need this week, just let me know."

"Calories." Dad patted his flat stomach. "I'm trying to gain back the weight I lost. And fresh air."

"You're in luck. We've got both in spades. Passed the kitchen on the way out. Dinner for tonight smells incredible." Curtis grinned, then looked to me and dipped his chin. "Miss Keller. Welcome."

"Thank you. Is West here?"

"He sure is. I'll go find him. Any plans for this afternoon?" he asked Dad.

"No, we'll get settled. Ellen is hooked on a book, so she wanted to read for a bit before dinner. I think tomorrow maybe we'll take a ride."

"I'll clear my schedule. Take you out myself."

"Thanks, Curtis."

"My pleasure." He shook Dad's hand again, then gave me a wink. "I'll go find West."

As he walked to the lodge, fitting the hat back on his head, Dad put his arm around my shoulders. "He's good people."

Dad made sure to tell me when he thought someone was *good people*. He didn't tell me when someone was bad people. Maybe we didn't know any bad people?

"Grant!" Mom called from the cabin.

"Yeah?"

She held up a bottle, shaking it so the pills inside rattled. "Did you take these?"

"Shoot." He sighed. "I forgot. Do you want to go play?"

"Yes." I stood on my tiptoes as he bent to kiss my cheek, then ran for the lodge.

"Stay close," he hollered.

"I will." I waved to him, then yanked the door open to the lodge, scanning the open space for West. The sound of voices drew me toward a hallway.

"You need to go play with the girl who's staying in Beartooth."

"Dad." West's groan hit my ears, and my smile dropped. "I don't want to."

"Tough," Curtis said. "We all pitch in around here. This is your job for the week."

West huffed. "Fine."

A job. I was a job? I wasn't exactly sure what that meant, but I knew I didn't like it.

I backed away before they caught me eavesdropping. Mom got mad at me when I eavesdropped. Then on silent feet, I crept to the door and slipped outside before running down the porch steps and across the stone path that led to the cabin.

My feelings hurt. I kind of wanted to cry.

I'd cried a lot this year. Usually when Mom and Dad were sad. If I cried, they cried. So I tried really hard not to cry.

Why wouldn't West want to play with me? Didn't we have fun last year? I was older now. I was nine. I could do more stuff. Weren't we friends?

The sound of a door opening and closing behind me made me turn, just as West came out of the lodge.

If he didn't want to play with me, then I didn't want to play with him. I slipped around the back side of the cabin, where he couldn't see me, then walked into the tall grass that hadn't been mowed.

There were small white and purple flowers everywhere. They were really pretty, so I started making myself a little bundle. I could give it to Mom later.

"Hey." West came up beside me with his hands shoved into his jeans pockets.

"Hey," I muttered.

"Want to play?"

Yes. "No. I'm picking flowers for my mom."

"Okay." He shrugged and turned to leave.

I stuck my tongue out at the back of his head. Then I bent to pick a purple flower, but it wouldn't break off. *Come on, stupid flower.* Wrapping my whole fist around the stem, I tugged as hard as I could. It broke with a quick snap, dirt flew into my face from the roots, and all the force of my pulling slammed me backward, sending me into the dirt with a plop.

"Ouch," I muttered and rubbed the sore spot on my butt.

"You okay?" West's hand came to my elbow, then hauled me to my feet.

"Yeah."

"Come on. Let's just play or something."

"I don't want to," I lied.

"Want to see my fort?" he asked.

Yes. "That's okay."

He rolled his eyes.

I got in trouble when I rolled my eyes.

West walked away, turning back when he made it to the short grass. "Are you coming or not?"

"Fine." I trudged after him, hurrying to keep up as he led me past the lodge and barn to a cluster of trees way past the fence. The farther we got from the resort, the more I checked over my shoulder to see just how far we'd walked. "I don't know if I should be all the way out here."

"I come out here all the time."

"But you live here."

He kept walking.

So I kept following, my picked flowers held firmly in my grasp.

West wove past small trees, some shorter than me, and when he reached the big trees, he pointed to a triangular structure, the roof covered in a green tarp. "That's my fort."

"Cool. Did you make it?"

"Yeah. My grandpa helped too."

All my grandpas ever did was golf.

West ducked inside and took a seat on a wooden bench.

There were two, so I sat on the other. The legs were a bit wobbly, but if I kept still, it didn't rock.

"I made these benches," he said. "And the table. And I hung up that light."

Above us, at the peak of the two wooden sheets that made up the walls and ceiling, was a camping lamp hung from a wire. He stood on his toes, flipping the button to turn it on. Then he picked up a tin on the floor, prying open the lid to reveal a deck of cards, a pile of broken toothpicks, and a wad of money.

"Want to play poker?" he asked.

"I don't know how."

"I'll teach you." He dragged over the square table, even wobblier than my seat, and positioned it between us. Then he shuffled the cards before dealing out five to us both.

By the time I heard my dad calling my name, I knew how to play poker.

"I better go," I told West and rushed out of the fort.

Dad was walking toward the trees with Curtis. He smiled when he spotted me. "Hey, pumpkin."

"Hi, Dad." I rushed to his side and threw my arms around his waist.

Mom said I should hug him whenever I had the chance. It was a good idea.

"Did you have fun? Curtis says that West has quite the fort."

"Yeah. It's really neat. Want to see it?"

"Sure."

I took his hand and led him to the fort, shifting out of the way so he could go first.

"Hello." West dipped his chin, something Curtis must have taught him to do, then waved Dad inside.

"I heard you built this," Dad said, hunching because he was too tall.

"Yes, sir."

"Very nice." Dad's gaze shifted to the cards and chips on the table. "Poker?"

"West taught me how to play," I said as Dad ushered me out to rejoin Curtis. "I lost twenty dollars. Can I borrow it?"

Dad chuckled and dug into his jeans pocket, taking out cash from his money clip to hand to West.

"That's all right." West waved it off. "You don't have to pay me. It was just for fun."

"I insist. If she placed the bet and lost, then Indya has to pay."

West looked to Curtis.

"It's fine." Curtis nodded.

"Thank you." West beamed as he took the twenty and slid it into his pocket.

"We'll let you get on with your evening." Dad shook Curtis's hand again, then put his hand on my shoulder to steer me away.

"Don't forget your flowers, Indya." West pointed to the small bundle I'd left tucked into the slit between boards on my bench.

"You can keep them." They looked nice in the fort. "Want to play again tomorrow?"

Even if I was his *job* for the week, I still wanted to play.

He shrugged. "Sure."

Dad lifted a hand to wave; then we made our way toward the lodge. The chime of the chef's dinner triangle rang through the air.

"You know what, Daddy?" I took his hand so he could swing it between us.

"What?"

"Tomorrow, I'm going to win back my twenty dollars."

He let out a loud, booming laugh. The kind of laugh I hadn't heard much this past year. "That's my girl."

Chapter 5
INDYA

8:32. Exactly one minute since the last time I'd checked my phone.

I had said eight, not eight thirty. Not 8:32. Eight. Where the hell was he? Where was Curtis? Or Jax?

I tapped my pen on the desk, the *tat-tat-tat* turning furious as I thwacked harder and faster.

"Damn it." I tossed the pen aside and shoved to my feet, pushing out of West's uncomfortable office chair—I'd ordered its replacement last night, but the chair I wanted was back ordered, and the company wouldn't do overnight shipping to Middle of Nowhere, Montana, so it wouldn't arrive for nearly two weeks.

He wasn't coming. That obstinate bastard. He wasn't going to make this easy, was he? Not that I'd expected anything about this situation to be easy.

Maybe I shouldn't have gotten so heated when he'd come to my room last night. But when he'd told me I didn't belong here, my temper had gotten the best of me, and I'd snapped.

No, I didn't belong here. But I *was* here. And I wasn't leaving.

Yet.

I blew out a deep breath and paced to the window. The meadow behind the lodge was overgrown. They'd always kept that space mowed short so guests could play horseshoes or yard games. Who was the groundskeeper?

Another item on another list. Another employee to hire—or fire if there was in fact a groundskeeper.

Too long, but pretty. The grass sparkled with morning dew. There were wildflowers in the field beyond the lawn. Maybe later today, I'd make a bouquet of white and purple wildflowers for my room.

The last time I'd picked wildflowers was, well . . . a long time ago.

Turning from the window, I studied the office for the tenth time this morning. West's office.

It didn't feel like him. It was too plain. Too dull. When I closed my eyes and thought of West, I saw rich color. Chocolate brown hair. Blue denim Wranglers. Gold flecks in hazel eyes.

West's office should have deep-green walls and leather armchairs. Instead, the walls were beige. I hadn't moved the folding chairs Curtis had brought in yesterday.

There was nothing to actually work with, not in the desk's drawers or cabinets. There wasn't a hint of his spicy scent lingering in the stale air. The only hint that West might have spent time here was that watercolor painting.

The room was also too neat and tidy. West wasn't a messy man, but he loved the outdoors. His boots were always dirty. He could usually be found with a pair of leather gloves or a coffee mug. There were no cup rings in the desk's layer of dust. No discarded items in the trash can.

Given the state of the business, maybe it shouldn't surprise me that the office had been neglected. Though I doubted Curtis had even given West a chance to help. Curtis had always been in charge. This was *his* ranch. Even I'd known that, and I'd simply been a spectator.

It was such a contrast to how Dad ran his business. Before his retirement, he'd treated me like a partner. He'd asked for my opinions and given me advice.

For all intents and purposes, West was Curtis's employee. Another man probably would have left. But West loved this ranch, and even if it meant taking orders and biding his time until Curtis's retirement, he'd stayed.

He'd stayed while his father had run their business into the ground.

It wasn't Curtis's problem anymore, was it? Now it was mine.

And it would be freaking great if the Havens could answer a few questions.

I checked the time again.

8:37. Apparently, I was on my own.

I'd pored through the ranch's recent tax returns countless times in the past month. I'd gone through them again last night, staying up until well past midnight to make sure I had a good understanding of the numbers.

They'd had a string of unprofitable years with the resort, and the reservation count for this summer was at an all-time low. In the past, when the resort income had waned, the ranch had made up the difference.

Except five years ago, they'd bought a piece of property to expand their cattle operation. They'd taken a loan from the bank to fund the purchase. I wasn't an expert on Montana land prices or how much a cattle operation could make from additional acreage, but the price point seemed high.

That expansion had depleted their cash reserves, making it nearly impossible to recover losses from the resort. And after four years, they'd fallen behind on bank payments. The only thing keeping them from bankruptcy was this sale.

The numbers told only part of the story. I still wasn't sure what exactly had happened, and without West or Curtis here to explain, I was guessing.

Why hadn't Curtis carved off some property to sell? Land prices had fallen over the past couple of years. Maybe he'd hoped to wait out the market until it swung the other direction.

I'd seen plenty of real estate investments fail because the owner had overpaid, then hung on too long.

By the time Curtis had been willing to bring in help, well . . .

It didn't matter now. The deal was done.

Curtis had millions of my dollars in his pocket.

And I had a resort to keep from crumbling to the ground.

Alone.

8:41. "Stubborn, stubborn man." I seethed.

The last thing I wanted was for this ranch to fail. We were both working toward the same goal. We were fighting on the same side. But West had cast me as the villain.

Fine. I'd play that role. And when I turned this place around, I'd revel in his apology.

My first order of business would be cleaning this office, so I marched down the hallway, opening every door until I found a supply closet. Fury and frustration fueled my cleaning. It took only thirty minutes to scour the room, wiping away dust and replacing the stale scent with the smell of lemon wood polish.

With that task complete, I closed the door and dived into phone calls, starting with the marketing agency in Dallas that we'd used for years at Keller Enterprises.

After thirty minutes of chatting with their CEO, I'd filled her in on why I was in Montana. She called a graphic designer into her office. Then we spent another thirty minutes brainstorming a rebrand for the resort.

"I've got some ideas," the designer said. "Let me work up a few new logos, and I'll email them over before the end of the week. Just to confirm spelling, it's h-a-v-e-n."

"Yes. Haven River Ranch."

"Great name."

It was a great name. "Thanks for jumping on this so quickly."

"Anytime."

After ending the call, I stood, rubbing the ache in my lower back from that damn chair. I collected the notebook I'd filled last night with lists upon lists, then squared my shoulders and left the office.

If West wouldn't come to me, then I'd track him down. There were only so many places he could hide. But before I could start my search, my phone buzzed, Blaine's name on the screen.

My lip curled. If I didn't answer, he'd just keep calling. "Hello."

"You didn't call last night."

Because I no longer needed to report my whereabouts. "I didn't realize I needed to check in."

"You drove across the country and didn't think I might be worried about my wife? Indya." Blaine had a wholly unique way of saying my name. He could turn those five letters into a verbal slap, crushing disappointment, or a scathing accusation.

And I'd foolishly assumed our conversations would stop now that the divorce was finalized.

"Ex-wife," I corrected. "No need to worry. I'm fine and in Montana."

Was he really worried for me? Or was he just making sure I still had a pulse? Making sure I was alive to sign his precious paperwork?

"We need to set a date," he said.

"Just pick one."

"When are you flying back?"

"I'm not."

He scoffed. "You're actually going to stay there? *Live* there?"

"For now."

I liked room 208, but it wasn't permanent. Eventually, I'd have to find a place to live. Maybe a house in Big Timber. Maybe one of the resort cabins. My plans were none of his business, not anymore.

The sound of his molars grinding made me pull the phone from my ear. "You're really doing this," he said.

"Why do you care?"

"I don't."

I rolled my eyes. "Anything else?"

"What happens when you fail?"

Then he'd find a way to rub it in my face. "Have a nice day, Blaine."

"Ind—"

I hung up before he could finish my name. Just a little while longer—then I wouldn't have to answer his calls. Then Blaine and his judgmental bullshit could go to hell.

Despite Blaine's insistence that I wasn't qualified or capable of running a multimillion-dollar business, I could do this. I *would* do this. For Dad. For me. And if that wasn't motivation enough, I'd do it simply to spite my ex-husband.

I'd been working for Dad since college, and if Grant Keller was anything, he was a savvy businessman. He'd made millions upon millions of dollars in his lifetime, and he'd personally mentored me after college.

Did I know anything about running a cattle ranch? No. But the resort was a different story. Sure, I had no experience in the hospitality industry, but I did know our target audience. The latest reviews were abysmal—probably why reservations were dwindling. Rich people wanted certain amenities, and it was time to offer more.

Whether West liked it or not, we'd have to work together. Somehow, I would figure out the resort. But I needed him to run the ranch.

I needed him to stay.

The reception desk was empty when I reached the lobby. It had been empty when I'd come down this morning too. Where was Deb? It was her job to be here, right? To answer the phone and help guests?

I rang the bell, then waited until its chime had faded before ringing it again. By the third time, there was still no Deb. So I dug my phone from my pocket and called the resort's number. It rang three times before she answered.

"Crazy Mountain Cattle Resort." Her voice was breathless, and the rush of wind made it hard to hear.

"This is Indya Keller. I'm at the front desk."

"Sorry. Be right there. Two minutes." She ended the call.

It took her five to blow through the front door, her black bob disheveled and her cheeks flushed.

"Sorry. My boyfriend is leaving for the weekend and came over to say goodbye."

Could this boyfriend not come inside to say goodbye? Or say fare-well before she came to work? I bit back the questions. Deb was a problem I'd deal with later.

"Please call Curtis and West. Tell them they're needed immediately at the lodge." There wasn't a chance they'd answer if I called. If this lodge were on fire, I had a feeling they'd let me burn with the building.

Deb's eyes narrowed. "Um, okay."

"I'll be in my office."

"I'm sorry. Your office?"

It had taken a month for Curtis to tell his sons that I'd bought this resort. I wasn't going to wait around for him to make an announcement to the staff.

"My office. I'd also like you to organize a staff meeting for this afternoon. Let's plan for one o'clock. Everyone who is not occupied with guests needs to meet here in the lobby."

Deb gulped. "W-what?"

"One o'clock. We'll discuss it all then." I retreated down the hallway but was still within earshot when I heard her on the phone.

"West, you'd better come to the lodge. Right now."

I wasn't holding my breath that he'd show, but ten minutes later, I heard the angry stomp of boots outside my office.

"What the hell do you think you're doing?" He stopped outside the door, but his scent wafted inside.

Leather and wind and soap. There was no smell on earth better than West Haven. It was rugged and real. The way a man should smell.

He'd been outside working this morning. The top button on his shirt was undone, and there was a sheen of sweat at the base of his throat. His hair was trapped beneath a baseball hat, and the longer strands curled at his nape.

The hat was embroidered with the ranch's brand. CMC, the letters stacked together. Too bad there wasn't an *H* for Haven. That would fit the new name better.

Still, maybe we could work the cattle brand into the new website. Was there a photo of it somewhere I could send to the designer?

"Indya," West barked.

I ignored him and took my phone, aiming the camera at his face. "I need a picture of your hat."

"My—what the fuck?" He scowled as I snapped the photo.

"Do you have any more of those hats?"

He crossed his arms over his chest, his legs planted wide. The scowl deepened.

"Never mind." I nodded to one of the folding chairs that Curtis had left behind yesterday. "You're late. I said eight o'clock."

He arched an eyebrow. "Baby, I do not answer to you."

Baby. He used that word like a weapon. It used to bring me to my knees.

Good thing I was sitting in his terrible chair.

"You do, actually." I folded my hands on the desk's gleaming, dust-free surface. "All I'm asking is for a bit of your time."

His jaw clenched beneath a layer of thick stubble. If he didn't shave soon, he'd have a beard. I'd never seen him with a beard.

"West." My voice gentled. "I'm not your enemy."

Those hazel eyes shifted to a window. "I don't know what to do here, Indy."

He wasn't the only person who'd ever called me Indy. But I liked the sound of my nickname best when it came from his lips.

"Just give me an hour," I said. "Tomorrow morning. Please. Let's talk."

The stiffness in his frame eased slightly. "Figured the last time you were here was the last time we'd talk."

That memory was the sharpest. A dagger through the heart. I swallowed hard as it sliced. "Me too."

"Fine." He dragged a hand through his hair. "Tomorrow morning at eight. This meeting needs to be short. I've got work—"

Deb flew down the hall, skidding to a stop before she crashed into West's frame. "Oh. Sorry. I didn't hear you come in."

He looked at her, lips pursed and arms still crossed. "Because you weren't at the desk."

"I was organizing the staff meeting."

West blinked. "What staff meeting?"

Deb's eyes darted to me, then back to West. A slow, malicious grin stretched across her mouth. "Hers."

Would she lose the attitude when she learned I was her boss? Doubtful.

I ignored her and met West's glare. It was lethal. The fragile truce we'd found just moments ago suffered a quick, painless death.

Shit. "There's an announcement to make," I said gently.

"What announcement?" Deb asked.

West didn't answer. He glowered at me, a storm brewing in those hazel eyes. Then he was gone, brushing past Deb and disappearing from sight.

If angry was a sound, it was the thunder of his boots on the floor.

"What announcement?" Deb repeated.

I held up a hand. "One o'clock."

She frowned and raced after West. With any luck, she'd go back to the desk and stay there to do her job.

I dropped my elbows to the desk and buried my face in my hands. "What the hell am I doing here?"

West was right. I didn't belong here.

Where did I belong?

I dropped my hands and reached for my phone, then called Dad's number. Voice mail. Again. "You've reached Grant Keller. Please leave a message, and I'll return your call as soon as possible. Thank you."

"Hi, Daddy." I didn't have the energy to muster false cheer. "Just calling to say hi and check in. The first day is going, well . . . like a first day. I'll catch you up on everything later. I love you."

Yesterday's headache had faded but hadn't disappeared. The throb in my skull warned it would be back in full force, likely before my staff meeting.

I stood and walked to the window, measuring deep inhales and exhales as I massaged my temples. When I opened my eyes, beyond the meadow of grasses and wildflowers was a man on a black horse, galloping toward the mountains.

West.

He looked as comfortable in the saddle as he did on his own two feet. It was like a dance, that man on a horse. Beautiful. Graceful. Sexy.

And definitely not coming to the staff meeting.

Chapter 6
INDYA

Age Eleven

I tapped Mom's shoulder, waiting until she looked up from her book. Then I pointed from the soccer ball tucked beneath my arm to the cabin's door.

She nodded with a smile, then gave me a wink.

Dad was asleep on the couch. His feet were on Mom's lap, and he was snoring. Loud. He'd never hear us if we whispered, but we stayed quiet anyway.

"I love you," she mouthed.

"Love you too."

Mom and I were good at reading lips. We'd had a lot of practice talking without a sound during Dad's naps, both at home in Texas and here in Montana. She said he didn't get enough sleep, and the reason she loved our vacations to the Crazy Mountain Cattle Resort was because they forced Dad to rest.

He always took naps when we were here.

Not me. I didn't want to miss anything on these trips.

I blew her a kiss, then tiptoed outside, careful not to let the door slam behind me. Then I ran down the porch stairs, bouncing the ball off my knee when I reached the ground. A curl fell into my face even though I'd pulled my ponytail tight. Not tight enough. I hated my hair.

I really wanted to cut it short. But whenever I asked Mom, she said no. She told me it was too pretty to chop off. I think she just didn't want me to look like a boy.

She already grumbled about my clothes. She wanted me to wear dresses and skirts. I hated dresses and skirts. I wore them only to church on Sundays.

I didn't like pink polka dots or purple ruffles. I liked shorts and T-shirts. And I wanted short hair. I was sick of it always getting in my mouth when I played soccer. During one of my games this spring, a clump flew into my eyes, and I missed a goal.

I usually missed kicking goals, with or without my hair in the way, but for sure that time I missed because of my hair.

Dad told me he thought soccer was helping me become more coordinated. I think he was just saying that to be nice. I still tripped a lot.

After tossing my ball to the ground, I kicked it along the stone path toward the lodge. We'd gotten in late last night and gone straight to the Beartooth Chalet, so I hadn't found West yet.

Did he play soccer? I was the worst one on our team, but I could still teach him how to play if he didn't know how.

The lodge door opened, and West's grandma walked outside with Jax.

He was a lot bigger now and the cutest little kid ever. He didn't really look like West or Curtis. Jax had blond hair and blue eyes. How old was he? The first time we had come to Montana, he was only a baby. This was our third vacation here, so he was probably four.

The grandma held his hand as they walked down the stairs. She smiled at me, her hazel eyes twinkling. "Hello."

"Hi." What was her name again? "Hey, Jax."

"Hi." He waved his whole arm, not just his hand. He had a pair of goggles on his head, pushed into his blond hair. His swimming trunks were neon orange and matched his flip-flops. "We're going to swimming lessons."

"That sounds fun." I giggled as he put the goggles on his eyes, giving me a smile that lit up his face.

"We'd better get to town," the grandma said. "Bye, Miss Keller."

"Bye. See ya, Jax."

"By-eee." He skipped to her truck, then stood on his toes to reach for the door's handle, but it was too tall.

I picked up my ball, then carried it up the porch stairs as they drove away.

No one was at the front desk when I walked into the lobby. The dining room doors were open. Inside, a waitress sat at a table, rolling silverware into white cloth napkins. But no West.

There was a hallway past the front desk. Guests probably weren't supposed to go down there, but on our last trip, West had shown me all around the lodge. We had been playing in his fort and had run out of snacks, so we'd sneaked into the kitchen to get granola bars from the chef.

I took a few steps down the hall, checking over my shoulder to make sure I was alone. The sound of raised voices made me freeze.

"I can't do this anymore, Curtis."

"Lily, please."

Curtis and Lily. West's parents. Lily was usually at the front desk. She was nice. She was really pretty, too, and I loved her silky dark hair.

"It's too hard." Lily sniffled, like she was crying.

Every time Mom and Dad caught me eavesdropping, I got in trouble. But I didn't move. I flattened my back against the wall and held my breath as I listened.

"What am I supposed to do?" Curtis asked. "He's my son."

Who were they talking about? West?

"I know," Lily whispered. "He's precious. He truly is. And I love him."

"But . . ." Curtis trailed off.

"I've tried. For four years, I've tried. But it's not working, and it hurts too much. I can't do this anymore."

There was a long pause, the perfect time for me to leave. But I stayed completely still, my heart hammering as I clutched my ball, making sure I didn't drop it to the floor.

"What are you saying?" Curtis asked.

"I want a divorce."

I gasped. Divorce? They were getting divorced?

"I'm going to find a job in town," Lily said. "I'll find a house."

"And West?"

"I'd like him to move with me."

"No. You can't take him from me. This is his home. This is where he belongs. Where you both belong."

Lily sniffled again, and when she lowered her voice, I couldn't make out the words.

I backed away, a sinking feeling making my stomach churn. I shouldn't have listened. That wasn't my business. I turned, ready to sneak outside, when I smacked into a body.

West's hands gripped my shoulders before I could fall on my butt. But the hold I'd had on my ball slipped. It bounced so loudly on the floor that I flinched.

The door behind us flew open, and Curtis stepped outside, a frown marring his face as he saw us in the hall.

"Sorry." I peeked up at him as I bent to snatch my ball.

He wasn't looking at me. He was staring at West, and the sadness in his gaze made me feel like crying.

Did West want to cry? If he did, his face gave nothing away.

"Go outside, son."

Lily emerged, her face splotchy. When she saw West, tears flooded her eyes, but she smiled anyway. "Hey, bud. Why don't you two go play? Let us finish talking."

"You're getting a divorce?" West looked between his parents. "And you want me to move?"

Lily's arms wrapped around her waist. "We'll talk about it, okay? We're not making any decisions today."

"I'm not moving." He scowled at them both, then turned and stormed down the hallway.

Following him seemed like the best idea, so I hurried to catch up, tripping on the toe of my new Nikes, but I caught myself on the wall before I could crash. And I didn't drop the ball again.

West was really tall now. Way taller than he'd been two years ago. When we made it outside, I had to run to catch up because he was walking so fast.

"Are you okay?" I asked.

He kept walking. "Yeah."

I knew what it was like to tell people you were okay when you really weren't. When Dad was sick, I lied all the time, even though lying was bad. Mom did too.

"Want to play soccer?"

"Nah." West walked faster, like he didn't want to be around me.

So I slowed, watching as he shoved his hands into his jeans pockets and walked down the road. Alone.

I kicked the ball back to the chalet.

Dad was still sleeping and Mom was still reading when I came inside, so I went to my room to play my Nintendo. I'd brought it only for the plane. Video games seemed like a waste of time on a vacation when we could be doing other stuff, but we weren't doing a trail ride until tomorrow.

Finally, after an hour of *Mario Kart*, Dad knocked on my door. "How about a game of horseshoes?"

"Okay." I leaped off the bed and followed him outside.

Other guests were outside, too, lounging in the chairs set up around the lawn and firepit behind the lodge. An older couple was playing cornhole. A group of men in fishing gear were visiting and drinking beers from an ice cooler.

As Dad and I played horseshoes, I kept looking for West. Was he okay? If Mom and Dad got divorced, I wouldn't be okay.

West didn't come back to the lodge. Not a single Haven was at dinner in the dining room.

It was still light outside when one of the staff members lit the evening campfire and brought out supplies for s'mores. After I ate three, I went to the cabin to get the paper I'd brought along for the trip. Sometimes I liked to color and draw. But tonight, I felt like making paper airplanes.

I was at an empty picnic table, making my first fold, when West slid onto the bench across from mine.

"What are you doing?" he asked.

"Making a paper airplane." I flipped the page over and made my second fold.

"You're doing it wrong."

"No, I'm not."

Mom had bought me a paper airplane book for my birthday. I'd been practicing this design—the flying ninja—because it was the best flyer.

West snatched a piece of paper and began folding.

His design was the dart. A classic, according to my book. "You didn't come last summer."

If he'd noticed, that made us friends, right? "Dad was too busy with work. Mom took me to London instead."

"London. Wow."

"It was fun." The telephone booths were cute. It had been exciting to explore the palaces and fancy buildings. Mom and I had spent hours shopping and even gone to a musical. "I like our Montana vacations more."

He nodded and kept folding.

"You got really tall."

West shrugged. "I guess. I'm thirteen."

"I'm eleven. How old is Jax?"

"Four."

"Oh. You probably can't play with him very much. But at least you have a brother." Being an only child was boring sometimes.

We finished our planes at almost the exact same time.

"I bet mine goes farther than yours," he said, climbing off the bench.

"No way." I followed him to the grass, then stood at his side as he lifted his plane and sent it flying.

West's plane soared straight before taking a nosedive into the lawn. "Your turn."

I pinched the bottom fold of mine, turning sideways as I lifted my arm. Then with a smooth motion and slight flick of my wrist—that was the best way to throw it according to my book—I launched my ninja into the air.

It floated way past West's dart.

His shoulders fell as he stared at them, two paper planes on soft green grass. Then without a word, he turned and walked away, past the campfire and around the lodge until I couldn't see him anymore.

I didn't see him again all week. Maybe he went to live with his mom. Maybe he just didn't want to play with me anymore. It kind of hurt my feelings, but I thought maybe West's were hurting more.

The morning that we left, while Mom and Dad were packing, I took the best paper airplane I'd made all week.

And left it in West's fort.

Chapter 7
WEST

A staff meeting.

Indya had organized a fucking staff meeting yesterday.

With our employees.

Her employees.

Curiosity was a real motherfucker. Had they reacted well to her announcement? Was the staff glad someone else was in charge? Or had they rioted against her? Had anyone walked out?

At this point, I wasn't sure which outcome I was rooting for. A good staff meeting. Or a bad.

While Indya had been conducting that meeting, I'd spent my afternoon and evening on a long, hard ride. It should have cleared my head. It should have calmed my frustration.

Instead, I'd spent those hours dwelling on the missteps, analyzing the mistakes. Those missteps and mistakes had kept me up most of the night, too, until finally, I'd crawled out of bed and brewed a pot of coffee.

Steam swirled from my mug as I sat on the steps outside my house, taking in the dawn. The air was cold against my skin and smelled of earth and pine. The grass glimmered with dew. Cattle bellowed in the distance.

It had been a while since I'd spent a morning just . . . sitting. Usually I worked at a breakneck pace from sunrise to sunset. Was that the problem? I hadn't spent enough time thinking? Reflecting?

I wished I had done things differently. I wished I had pushed harder on Dad. Fought harder. If I had known that our mistakes would line up like dominoes, waiting for one tiny push for it all to collapse, well . . .

Damn, what I wouldn't give to go back. To do things differently. To make a single other choice that would have taken us on another path.

Maybe if I had never spoken to Indya Keller, she wouldn't be holding staff meetings.

No matter how hard I tried, it was impossible to regret my time with Indya.

Was she awake? Was she in the office already? Would she be waiting for me at eight o'clock?

We both knew I wasn't going to show.

She could have that office. The desk was too short, and I was constantly knocking my knees against the edge. And the chair Courtney had bought me as a Christmas present years ago was uncomfortable as fuck.

Indya had taken that chair. The office. She'd taken it all.

Dad had played his part. We hadn't spoken since the day Indya had arrived. There was nothing to say. He'd gone behind my back to sell the ranch, and at the moment, I wasn't sure I'd ever forgive him for it.

What were the stages of grief? Denial. Yep. Anger, definitely. Bargaining—maybe I needed to revisit that one and start begging Indya to reconsider selling it back. Depression, not yet.

Acceptance? Never.

Even if she took over the ranch and resort. Even if she forced me from my home. I would never accept Indya as the owner of Haven land.

The crunch of gravel pulled my gaze to the road as Mom's white SUV crested the hill and rolled down my driveway. I shoved to my feet and set my coffee aside.

Mom waved from behind the wheel, a smile stretching across her face. Not a chance she'd be smiling if she knew about the sale.

Maybe I should have called her last night, but this was Dad's mess. I'd given him a couple of days to tell her himself. He should be the one to bear the brunt of her disappointment.

Except he'd stayed quiet, hadn't he? He was saving himself another painful conversation. Either because he knew I'd do it eventually, or he figured she'd hear about it through the rumor mill.

Most of our employees lived in Big Timber. If Mom hadn't heard yet, it was just a matter of time. Gossip traveled faster than a shooting star in our small town.

Coward. My father was a goddamn coward. How was I supposed to respect him now?

Mom deserved to hear the truth from Dad. But she'd get to hear it from me. *Fuck.*

I opened her door as soon as the car was parked. "Morning."

"Hi." She climbed out and offered her cheek for a quick kiss.

"Want coffee?"

"No. I'm going home and going to bed." Mom was dressed in teal scrubs, her dark hair pulled into a tight knot. She worked as a nurse at the hospital in Big Timber and, a year ago, had taken over the night shift in the emergency room.

It wasn't what I wanted for my mother, sitting alone in the dead of night. But the shift paid more per hour, and she was determined to save a stash for an early retirement.

"You're up early." She covered a yawn with the back of her hand, then bent to grab a stack of mail bound by a rubber band from the car. "I've been meaning to drop this off. For your father."

Dad's house was half a mile past mine. She could be there in a minute. But it wasn't the first time I'd deliver his mail because she refused to go to that house. For years, I'd been playing the go-between for my parents.

If I were as good at managing a resort as I was at keeping my parents out of each other's sight, maybe my family would still own the ground beneath my feet.

"I could have picked it up the next time I was in town." I took the bundle and tucked it under an arm.

She shrugged. "It gave me an excuse to come see you."

"Glad you did." I threw an arm around her shoulders, hauling her into my side. "Need to talk to you about something important."

"You're getting married and giving me grandbabies."

"No." I chuckled. "Sorry to disappoint."

"A mother can dream." She looped her arm around my back as we walked toward the house. "What's up?"

It took an effort to form the words and force them off my tongue. Telling her felt a lot like admitting defeat. But I'd be a shithead of a son if I let her leave without an explanation.

"Dad sold the ranch." Whoosh. Out it came.

The bandage ripped free, and the wound started gushing again.

Mom's footsteps faltered. "W-what?"

I let her go and faced her. "Dad sold the ranch. To Indya Keller."

The color drained from her face. Her hazel eyes blew wide as her jaw dropped.

There was probably a gentler way to break the news. Indya had probably given an eloquent speech at yesterday's staff meeting. But I wasn't an elegant man, and this truth was brutal.

Luckily, Mom was a strong woman. She could handle blunt.

"He didn't." The shock in her gaze shifted to fury.

"He did." I nodded. "We're broke."

She swayed a bit, and I held her again until she was steady. It didn't take long for her to recover. Then she stepped away and planted her fists on her hips. "You never told me you were having financial problems."

"I didn't realize how bad it was. You know Dad."

These were *his* problems. This was *his* business. Was it pride that made him so secretive? Or shame?

"Not good enough, West." Her glare was lethal. "You should have known."

Yes, I should have. She was right to be angry. She was right to put some blame on me.

Without Dad around to catch her wrath, I was going to receive that first wave. But I had a hunch he'd get the rest. It had been five years since my mother had spoken to my father. For this, she might break her streak.

This might be the final slice that severed their relationship for good. And I'd just handed her a knife.

"I can't believe this." She blinked rapidly, shaking her head. Mom loved this ranch. It might not be her home anymore, and she might have lived in town for years, but her heart would always be tethered to Haven land. "Are you sure?"

"I'm sure." This was real.

"West." The crack in her voice was like a punch in the gut. "He sold it? Why?"

As pissed as I was at my father, I didn't like throwing him under the bus like this, not while he wasn't here to defend himself. "I think you'd better talk to Dad."

"West Robert Haven. I'm not going to that house."

The last time she'd scolded me with my full name, I'd still been in high school. "Please, Mom. Go talk to Dad."

Her mouth pursed in a thin line. "No."

She hadn't set foot there since the day she'd moved out when I was eleven.

It was a curse, loving someone the way my parents loved each other. Mom might never forgive Dad for his drunken affair, but she hadn't stopped loving him either.

They were divorced. They had separate lives. But she loved him all the same.

They used to be on speaking terms. But five years ago, Mom and Jax had gotten into a huge blowup. Jax had stopped talking to Mom. Mom had stopped talking to Dad.

He'd taken Jax's side in the argument.

It burned to admit he was right.

Still, Mom punished Dad with her silence. And Dad punished himself with solitude.

"Are you going to talk to him?" I asked Mom.

She dropped her gaze to the dirt. "I don't know. It's not really my business anymore, is it?"

Mom had never owned the ranch. When my grandparents had passed it down to Dad, it had always been his. But Dad had never acted like her opinion didn't matter. She was the only person who stood a chance at giving him input. Hell, he didn't even listen to Grandpa these days.

But after the divorce, Dad had withdrawn from us. All of us. I doubted even Mom could get through his thick skull these days.

"You need to fix this, West. Fix it."

She might not be talking to Jax, but damn if they didn't sound alike.

"I would if I knew how."

"Figure it out." Mom retreated to her car and yanked the door open. Then she shot me a warning look.

Fix it.

Without a wave or goodbye, she turned her car around and headed down the road. The road that would take her off the ranch, not to Dad's.

I blew out a long breath, waiting until her car vanished from sight, then trudged inside, Dad's mail still tucked under my arm.

Fix it. How the hell did I fix it?

Indya. She was the only way out of this clusterfuck.

Which meant it was time for more bargaining.

~

The parking lot at the lodge was packed.

If all the license plates had been from out of state, I would have been elated to see so many guests. It had been a few years since we'd been booked to capacity.

But the cars were all from Montana. Every number started with forty, meaning they were all from Sweet Grass County, and most of the rigs I recognized from the staff.

Another meeting?

If so, this was absolutely the last place I wanted to be. But I slammed the door to my truck and headed inside, the pit of dread in my gut doubling as I opened the door.

It smelled . . . different. It smelled good. Clean, like floor polish and apples. It was brighter too. The bulbs that had burned out on the chandelier had been changed, their replacements glowing white.

The scents of syrup and coffee and bacon drifted from the open dining room doors. The clatter of silverware on plates mingled with the murmur of conversation.

"Morning, West." Deb smiled from behind the desk.

"Morning," I drawled, checking the time.

Eight fifteen. She was here at the start of her shift. And at the desk. When was the last time I'd come into the lodge and she was where she was supposed to be?

"What's going on?"

"Um, a lot." She blew out a deep breath, her cheeks puffing. She blinked too fast, like she was fighting tears. So help me, if Indya was upsetting the crew, I'd haul her ass off this ranch whether she owned it or not. "Why didn't you tell us you sold the ranch?"

It wasn't Indya making her cry. It was me. *Shit.*

"I'm sorry. It, uh, happened quickly."

Another instance when Dad should be here in my place. When he should be dealing with the fallout from his decision.

Whatever. I'd told Mom. I'd handle the staff. But not a chance in hell was I telling my grandparents. That, he'd have to do himself.

Tara came from the hallway carrying a caddy of cleaning supplies. Her round cheeks were flushed, and her auburn hair was pulled into a knot. She was smiling—Tara was always smiling. But it dropped the moment she spotted me at the desk. A snarl curled her lips.

Today was the day that all the women in my life were going to be pissed at me, wasn't it?

I held up a hand. "I'm sorry."

"That you sold the ranch and didn't have the balls to tell us?" She huffed. "You should be sorry."

"I am."

"Did you tell your mother?"

I nodded. "This morning."

"Then I'd better give her a call." Tara breezed past me, heading for the stairs.

She was Mom's best friend. Tara had always been more of an aunt than an employee. She'd started working here when I was a kid, and even though she loathed Dad for breaking Mom's heart, she'd stuck it out at the resort as head housekeeper, even after Mom had moved away.

In part, I thought Tara had stayed to act as Mom's eyes and ears. To be here for me and Jax on the days when Mom couldn't.

Tara was the best employee we could have asked for. She worked tirelessly to ensure the rooms were clean. She managed the housekeepers with kindness and fairness. But she was only one woman, and we'd stretched her budget thin. Finding housekeepers who wanted to drive out here each day and work for less than they could get at the hotel in town was basically impossible.

When I was a kid, Mom used to pitch in to clean when we were short staffed. She'd managed the resort and worked the front desk, but if there was work to be done, Lily Haven had been the first to volunteer.

The image of Indya in yellow rubber gloves, hunched over a toilet, scrubbing with fury popped into my mind.

I scoffed. Not a chance she'd get her hands dirty.

"So now what?" Deb asked. "Are you guys, like, leaving?"

"No." Maybe. I didn't have a damn clue.

"Okay, good." She sighed. "It would be so strange here without you."

Two guests walked out of the dining room, both carrying to-go cups of coffee.

"Morning," I said, dipping my chin. "How was breakfast?"

The man, a tech guy from Seattle who'd come two years in a row, patted his gut. "Delicious."

"I'm glad you enjoyed it. Plans for today?" I asked.

"Hiking," the woman answered. "We're going up Rustler's Trail."

It was one of four hiking trails we had mapped out for guests. "I rode up that way yesterday. It's beautiful. Have a nice time."

They went to the stairs, heading for their room on the second floor. I waited until they were gone before dropping my smile. "What else?" I asked Deb.

She picked up a piece of paper with a list written from top to bottom in unfamiliar handwriting. The first two items were crossed off.

Dust and mop lobby

Fix chandelier light bulbs

"She gave me this list." Deb sneered the word *she*. Apparently, Indya hadn't won her over yesterday. "And she told me that unless I was using the bathroom or taking a break, I had to be at the desk."

I snatched the list, scanning the tasks.

Sweep porch

Organize desk

Input reservations into software system

It went on and on. Somehow, in just days, Indya had identified all the items that Deb should have been doing all along. Duties I should have enforced. Instead, I'd let Deb's mistakes fly because I didn't have time to babysit her or spend my days at the lodge.

Hiring desk clerks was just as difficult as hiring housekeepers.

"Do I really have to listen to her?" Deb whined. "Aren't you still my boss?"

"Yes, you do have to listen." And as for her second question, I wasn't sure. "Is she here?"

"In your office."

"Thanks." I handed her back the list. "Lobby looks great. Smells good too."

"She threw away my candle."

"Sorry." Not sorry. Deb's candles reeked.

With a nod, I squared my shoulders and left the desk. Not in a million years would I have expected to feel uncomfortable in these halls, but every step was pained. Like my body was screaming at me to turn around. Run away.

Except this conversation was inevitable, so I kept walking.

Indya was behind the desk, wearing earbuds, her eyes locked on her laptop's screen. Her hair was a wild mess piled on top of her head. She was dressed in a cream T-shirt and jeans.

The casual clothes suited her, more than the slacks and blouses she'd been in for the past two days. The jeans and tee reminded me of the girl she'd been, the tomboy who'd loved soccer and neon green and paper airplanes and five-card draw.

Her gaze was narrowed in concentration. She nibbled on her lower lip. Her face was perfectly symmetrical, centered on the line of her classic nose.

I'd spent more time than I was willing to admit tracing the delicate line of her jaw with my fingers. With my tongue.

God, she was beautiful. Sparkling eyes. Dark, sooty lashes. Soft pink lips. Her beauty rocked me on my heels every damn time.

I leaned against the doorframe, feet firmly outside the threshold.

The movement caught Indya's attention, and her caramel eyes shifted. Her fingers remained over her keyboard. She didn't move to withdraw her earbuds.

We just stared at each other, like we were catching up from the years apart.

It had always been like this. No matter how much time had passed, all it would take was a look. The years would fast-forward, shortening, disappearing until we were right back where we'd left off.

Except not this time.

Too much had changed.

She plucked out the headphones, setting them beside her mouse. "Hi."

"Sounds like you're riding herd on my staff."

"My staff," she corrected. "They're my staff."

It was an effort to keep my mouth shut and not argue. She wasn't wrong.

"You missed the staff meeting yesterday," she said.

"You had it covered."

She waved a hand toward the folding chairs across from the desk. "Would you like to come in?"

I didn't move.

"Stubborn," she muttered, crossing her arms over her chest. "Are you here to glower, or is there a point to this visit? I'm busy."

Doing the job I'd failed to do. The words went unspoken. Again, she wasn't wrong.

"Sell me the ranch." I swallowed hard. "Please."

"Did you not hear me the other night? I'm not selling it."

"We'd work out a contract. A payment schedule."

"Not interested."

Fucking hell. "Do you always have to be so goddamn difficult?"

"That's priceless, coming from you."

"I'm trying to fix this." I tossed out a hand and crossed that invisible barrier of the doorway.

"There's nothing to fix, West. It's done. The sooner you accept it, the sooner we can turn this place around. You know what I've been doing since four o'clock this morning? Trying to figure out why every guest is charged a different price. Why two identical double-queen rooms go for two random rates. Care to enlighten me?"

"Dad doesn't raise prices for repeat customers."

Indya blinked. "So if someone has been coming here for ten years . . ."

"Then they pay the same rate they did ten years ago." It wasn't my decision. Costs had only gone up. But after Mom had left, it was something Dad had been adamant about. And I'd had bigger battles to fight.

Besides, we hadn't raised prices that much in the past ten years. A bit here and there, but the difference wasn't outrageous.

"When was the last time you compared your rates to other resorts? They're charging two, almost three times your prices."

"I don't know, Indya." I dragged a hand through my hair. "Dad set the prices. He felt like they were fair. When I told him we should bump them up a bit, he told me it wasn't my decision."

And I hadn't pushed. I hadn't made a strong enough argument to change his mind.

Instead, I'd kept my focus on the ranch. If she wanted to know about the cattle market and current operating costs per head, I could give her numbers for days. But I was half-removed from the resort, leaving Dad in control. Just the way he liked it.

Just the way *I* liked it.

But if we really were undervalued by that much, why weren't we overrun with guests? Probably because we were falling apart.

We'd marked two cabins as unavailable because they needed some major overhaul. Flooring. Roofs. Furniture. None of us had the time to do construction. And we hadn't had the extra cash either.

Balancing on a tight budget was a double-edged sword. Yeah, we could have rented out refurbished cabins. But it would take years to recuperate the costs and turn it into a profit. So we'd decided to just shut them down.

Given the flat look on Indya's face, she would have made different decisions. "Would you come inside and sit down? You're making it weird by standing in the hallway."

I stayed put.

"Fine." Her nostrils flared. "I'm taking over all operations for the resort. Effective immediately, every decision must be run past me. If an employee comes to you with a question, I'd appreciate it if you'd send them my way."

"They're used to asking me or Dad. You're not going to change habits overnight."

"All I'm asking is that you send them to me."

"Look, we might not have done everything perfectly, but we have been running this place for decades. I'm not going to—"

"Stop." She sliced a hand through the air, cutting me off. This was a different look for her, bold and in charge. It was sexy. Not that I'd admit that, to her or myself. "Stop fighting me."

"Then stop trying to run my business."

Her expression gentled, and before she spoke, I knew what she was going to say. "It's not yours. Not anymore."

No, it wasn't, was it? How long would it take for the reality of this to sink in? More than a couple of days, apparently.

What was happening? What were we going to do?

"What about our homes?" What about the house where Grandma and Grandpa had planned to spend their final years? What about my childhood home?

"I didn't take them," she said. "You left before your dad could get into the specifics, but you all have your homes and twenty acres around them."

Thank fuck. The relief was crippling. "At least Dad did something right."

She dropped her gaze to the desk. "I'd like you to stay and manage the ranch."

"Stay."

"I don't know anything about cattle."

I scoffed. "No shit."

"You'd be paid a salary. I'd leave the decisions to your discretion."

A job offer. She was making me a job offer. I opened my mouth, about to tell her to shove it, when she held up a hand.

"Don't tell me to shove it."

This woman. She'd always been good at reading me.

"Think about it. Please."

"Fine," I muttered. "What about the resort? Will you hire a manager too?"

"No. I'm staying. I'll manage it myself."

She was staying. I wished I didn't like the sound of that. "What about your life? Don't you need to get back to it? To your husband?"

It was a dig, but damn it, I wanted to know what had happened with *Blaine*. Why she wasn't wearing that monstrosity of a diamond ring.

Indya glanced to the window, giving the slightest headshake. "No. I don't have anywhere else to be. And as far as a job, this is it for the foreseeable future. I'm not here on vacation. This isn't a hobby or a phase. I'm moving here. The rest of my things arrive in two days."

Moving to Montana. Once upon a time, that would have been a dream. Now, I wasn't so sure.

"And where exactly are you going to be living?"

Big Timber. *Please, say Big Timber.* It would be so much easier if she was sleeping thirty miles away.

"Beartooth Chalet. There are only two reservations for the rest of the summer. I've made arrangements for those to be moved, so the chalet is mine."

Beartooth Chalet. My molars ground so hard they nearly cracked. Was this a joke? Was she trying to torture me?

"It's the nicest property on the ranch," I told her. "It should be for guests."

Indya stayed quiet, her gaze locked on mine in a silent dare for me to forbid it. We both knew it wasn't my decision. And she'd just played her cards. If I wanted to run the ranch, I'd have to butt out of resort affairs.

Sure, I could leave. I could find another job somewhere else.

We both knew I wasn't going anywhere.

Trapped. I was fucking trapped in whatever game she was playing.

Without a word, I turned and walked away. I breezed past Deb, whose fingers were flying over the keyboard of the front desk's computer. The moment I was out the door, I sucked in a deep breath to keep my head from spinning.

My gaze shifted to the Beartooth Chalet.

It was the best cabin on the ranch. I'd made sure of it. If there was anything extra, I'd poured it into that building. A new roof. Updated plumbing. Fresh paint. New hardwood flooring.

Most of that work, I'd done myself in the winter when the resort was slow.

For Indya.

I'd wanted that cabin to be nice in case one day she came back.

I should have saved that money.

And let the Beartooth rot.

Chapter 8
INDYA

"Vegetarian?" The chef's eyes bulged. "This is Montana."

"I'm aware of our location. We need at least one vegetarian option on the menu for every meal."

Reid scoffed. "I won't cook vegetarian."

This man was so freaking difficult. He must have taken lessons from West. Reid should count himself lucky that I wasn't requiring a vegan option too.

We'd had this argument every day for the past week. I'd asked him to revise the menu, and each afternoon when I came into the kitchen to check on his progress, he'd tell me no.

I was done debating.

"Either you add a vegetarian option, or you won't cook at all. This is nonnegotiable. Unless the reason you're dragging your feet is because you're unable to come up with meatless recipes." It was a baited statement.

He took it without a blink. "I can cook anything."

"Great. Then tomorrow, I expect to see the updated menu." And if he wouldn't cooperate, then he'd be replaced. I didn't have a clue how to feed the guests, but somehow, I'd figure it out. If I had to beg Mom's personal chef to spend a summer in Montana, so be it.

Reid huffed and threw a mixing bowl in the sink, the metal clanking against the other dishes.

I took that as my cue to leave. Not bothering with a goodbye, I slipped through the swinging door that led to the dining room.

There was still an hour before dinner, but the waitstaff bustled around the room, setting places and prepping for guests. The bartender, Lisa, was behind the bar in the corner, setting up her station.

She stilled when she spotted me and sent a scowl sailing across the room.

I didn't have the energy for her today. She hated me because . . . well, I wasn't exactly sure why. Lisa and I'd had a single conversation, in which I'd told her I'd like to bring in some different wines. She'd sneered and told me their current selection was fine.

If *fine* meant cheap and bitter.

Her hatred probably wasn't about the wine. I was fairly certain Reid was turning everyone against me, the mutinous traitor, and she'd sided with her boss.

Apparently it didn't matter that I was her boss's boss.

The lines of loyalty had been drawn long before I'd returned to Montana, and my side of that line was severely outnumbered. But I kept trying. I'd keep trying.

There was a job to do. Dad always said that running a business was a lonely job. You didn't get the luxury of friends when you were the captain of the ship.

So I'd endure the scowls and glares and sneers.

I'd survive it all until this year was over.

I walked over to a waiter setting out water goblets. "Hey, Ron."

"Uh, hey, Miss Keller." Ron was young, in his early twenties, and always had a deer-in-the-headlights look when I spoke to him.

"You can call me Indya," I corrected.

"'Kay." He nodded, his mop of blond hair falling into his eyes.

"Would you mind bringing a dinner to the Beartooth Chalet tonight instead of my office?" If I was going to eat alone, tonight I was going to do so in my pajamas.

"What would you like?" he asked.

"Whatever the special is would be great."

For the past week, I'd ordered Reid's special every night to get a feel for his cooking. He was a good chef. His dishes had flavor and character. But there wasn't much variety. Every special this week had been beef and potatoes. There was a single chicken option on the menu, no fish, and no vegetarian.

"What time?" Ron asked.

"Just bring it over whenever you have a moment. Don't prioritize it over serving the guests."

"All right."

"Thanks." I gave him a smile that went unreturned, then headed for the lobby, only making it two steps before Deb's voice drifted into the dining room.

"She's such a bitch."

Nice. There was no doubt she was referring to me.

"Sorry, babe," her boyfriend said.

What was his name? Didn't it start with a *C*? Allegedly, he was an employee. But he hadn't shown up at the staff meeting or subsequently come to find me to complete his employee paperwork.

So as of now, he wasn't on the payroll. And if he ever bothered to approach me about his job, I wouldn't be extending an offer.

Over the past week, I'd rehired every person on staff, so they worked for my corporation. There were people who may or may not work out, like Reid, but I hadn't let anyone go.

Deb's boyfriend would be the exception.

And unless Deb's attitude changed, she was going to be the first person I fired. The six-month probationary period I'd instituted for all employees was going to be my saving grace.

I squared my shoulders and emerged from the dining room.

Deb at least had the decency to look guilty as she smiled too widely. "Oh, hey, Indya."

"Hi." I shifted my attention to the boyfriend, extending a hand. "Indya Keller."

71

He jerked up his chin as we shook. "Casey Lawrence."

"Nice to meet you."

When I glanced to Deb, she was noticeably paler. "We were just talking about, um, Tara."

She was a horrible liar.

"Ah." It was on the tip of my tongue to reprimand her for doing that at the desk, where any guest could overhear, but tonight, I didn't have the energy. She knew she'd been busted, and she'd get away with calling me a bitch. For now. "Good night."

"See you in the morning." Deb's voice was too bright, especially considering I'd declined her request for a two-week vacation. Probably why she was calling me a bitch.

That, or because I made her work.

That girl didn't want to do anything. I'd been hounding her all week to finish the list I'd given her *last* week. But beyond cleaning the lobby, changing a few light bulbs, and updating the reservation system, she'd done next to nothing else. For a week.

I had help wanted ads in the local paper and online, but they'd only gone up yesterday. For now, Deb was better than the alternative—me. I didn't have time to sit at the desk all day.

The weight on my shoulders felt heavier than it had this morning. Heavier than it had yesterday or the day before that or the day before that. It was so heavy that picking up my feet was difficult. I shuffled more than walked from the lodge to the Beartooth.

The moment I walked through the chalet's door, I went straight for the bottle of wine I'd opened last night and poured myself a glass.

Coffee would be the smarter choice. There was still a pile of work to plow through before the end of my day, and the sun was already dipping toward the mountain horizon beyond the cabin's windows.

Never in my life had I been this tired. Never in my life had I worked this hard. My entire body ached. At one point this afternoon, before I'd caught a second—or maybe it had been the third—wind, I'd struggled to keep my eyes open. Whatever pace was faster than frantic, that's where my dial was set.

A year. I just had to endure this for a year. Maybe less, if everything went according to plan.

My attorneys had advised me to keep my long-term plans private. To the world, I was in Montana to stay. Indefinitely.

Only a handful of people knew that in a year, I'd be gone. To where, I had no clue. But gone from Montana.

In the meantime, I'd learn to live with the exhaustion and anxiety.

Maybe I'd feel better if West decided to take the job I'd offered.

He had to stay. He couldn't leave. Somehow, I had to convince him to run the ranch and stay.

Which would be easier if he weren't avoiding me. I hadn't seen him once this past week—not that I'd gone searching.

I was giving him time to let this new reality sink in. And meanwhile, I was working myself to the bone.

For the past week, I'd worked nonstop to learn every aspect of the resort's operation. From the finances to marketing to housekeeping to guest services, I'd crammed my brain so full of information it was about to explode.

I'd earned every sore muscle and weary ache in my bones.

On Monday, I'd shadowed Deb at the reservation desk. That was probably when she'd decided I was a bitch, because each time I'd asked her to explain in detail her process, she'd get annoyed.

Tuesday, I'd spent a day cleaning rooms with Tara and doing laundry. Of all the employees, she seemed the most receptive, though maybe that was just wishful thinking. But she had seemed surprised when I'd volunteered to scrub the toilets.

Wednesday, I'd stood in the corner of the kitchen, watching the chef and waitstaff prepare and serve the evening meal. The corner had been the safest place, far from the knives. When I'd told the chef he had to come up with a vegetarian menu, he'd told me he hated me.

Yesterday, I'd gone on a trail ride with Wyatt. He'd been a guide here when I was a kid—not that he remembered me. But it had been comforting to see a familiar face. Wyatt was our only guide at the moment. Jax was normally on the rotation, but he hadn't taken a group since before I'd come to Montana.

I owed him a phone call. I owed him a job offer. But as with West, I was giving Jax time.

Next week, I'd seek them out. Until then, I was focused on my own to-do list. Any hour not tagging along with a staff member, I'd been in the office, poring over plans and budgets.

I'd already hired a contractor out of Big Timber to renovate three cabins. He'd told me his schedule was packed for the summer, and I'd have to wait until next spring. Then I'd written him a check, paying three times the current market rates.

He'd started work this morning.

With any luck, we'd have the cabins back in the reservation rotation before the end of the month. Which was critical, considering I'd taken over the Beartooth.

It was selfish, staying in the nicest cabin. But this chalet was mine. If I was going to stay on the ranch and turn the resort into a profitable business, then this would be my home.

Even if that meant facing old memories.

At least it wasn't exactly the same. The other cabins might have fallen into disrepair, but someone had taken care with the Beartooth.

The cabin's old couch had been replaced with a new piece. The rich brown leather was supple and soft. Studded with brass fittings, the style fit the rustic decor.

Dad would hate that new couch. It would be too firm for his afternoon naps.

He'd like the other changes, though. The stainless steel refrigerator was new. The black faucet fixtures added a modern touch with clean lines. And the white oak herringbone floors were a dream.

Had West been the mastermind behind these changes? Did he ever think about this cabin? Did he ever think about us?

I did.

Every day. Every hour.

It was beautiful torture. Torment I had to endure for only a year.

Then I could leave Montana, for good this time.

I carried my wineglass to the living room window, staring out to the meadows and mountains. Then I pulled my phone from my jeans pocket, about to call and check in with Dad when a knock came at the door.

Dinner. Bless you, Ron. It was earlier than I'd expected, but I was starving.

The few groceries I'd bought on last weekend's trip to town had dwindled. Another run to the store was on tomorrow's list.

My stomach growled as I rushed across the room. Except it wasn't Ron on my porch.

It was West.

"Hi." I tucked a lock of hair behind my ear. The last time I'd looked in the mirror was hours ago, and I was probably a mess. The little bit of makeup I'd put on at dawn, enough that I wouldn't look like a corpse, had long since worn away.

"Hey." He dipped his chin, the brim of his black cowboy hat tilting.

How did he do that, look better and better each time I saw him? The ends of his hair were damp, not from a shower but from sweat. His gray pearl-snap shirt was rumpled from a day of work and wear, its sleeves rolled up his forearms. The collar was undone a couple of buttons, revealing a hint of dark hair that dusted his chest. There was a sheen of sweat on his face, and he smelled like horses and wind and masculine spice.

He'd worked all day, hadn't he? Of course he'd keep working. That was the type of man he was. The type who would do it for the land, for the animals, for his family's legacy, whether he was being paid or not.

For me, the physical labor was a new experience. For West, this was life.

It wasn't fair that he'd pushed so hard. That in the end, his hard work hadn't mattered.

Curtis had sold the ranch anyway.

I set my wineglass on the table beside the door, then waited. West would speak when he was ready.

It took nearly two minutes. I counted the seconds as they passed.

"I don't know if I can work for you." His throat bobbed as he swallowed and reached for his back pocket, then took out a fold of white papers. "But I'll try."

I took the papers and opened them to see the employee code of conduct I'd printed for each employee to complete.

West's name was signed at the bottom.

My heart splattered on the pretty herringbone floors. My hand trembled with the urge to crumple the pages into a ball and toss them in the trash.

This wasn't right. This wasn't fair. He shouldn't have signed this paper.

West stared past the porch and into the distance. He looked tired. Humiliated. He'd come here to deliver this paperwork so he wouldn't have to bring it to the lodge.

The papers in my grip felt slimy. A wash of shame rolled over my shoulders. This was wrong. This was all wrong.

I was here to do the right thing.

Except it was all wrong.

I was doing it wrong.

Dad would have handled this better. He would have known what to say.

Why had I made West a job offer? Why had I phrased it like that? I had no intention of treating West like the other employees. This was his land, regardless of if my name was on the title or not.

But my name *was* on the title.

And I'd made it a point to remind West of that fact, hadn't I? He'd made me mad last week, so I'd tossed his family's failure in his face.

But he was staying. I'd needed him to stay. And he was staying.

"We'll work out the details later, yeah?" He took a step away.

I tore my gaze from the paper. "Wait."

He waited.

"Why?"

West sighed, his shoulders falling. "Because you need help."

Yes. Yes, I did.

"This is my home. If the only way I get to stay is through this"—he waved a hand to the page in mine—"then this is what we'll do."

His voice dripped with disdain.

West would hate me before that year was over, wouldn't he?

I'd been irritating West since we were kids. Since the days his father had insisted he entertain me on our vacations to Montana. As I'd grown older, I'd learned to enjoy pushing his buttons. I'd liked leaving a lasting impression so that when those trips were over, I wasn't immediately forgotten.

But the thought of him truly *hating* me made my insides churn.

The bridge between us was crumbling. I wouldn't—couldn't—let it fall.

"Your staff respects you. They value your input. They look to you as the leader here."

He crossed his arms over his chest. "So?"

"I'm not making many friends." I shrugged. "Not that I'm here to make friends. I'm fairly certain Deb is plotting my murder. Reid will likely poison my next meal. But I'm trying to help. I'm pushing them to make some changes, and they don't like it. It would go a long way if they knew you supported me."

He arched an eyebrow.

"If you pretended to support me."

A blink. That was all he gave me. *Stubborn, stubborn man.*

"You said you want to fix this."

He nodded. "I do."

"West," I whispered. God, he was going to hate this. It had to be said. And he'd hate it. He'd hate me for it. "You can't fix it. But I can."

A flash of rage crossed his face. Those hazel eyes blazed. His arms dropped to his sides, and he spun around, then stomped down the stairs.

"West, please." I chased after him, stopping on the last stair as he whirled around. It put us eye to eye.

"What, Indya? Just let me go."

Never. No matter how hard I tried, I could never let him go.

And damn it, my life would be so much easier if I could just watch him walk away.

"There are things to say," I said. "Things I've put off too long."

"Not tonight. I'm taking your job. I'm filling out your forms. I'm swallowing my pride. But I've hit the limit for today."

"Please," I whispered.

It wasn't the first time I'd said *please* from this very spot.

Like the memory slapped him in the face, he winced.

But he didn't go.

"I'm on your side, believe it or not."

"I don't." He scoffed. "If you were on my side, you would have come to me before buying this place out from under my feet."

"You're putting all the blame on me? What about your dad? He sold it."

"I'm aware he sold it." West tossed a hand to the side. "I'm very fucking aware. But you could have come to me, Indya. After all we've been through, you should have come to me first."

No, I couldn't have gone to him first.

The sale was inevitable. Even if West had been able to squash the sale, if he had convinced Curtis to back out of the deal, it wouldn't have changed anything. Within a year, they would have been in over their heads with the bank. Foreclosure would have been next. And there was no way they would have been able to fend off the sharks.

"I'm sorry." For the betrayal. For the pain this was causing.

He pulled off his hat and dragged a hand through his hair. "What do you want from me?"

Everything. The answer to that question used to be *everything.*

Now, I just wanted him not to hate me.

When I didn't answer, he stared.

I stared back. I stared because I knew how fleeting it was to see his face. How much I missed it when he was gone.

Collisions on crossroads.

West and I were nothing but collisions on crossroads.

Sooner or later, our paths would drift apart again. We never seemed to be going in the same direction, and this time was no different.

He'd stay because he belonged.

I'd leave because I didn't.

West broke away first, dropping his gaze. Then he turned and, without another word, walked across the flagstone path around the chalet until he was out of sight.

I retreated inside, fetching my wineglass to sip my cabernet. Then I stood at the living room window, watching as the sun dipped below the jagged mountain edge. When the sky was a riot of pink and purple and gold, I took out my phone, then pulled up Dad's name. It went straight to his voice mail.

"Hey, Daddy." Maybe it was the exhaustion. Maybe I was just being emotional. But the sting of tears made me glad I only had to leave a quick message. Then I could go cry into my pillow. "You're probably watching TV. I hope whatever show you picked is making you laugh. Just wanted to say I love you. Talk to you later."

I tucked my phone away and drained my wineglass. Then I balled up West's code of conduct for the trash and went to bed.

Ron never did show up with my dinner.

Chapter 9
WEST

You can't fix it. But I can.

Indya knew how to deliver a blow. Every time I replayed her words from last night, they hit square in the chest.

Maybe they wouldn't have hurt so much if they weren't true.

I couldn't fix this. But she could.

From the moment she'd offered me that job last week, I'd spent countless hours trying to see a way forward. To weigh my limited options. And the best solution I'd come up with was . . . nothing.

Maybe the way I fixed this was to let Indya take control. To become her employee and take my marching orders. Because we'd had our chance, and we'd failed.

Would Indya?

No. She wouldn't fail.

The stubborn, arrogant part of me wanted to walk away. To let her handle everything on her own. But when it came to Indya Keller, she'd always been the one to walk away. Not me.

I couldn't fix this.

But she could.

If I wanted the Crazy Mountain Cattle Resort to succeed, it wouldn't be through my efforts. Not anymore. Was this acceptance? It had taken only a week for me to get to that last stage of grief. Should it have taken longer? Probably. But I was too tired to fight it, and there was too much work to be done. Work that I wasn't going to do all on my own.

I raised my fist and pounded on Jax's front door. Again. I'd been knocking on this damn door for five minutes.

"Jax!" I bellowed. His truck was parked outside, and I was sure he was home.

"Coming!" His voice was muffled as footsteps pounded my way. Then he ripped the door open with one hand as the other zipped up the fly on his jeans. His torso was bare besides the fingernail scratches raking over his pecs.

"Nice hickey."

"Shit." He slapped at his neck, like he could bat it away. Then he scrubbed both hands over his face. "What's up?"

"Did you just roll out of bed? It's five o'clock."

"Yeah." His voice was hoarse, and he reeked of booze. "Got in late last night. Or early this morning."

"Shower. Then get your ass to the lodge, and fill out the employee paperwork. There's a ride tomorrow at first light, and you need to be the guide."

"What?" He squinted at me.

"Work, Jax. You need to get back to work. Wyatt can't manage it on his own."

"You want me to work for her?"

"Yes. For her."

He scoffed and crossed his arms over his chest. "Why?"

"What else do you have to do? Drink and chase women?"

"Well . . . yeah."

"For fuck's sake, Jax. At least you're honest." I'd forgotten what it was to be twenty-two. To shuck your responsibilities for a good time and a quick fuck. But Jax could party on his own time.

"Why would I work for her?" he asked.

"Because she needs help."

"Then she can hire it."

"She did. She hired me."

He blinked. "Wait. What? You're working for her?"

"Yes. I'm going to manage the ranch."

"Are you fucking kidding me?"

"No."

His jaw dropped. "Why?"

For Indya. That answer would lead to more questions than I was willing to answer, so I gave him a different version. "I don't know what the hell Dad was thinking. I haven't talked to him. But this is our home. This is our land."

"Technically, it's—"

"I don't give a fuck about technicalities. I'm not leaving this ranch. I can't. Can you? Can you walk away?"

He stayed quiet.

"Could you live here and watch someone else work our property, manage our cattle, ride our horses?"

His jaw flexed as he considered my words.

"It's not just the ranch. Think about the resort. The employees. Tara has worked here for as long as I can remember. So has Wyatt. Are you really going to leave them to do their own jobs, plus ours?"

Jax loved Wyatt. And Tara. They were family, and I knew before he answered what he'd say. We couldn't abandon our responsibilities, because it would royally screw them over.

He blew out a deep breath. "No."

"Neither can I. And that's why I'll give her a chance. That's why I'll work for her."

"Damn it." Jax groaned. "Did you read that stuff she's making everyone agree to?"

"Yes."

The employee code of conduct was . . . thorough. By signing it, I'd agreed not to pursue romantic relationships with guests or take ranch equipment for personal use or disparage the resort on social media. The document had clearly been drafted by lawyers and was over the top, as far as I was concerned. But maybe we needed a little over the top. So I'd signed the damn thing and taken it to her last night.

"This sucks," Jax muttered.

"It does."

"I heard she's a real bitch."

"Watch your fucking mouth," I snapped, pointing at his nose. "Only warning I'll give you. You do not talk about her like that."

"Whoa." He held up his hands, looking at me like I'd grown two heads. "Jesus, West. I was just relaying what Deb said at the bar last night."

"I don't give a shit what Deb says. You'll respect Indya. Understood?"

He nodded. "Fine. Fuck."

"Good. Now get in the shower. You stink."

"Thanks, brother." He stepped away from the door to slam it in my face.

But I was already gone, walking away from the small cabin where Jax lived. It was one of two cabins my grandparents had built ages ago for employees. At one point, when my dad was a kid, they'd had two employees who'd lived on the ranch full time.

We hadn't had employees who'd wanted to live out here since, and the cabins had been mostly forgotten. Until Jax had come home from college and decided to take one over as his place. The other was still forgotten, but Jax had been working hard to fix up his house.

This spring, I'd helped him put on a new roof, and he'd just finished remodeling the bathroom.

He'd need money to finish his projects. Money he could earn from Indya.

Because who the hell knew what Dad was planning to do now that he was a multimillionaire.

My stomach knotted as I climbed into my truck. The last place I wanted to go today was my father's house, but I'd delayed this visit long enough.

With my elbow propped on my open window, I bounced along the dirt road that led to Dad's house. The evening breeze was cool as it blew across my face.

It had been surprisingly easy to explain to Jax why I was going to work for Indya. I'd meant every word. When I could manage to spend more than five minutes around her, maybe I'd tell her too.

God, she'd looked tired last night. I'd never seen such dark circles under her eyes. And sad. She'd looked so damn sad.

I'd had to leave the Beartooth before giving in to the temptation to haul her into my arms.

Where was Blaine? Shouldn't her husband be here, arms ready, when she had a rough week?

Not my problem. I had enough to worry about without that mess, so I shoved it aside and continued down the road, then pulled up to Dad's.

I'd expected to find him inside, clutching a bottle of whiskey, drinking his sorrows away like Jax. Instead, he was mowing the lawn.

The buzz of the engine and the scent of cut grass filled the air.

When he spotted me, he slowed the rider to a stop and killed the motor. When he hopped out of the seat and picked up a glass from the cup holder, the amber liquid inside sloshed.

Ah. There was the booze.

"Drinking and driving is illegal," I said as he walked over.

"Then I guess you can finish with the lawn." He gulped the last shot, the slight curl of his lips the only sign that it burned as he swallowed.

"You look like shit," I said.

Dad's hair was greasy, like he hadn't bothered with a shower all week. His whiskers were thick, and the circles under his eyes were as dark as Indya's.

"I feel like shit. Might as well look the part." He trudged to the house, then held open the screen door for me to follow.

I grimaced as I stepped inside. What the fuck had died in here? The burnt, putrid scent stung my nose. "What the hell happened?"

"Forgot a pizza in the oven this morning," he said, walking through the entryway.

"Pizza for breakfast. Okay."

This was a man who'd insisted on eggs, bacon, and toast every day of the week. Guess he'd changed his diet now that he was retired.

I followed him into the living room, then bypassed the couch for the windows, popping them all open to let the breeze clear out the stench. "Dad—"

The sound of a bottle's lid spinning cut me off.

Dad was in his recliner, about to refill his glass from a bottle of Jack. I snatched it away before a drop landed in the tumbler.

"Hey," he protested.

"You've had long enough to sulk. Time's up. There's work to do."

Dad blinked. "What are you talking about?"

"Tomorrow I want to get the cattle moved to the north meadow. Jax is taking guests riding all day. So you get to help me."

"Excuse me?"

"What was unclear about that?"

His forehead furrowed. "You're working for her? Both of you?"

"Well, you might have been paid millions, but I sure as fuck wasn't. And I'm not about to let my ranch and my cattle suffer because of your decision."

"It's not your ranch."

"So I've been told," I muttered. "Indya doesn't know how to run a ranch. It's not fair to the animals living here to force her to learn. So unless you want to watch the cattle die, seven o'clock tomorrow. Be ready to go."

Indya wouldn't let the cattle die. But I also wasn't giving up control. She'd have to hire someone else to come help, and I didn't feel like having another person waltz onto our property and fuck it up.

"I'm not helping." He held out a hand. "Give me back my whiskey."

"Not a chance."

There was probably another bottle in the kitchen, but he could get his ass out of that chair and get it when I was gone.

Dad sighed, sagging into the chair. He looked smaller than I'd ever seen him before. "It's good you're working. Staying. Helping Indya get on her feet."

Was he drunk? He wasn't slurring, but damn, he was all over the place. "So you're glad that I'm helping her out. But you refuse. Do I have that right?"

He lifted a shoulder. "Have you, uh, talked to your mother?"

"Not since last week. She brought out a stack of mail." Which was still on my kitchen counter.

"Did you tell her?"

"Yes."

He gulped. "How'd she take it?"

"Not well."

Mom hadn't spoken to me since.

"Thanks for telling her," Dad said. "I would have, but . . ."

But she wouldn't have given him the chance.

"Your grandparents have disowned me." He let out a dry laugh and turned his gaze to the windows. It didn't hide the sheen of tears. "Can't say that I blame them. They aren't speaking to me at the moment. Do me a favor, and swing by from time to time? Make sure they don't need anything."

"All right." I went to the couch, then sat on the edge with my elbows to my knees. "What are your plans for the money?"

We'd owed the bank, but not fifteen million dollars.

"Pay off our debts. Set up your grandparents so they'll be comfortable as they get older."

"Well, at least we've got our homes and some acreage. That should have made them happy. Glad you were able to negotiate that with Indya."

He shook his head. "I didn't negotiate that. She presented it with her initial offer."

"What? It was her idea?"

"Yeah."

What the hell? I'd assumed it was Dad. She'd let me make that assumption. Why?

If she hadn't done that, would Dad have pushed for it? I wasn't sure I wanted the answer to that question, so I didn't ask.

"Once everything is paid, you and Jax will get the money. Congratulations. You're rich."

"I was rich before." Rich in everything but cash.

Dad closed his eyes. "If there'd been another way—"

"I know." I wasn't here to punish Dad. He was managing that all on his own. "If I can convince Indya to sell the ranch back to me, even just a part of it, I'll need some of that money."

He shrank even deeper into that chair. "She won't sell it back."

"She might."

He hummed. The hum I'd heard my whole life.

The hum that meant this conversation was over. He had his mind made up, and nothing I said would change his mind.

What wasn't he telling me? What had happened during their negotiations for the sale that made him say that? Had she mentioned specific plans?

"Dad—"

"Let it go, West. It's done. Trust me." He shoved out of the chair and disappeared from the room. A moment later, his bedroom door slammed shut.

Trust me.

He'd said that the day Indya had shown up too.

Did he even know what it meant to trust?

I took Dad's whiskey when I left the house, a new wave of anger coming with me as I stormed outside. So that was it? Let it go?

Why wouldn't he want me to buy the ranch back? He'd never loved that side of the operation. He'd always preferred spending days at the resort, taking guests on rides, and bullshitting with visitors over dinner and drinks.

Maybe that was why I'd always focused on the ranching operation. It was the area where I'd had some semblance of control, most days.

How fucked up was it that I'd probably have more autonomy running the ranch for Indya than I would for my own father?

After I climbed in my truck, I slammed the door too hard, then started the engine and drove home. It was Saturday. The tradition was to spend the evening at the lodge, entertaining guests and helping kids cook hot dogs over the campfire. Reid would set up a burger bar, and after dark, we'd roast s'mores.

I didn't want a hot dog or a burger or a s'more. Dad's whiskey seemed rather appealing, though.

"Damn him." I was about to go inside and work on tomorrow's hangover when my phone rang, the chime filling the cab. "Hey, Tara."

"Hi, West. You got a minute?"

"Of course."

"It's about Indya."

"Figured as much." I pinched the bridge of my nose. Did Tara not feel like signing the code of conduct? "What's up?"

"She hired Jonathan Lee to remodel the cabins."

Son of a bitch. "Are you sure?"

"Yeah. I saw him myself when I was leaving tonight. He was at one of the cabins."

"Shit." I sighed. "I'll handle it. Appreciate the heads-up." I ended the call and immediately pulled up Jonathan's number. He answered on the second ring.

"West."

"You're not welcome on my property. I made that clear the last time we spoke. Don't come back."

"Is it your property? According to Indya Keller, that's her cabin I'm remodeling."

"I'll say it one last time. You're not welcome." Before he could reply, I ended the call and pulled up Mom's number.

"Tara already called me," she answered. "I know about Jonathan."

"I'll handle it. It won't be an issue."

"Okay." She sighed. "I can't believe she hired him."

"How would she have known, Mom?" Indya wasn't from around here. She didn't have any context to know who to hire and who to avoid.

"She could have asked around. Tara would have told her in five seconds not to hire that asshole."

Yeah, Indya could have asked. She probably would have asked me if I'd bothered to meet with her.

"Just . . . put it out of your mind. I'll take care of it."

"All right. You doing okay?"

"Not especially. You?"

"No. Still reeling over all this, you know?"

"Yeah, I know. I'll call you later."

"Bye."

With that call finished, I put my phone on the dash, leaning my head against the rest. "Shit."

While I'd called Mom, Jonathan had probably already dialed Indya. I'd have to explain why I'd just fired her contractor.

So much for that drink.

I put the truck in drive and sped to the resort, then parked in front of the Beartooth beside Indya's Defender.

The sound of guests laughing at the campfire drifted from behind the lodge. Chances were, Indya was with the guests, but I went to the cabin first, not wanting to get caught up in small talk if I could avoid it.

I marched up the steps and rapped my knuckles on the door.

Silence. I knocked again. "Indya."

Nothing. Damn. Guess I'd be making it to the campfire tonight, after all. I turned, about to make my way over to the lodge, when the door cracked open at my back.

"West?" Indya was dressed in a chemise the color of blueberries. Her hair was undone, the curls cascading around her shoulders.

God, that hair. I used to love threading it through my fingers. Was that what she slept in? Nightgowns? The few times I'd slept in her bed, we hadn't bothered with pajamas. There hadn't been much sleep either.

It was strange, discovering a part of her that I didn't know. Blaine had known this part. He'd gotten the Indya who wore sexy negligees that barely covered the curve of her ass.

"What's wrong?" She opened the door wider, the night air pebbling her nipples beneath the satin.

I swallowed hard, forcing my gaze to an invisible spot over her head. "Jonathan Lee. You hired him."

"Yes." She stood taller, her expression sharpening. "He's remodeling the cabins."

"Not anymore. He's not welcome here."

"But—"

"He's got an unhealthy obsession with my mother. She has no interest in him, but he's been relentless. Calling and texting so often she changed her number. Started showing up at the hospital while she was working. He'd send her expensive, inappropriate gifts like jewelry and clothes and lingerie. It's gone on for about a year. Every time, she'd send the stuff back and tell him to stop. He didn't stop. About four months ago, he came to her house drunk. Tried to force his way inside. She got a restraining order. But since she doesn't live out here . . ."

"It doesn't apply," Indya said, finishing my sentence. "I'll take care of it. Please pass along my apologies to your mother. I didn't know."

"Thanks."

She closed her eyes, her shoulders sinking. "I need a new contractor. Any recommendations?"

"I'll make a few calls. A couple buddies of mine have businesses in the area. They might be able to fit in a side job or spare one of their craftsmen. I'll have them reach out to you."

"Thanks." She eased away from the door, about to slip inside, when I stopped her.

"Why didn't you tell me it was your idea for the twenty acres and our houses?"

She lifted a shoulder. "I'm sure your dad would have asked for it. So I just made it part of the deal from the start."

Would Dad have asked for it? I hated that I had my doubts. "Thank you."

"Of course." She gave me a sad smile. "Good night, West."

My hand reached out without permission, gently wrapping around her elbow before she could disappear. "Indy."

Her eyes lifted slowly.

There were questions to ask. Things to learn. Why had she come back? Why had she bought the ranch? Where was Blaine?

"Is this what you wear to sleep in every night?" It seemed more important than the other questions.

My hand released her elbow, and my fingers drifted over her skin, trailing up and over her shoulder to the thin strap that would take no more than a tug to snap.

"Yes." Her breath hitched as I looped a finger beneath the satin strand.

Our gazes clashed, and as my eyes searched hers, the years between us seemed to unfold, swirling around us like a tornado, dragging us into the past.

To the days when I'd been a young fool. And she'd been brighter than the sun and the stars.

I wasn't sure which of us moved first. Maybe me. Maybe Indya.

One minute I was lost in those caramel eyes; the next, my hands were in that wild blonde hair, and my mouth was crushed against hers.

A single lick across her bottom lip, and she parted. Our tongues tangled in that familiar, beautiful dance. She tasted the same. Sweet, like summer strawberries on a woolen blanket in a mountain meadow.

Damn, this woman. How I'd missed her mouth.

We sank into the kiss, clinging to each other. Her tongue flicked against mine as I nibbled on her lower lip, just the way she liked it.

I groaned, the sound deep from my chest as my arms wrapped around her, hauling her close.

Kissing Indya was as natural as breathing.

It should be. I'd been kissing her since I was a kid.

She leaned into the kiss, rising up on her toes as her arms banded around my shoulders so she could climb higher. Her fingers dived into my hair, tugging at the roots.

I slanted over her, devouring her mouth, licking and sucking and plundering.

She mewled as I nipped the corner of her upper lip.

It was good. It had always been so fucking good. We were like kindling. All we needed was an ember, and we went up in flames.

One of my hands slid lower, finding that lace hem of her chemise. I slipped beneath the satin, fitting my palm to the smooth curve of her ass.

She gasped, tearing her mouth away, as I squeezed.

Our breaths were ragged between us as we stared, still holding tight.

Then Indya sank onto her heels. Her hand drifted down my chest, stopping over my thundering heart. One moment, she let the beat soak into her palm. This was the moment when she'd fist my shirt and drag me inside. When I'd carry her to bed.

Except she didn't pull.

She pushed.

One shove, and I rocked back on my heels.

While she slammed the door in my face and flipped the lock.

Chapter 10
INDYA

Age Thirteen

Mom fluffed my hair for the millionth time.

"Stoooop. It's fine." I swatted her away.

"Sorry." She held up her hands, surrendering the battle against the frizz. "I'm sorry I forgot your product."

"It's okay. I'll just wear it up." I pulled the hair tie off my wrist and quickly tugged my curls into a half updo. Since I'd chopped it all off last week, this was as much as I could get into the band. The ends at my neck bugged me a little, but at least it was mostly out of my face.

It usually looked cute when it was down. My stylist had taught me how to fix it and given me a special product, except Mom had forgotten the balm when we'd been packing.

Dad clapped his hands together as he walked out of the bedroom. "Who's excited for dinner?"

"Me." Mom smiled as he walked up behind her and pulled her into a hug. "I'm starving. So is Indya. She's hangry."

I scrunched up my nose. "No, I'm not."

"Yes, she is," Dad whispered to Mom.

"You guys are being annoying." The moment the words were out of my mouth, my stomach growled so loudly that they both laughed. "Fine, I'm hangry. Can we go?"

"Yep." Dad tossed one arm around Mom's shoulders and the other around mine, tucking us both into his sides. Then the three of us walked in tandem to the door. Rather than let us go, he held on tighter and spun us sideways so we had to shuffle outside.

"Dad. Seriously?" I giggled but didn't let him go either. I stayed nestled into his side as we descended the stairs and started along the stone path.

"Left." He swung his left leg wide. "Right. Left. Right."

We marched, our bodies jostling as our smiles widened, until we made it to the lodge, and only then did he let us go.

Dad clasped Mom's hand, bringing her knuckles to his mouth for a kiss. They kissed *all* the time.

"What if we quit our jobs and moved to Montana?" he asked.

I gasped. "W-what? You want to move?"

"Grant," Mom chided. "Be serious."

"Think about it, Ellen. Every night, we'd get to see this." He swept out his free hand toward the mountains.

I stopped walking. My heart hurt from beating too fast. "What about my friends? And my school? What about our house?"

Mom shot Dad a frown and elbowed him in the ribs.

"No, pumpkin. I'm just teasing. Forget I said it."

The air rushed from my lungs. "Are you sure?"

"Don't worry." Dad squeezed my shoulder. "We're not moving."

"Good." Montana was fun for vacations, but I didn't want to live here.

"Come on. Let's eat." He guided us inside the lodge and through the lobby to the dining room.

Nearly every table was occupied with guests. Most people were dressed like us, wearing hiking boots and shorts. Some were in jeans and casual shirts. After we'd gone up Rustler's Trail, I'd traded my hiking gear for my Air Jordans, a pair of running shorts, and a boxy neon-green T-shirt.

Mom hated my love for neon. The only version she liked was pink, but since I loathed girly colors, she was stuck with my greens and yellows and blues and oranges. At least in Montana, she never cared what I was wearing as long as I put on sunscreen.

She said that she loved my independent spirit, but sometimes, usually at school functions when there were other moms around, she'd give my clothes funny looks. I think she wanted me to be more like the other girls in my grade and not so independent.

Too bad. The girls who liked dresses and makeup were mean, and all they did was talk about boys. Even the girls on the soccer team were boy obsessed right now. It was annoying.

"Good evening, Mr. and Mrs. Keller," the hostess greeted us, plucking three menus from a stack. "Right this way."

It was cool that some of the staff members remembered us, even though we hadn't come last year. Dad had had another busy summer with work, so Mom and I had gone to Paris.

That's when she'd finally agreed to let me cut my hair. We'd been shopping at Chanel, and our associate had had short curly hair. Mom had said it *inspired* her.

Mine didn't look like that pretty French lady's hair, but it was okay. I missed being able to pull it all into a ponytail. Every time I'd complain, Dad would tell me not to worry, that our hair grew fast.

I tucked a lock behind my ear as the hostess led us to our table.

"Enjoy your meal," she said.

Dad pulled out Mom's chair and mine at the same time. And when we were all seated, we reviewed the menu card and the three options for tonight's dinner.

"I'm getting a steak," Dad said.

"No fish." Mom frowned. "Or chicken. Or vegetarian. Guess I'll go with spaghetti and skip the meatballs."

Mom wasn't a vegetarian, but lately, she'd been cutting down on red meat. Our chef hadn't made us burgers or steaks in ages. But beef was a big part of the menu here, and she'd been grumbling about it for days.

"I'm getting a steak too. You can have my veggies," I told her.

"Nice try. You'll eat your own vegetables, young lady."

"Fine," I grumbled.

Vegetables were gross. The only kind I liked was squash loaded with butter.

While Dad and Mom talked over the wine list, I glanced around the room, searching for West.

I hadn't seen him yet, and we'd been here for three days. Maybe he was gone this week? I had seen Jax playing with some other little kids yesterday. They'd all been chasing each other around by the swing sets. But no West.

"I forgot my book," I said. "Can I go back and get it?"

"You're going to read at the dinner table?" Dad asked at the same time Mom said, "Sure."

Whenever they both talked at the same time, I always picked the answer I liked best.

So I stood and smiled at Mom before weaving through the dining room.

My love for reading was the only hobby Mom and I had in common. She always let me pack extra books on our trips. In Paris, she'd shopped for handbags at boring designer stores. I'd insisted we go to Princes' Park, where the Paris Saint-Germain football club played. But the day we'd had the most fun was when we'd bounced from bookshop to bookshop together.

Mom and Dad could talk to each other while I was reading. I was nearly finished with this book and didn't want to quit with only fifty pages left.

I skipped down the porch stairs, about to hop off the last when a laugh stopped me.

A girl who looked to be about my age, with long strawberry blonde hair and wearing a hot-pink sundress, disappeared around the corner of the lodge.

Who was that? Was she another guest? Maybe she'd want to hang out tomorrow or something. Did she like to swim? Dad had promised I could go float on a tube in the river tomorrow. She could come along too.

I changed paths, walking to catch up and introduce myself. But just as I peered around the building's edge, I heard another voice. A boy's voice.

West.

The girl was holding his hand as he pulled her toward the barn.

He was wearing a pair of jeans and a button-down shirt. His hair was longer and sort of messy on top. He looked . . . older. Taller. A lot taller.

He was fifteen now and in high school.

The girl kept giggling as they walked toward the barn. She leaned away, smiling the way I saw girls at school smile at boys.

He grinned at her and tugged hard on her hand, hauling her into his side. Then he bent and kissed her.

It wasn't like the kisses Dad gave Mom. It wasn't a quick peck.

West's mouth moved over the girl's. He wrapped his arms around her and slid them down that hot-pink dress to her butt with both hands.

The sound of a car door slamming in the parking lot broke them apart.

The girl wiped at her lips as West's gaze flicked toward the noise.

Before they could catch me, I slunk backward, pressing my body against the lodge's log exterior. Then I inched away until I was out of sight.

My tummy felt strange as I climbed the porch stairs and trudged to the dining room. Was that West's girlfriend? Did they kiss a lot?

I knew about kissing. Sort of. A few of the older girls on my club soccer team had boyfriends. I'd overheard them talking about tongues and getting fingered—I'd been too nervous to google what that meant, and no way was I asking Mom.

Did West and that girl kiss with tongues?

"Where's your book?" Dad asked when I reached the table.

"I changed my mind. I don't feel like reading."

His eyes narrowed. "Are you okay?"

"Yeah." I sat with a plop, grabbing the glass of root beer the waiter had delivered with my parents' bottle of wine.

It was either the vegetables or too much soda, but my stomach felt icky all through dinner. And I couldn't stop thinking about West and that girl.

She was pretty. Really pretty. I liked her straight hair. And I even kind of liked her pink dress.

Who was she, anyway? She wasn't at the guest campfire after dinner. Maybe she lived in Montana and went to school with West.

"Do you want a s'more?" Dad asked from our chairs around the firepit. The other guests were passing around a bag of marshmallows.

"Nah. I'm not really hungry."

"You okay?"

"I think I had too much root beer. Can I go inside?"

"Of course." Mom put her hand on my forehead, something she always did when I wasn't feeling well. "You don't have a fever."

"I'll be fine." I stood to kiss Dad's cheek and hug Mom. Then I went to the cabin and got my book from my room. But it was too stuffy, and even with the window open, after ten minutes on the bed, I felt sweaty. So I took my paperback to the picnic table beside the lodge.

It was the same table where I'd made paper airplanes with West on our last trip. Had he ever found that plane I had left for him at the fort? Did he even play in that fort now that he was fifteen?

"Hey, Indya." The table rocked as West took a seat on the opposite bench.

"Hey." I tore my gaze from my book and met his hazel eyes.

He had pretty eyes. My stomach did another weird twist.

"How's it going?" he asked.

"Good." I tugged at a hair that tickled my neck. "How are you?"

"Not bad. It's been a good summer."

"That's good." I fiddled with the corner of a page, not sure what else to say.

Why was it harder to talk to him? He was just West. Maybe because I'd spied on him kissing that girl? Why wasn't he with her right now? Had his dad told him he had to come hang out with me again?

West shifted to dig something from his jeans pocket. He slapped a deck of cards on the table. "Do you remember how to play?"

"Yeah, I remember."

He shuffled the deck, the cards fluttering as he threaded them together. After he'd dealt us each five cards, he took out a small container of toothpicks we could use to place bets. "Think you can beat me?"

"I guess we'll find out."

After ten hands, he still had yet to win. And the strange twist in my stomach had moved higher, to my heart.

"You've got all the luck tonight." He sighed, trading three cards from his hand with the deck.

"Or maybe you're no good at poker."

One corner of his mouth turned up. "Maybe."

"We could play another game. Or do something else."

"Like what?"

I shrugged. "I don't know. I, um, saw you with that girl earlier. She could play a game with us."

"She had to go home."

"Oh."

He stared at me from over the edge of his cards. "I saw you earlier."

"You did?" My cheeks flamed.

"That's a bright shirt."

Great, he'd caught me spying. There was no point in denying it. "Is she your girlfriend?"

West shrugged.

Was that a yes or a no? I didn't know what that shrug meant.

"Do you have a boyfriend?" he asked.

"I'm only thirteen. Dad says I can't have a boyfriend until I'm thirty. But some girls on my soccer team have boyfriends. They're fifteen."

"Vanessa is fifteen." Vanessa. Her name was Vanessa, and she was fifteen.

That odd feeling in my stomach was back.

And I kind of wished I was fifteen.

Chapter 11
INDYA

"Expect to hear from my lawyer," Jonathan Lee said, his voice so loud I had to pull the phone from my ear.

"You can give him this number. Goodbye, Mr. Lee."

Hanging up was pointless. He'd already ended the call.

"Shit." With my elbows braced on my desk, I dropped my head into my hands and groaned.

So much for a productive, quiet Sunday morning in my office to catch up on emails. Not only had I been taking calls since six, but I couldn't focus to save my life. Every ten seconds, my mind kept wandering back to West.

What the hell had I been thinking kissing him last night? As if things between us weren't complicated enough. Maybe if I pretended like it hadn't happened, he'd go along with it too.

I was blaming my complete lack of common sense on exhaustion and shock. West had woken me up from a dead sleep to drop the news about Jonathan. Then he'd touched my arm, and it was like we'd been tossed into the past.

Back to the times when I'd wanted nothing more than a touch from West. When I would have given anything for just one more kiss.

So I'd let him kiss me. And God, it was good. I'd forgotten just how good it felt to be kissed by a man who knew how to use his tongue.

West tasted the same. Spicy and masculine with a hint of wintergreen mint. Did he still carry Altoids in his truck console? I couldn't eat an Altoid without thinking of West and a beat-up old truck.

What would have happened if I hadn't stopped us? Would he have fucked me on that new couch in the Beartooth?

Probably. And I probably would have let him.

But my brain had engaged for a split second, long enough for me to slam on the brakes. And because I clearly couldn't be trusted around West, I'd slammed the door in his face and bolted the lock.

What was wrong with me? Why couldn't I resist that man? The last thing I needed was a messy affair with West Haven—my personal life was already in shambles.

There could be no more kissing. I was here to do a job for Dad; then I'd move on. And I wouldn't be returning to Texas. It wasn't home, not anymore. Maybe I'd move to California next. Or New York. Or Paris.

Not that I loved Paris, but at least Mom would visit me often.

And I was guaranteed never to see West Haven.

But dreams of running away to France would have to wait. I was swamped. A slew of guests were leaving today, and a pile were arriving tomorrow. The housekeeping staff could use a hand, and I had two to spare. So as soon as rooms started being vacated, I'd pitch in.

But first, I called my lawyer and left a long message about Jonathan Lee. The idiot hadn't read the contract in detail. Part of our general terms was a probationary period, exactly like the one I'd put into place with employees.

Jonathan would be paid for his time thus far, but not a chance I wanted him around this ranch. I hadn't seen or spoken to West's mother in years, but I wouldn't have a man who made Lily uncomfortable on this property.

I pulled up Dad's contact, about to unload my stresses to him, but nearly dropped my phone when West strode through my office door.

It was the first time he'd crossed the threshold. Usually, he just glared at me from the hallway.

"Nice chair."

"Um, thanks?" My replacement had finally arrived. My lower back was rejoicing.

He plopped into a folding chair, crossing his arms across his chest. Then in true West fashion, he stayed silent and stared.

"Did you need something?" *Please, please don't bring up the kiss.*

"Thought we should talk."

Ugh. "Fine."

"You hired Jonathan Lee."

"Um, yes. We covered that topic last night." Before he kissed me. Before I kissed him back. "I also fired Jonathan Lee."

"After I fired him."

"Can you really fire someone when they don't work for you?"

One corner of that delicious, talented mouth turned up.

He had this way of kissing hard and soft at the same time. Firm but gentle. It was the strangest conundrum that I never had figured out. No other man I'd kissed could do it either. Only West.

"Indya."

I blinked. *Shit.* I'd been staring at his lips. "West."

"Jonathan Lee. He's a bastard."

"Hence why he's been fired and is now threatening to sue me. Tell me something I don't know."

"You don't know the people in this community."

"Actually, I did know that." Still, it prickled to have it hurled at me like an accusation. "Your point?"

"The point is I can't blame you for hiring Jonathan Lee when I wasn't around to offer background information."

"Oh." Not at all what I'd expected him to say.

He blew out a deep breath, shifting forward to lean his elbows to his knees. No cowboy hat today. Just that dusty green baseball hat with the CMC brand and a brim bent down into a perfect U shape.

West had always looked sexy in a hat. Any hat. But I liked the baseball hat a lot.

He'd shaved today. The stubble that had scraped against my mouth last night was gone. It had been a long time since I'd kissed a clean-shaven West. I couldn't remember it well enough to judge which version I liked better.

And I would not, under any circumstances, let myself find out. The kissing was over. Done. Never ever again.

Damn it, I wanted him to kiss me. Right now. On this desk. I wanted him to haul me out of my new chair and devour me whole.

I focused on an invisible spot on the desk, glad it was between us. Then I crossed my legs, doing my best to block out the pulse blooming in my core.

"I don't know where to go from here." He spoke in a voice so low it made me hold my breath so I wouldn't miss what he said next. "I never thought this would happen."

It shouldn't have happened.

That statement was on the tip of my tongue, but I held it back.

It wasn't West's fault. During the negotiations, Curtis had made it abundantly clear that this was his ranch. His resort. He was making the decisions for his family.

He'd always shoved West out, long before the decline of the business. Maybe if he had taken West's input, I wouldn't be sitting here today.

The trouble had started after they'd bought that neighboring property. Curtis should have known better. Had West agreed? Or had he tried to convince his father otherwise?

"I can see the questions spinning in your head, Indya. Go ahead. Ask."

Oh, I had questions. Lots and lots of questions, most about the logistics I was struggling to figure out on my own. West could probably answer them in less than two minutes.

How many guests can go on an excursion at one time?

Do you have a fly-fishing guide anymore?

What paperwork do guests need to go hunting in the fall?

Except they weren't what came from my mouth.

"Why did you buy the neighboring ranch?"

West's face hardened, his jaw clenching. I regretted the question immediately. "Land is the one thing they aren't making any more of."

"That's not a reason."

"Reason enough."

End of discussion. I held up my hands. "Okay."

"Did Jax turn in his paperwork?"

"Yes." I nodded. "I assume you encouraged that, so thanks."

"Welcome. He hasn't been around as long, but he can answer your questions too. Tara's a great resource. So is Wyatt. And I'll help, where I can."

Could we work together? With all our history, could we survive it? "I'd appreciate your input on a few things with the resort."

"Shoot."

Before I could start through my litany of questions, my phone rang. Mom's name flashed on the screen.

"We'll talk later." West stood, and before I could stop him, he walked out of the office.

When the sound of his footsteps faded, I sagged in my chair and sighed, declining Mom's call. I'd catch her later when my heart wasn't racing.

Well, at least he hadn't brought up the kiss. He probably regretted it. Did I regret it? Maybe. No, not really.

It had felt nice to be kissed.

I missed being kissed.

A yawn tugged at my mouth. The idea of sitting here for another moment, even in my new, comfortable chair, made my skin crawl. Coffee. I needed more coffee. Then maybe I'd go through the website mock-up my graphic designer had sent over this morning.

We'd gone for vintage-style branding, inspired by old rodeo posters and Western art. It was impossible not to love.

I headed for the lobby, too tired to deal with the kitchen staff today. Every time I walked into Reid's space, I felt like I was going to war. Instead, I'd raid the coffeepots set out for guests. Maybe visit with Marie, the weekend and evening desk clerk.

At the moment, she seemed to be my only ally.

Marie was a senior in high school and working here for the summer until she went to college this fall. Of all the employees, Marie was my favorite. Mostly because she smiled a real smile when I came into a room.

I missed real smiles.

But as I walked down the hall, voices caught my ear from the lobby.

"I'm quitting."

I froze. Who was quitting? Marie? No, not Marie.

"Deb," West warned.

Oh, thank God. Marie wasn't quitting. Wait. Why was Deb here? It was her day off.

"Don't do anything impulsive," West told her.

"She took away my lunch break."

Excuse me? No, I didn't take away her lunch break. I told her she had one hour, not two.

"Take it up with Indya," he said. "I'm not getting in the middle of this."

"Whatever," Deb muttered. "Vanessa was just looking for you."

Vanessa. As in West's teenage girlfriend who he had been kissing at fifteen, Vanessa?

A surge of old memories, of feelings I hadn't been old enough to understand, swelled so fast they made me dizzy.

"Okay. I'll go find her," West said. "What are you doing here anyway?"

"I ran out of eggs at home. I came to steal a few for breakfast."

"What?" He huffed. "No. Go to the store."

"What do you care? It's not like you had to buy them."

"I don't give a damn who pays for the food around here. If you're not on shift, it's not for you. Understood?"

"God, you're grumpy."

"Go home." The lodge door opened and, a moment later, slammed closed.

"Do you think he's fucking her?"

I cringed. A guest could have heard Deb's question.

"Who?" Marie asked.

"Indya. Ron said that when he went over to take her dinner Friday night, West was there."

Was that why I'd gone to bed hungry? So Ron could gossip with Deb?

"Oh, um . . . I don't know," Marie muttered. "I'm just minding my own business."

"You're so lucky you get to quit soon," Deb whined.

"I know. I kind of hate this job," Marie said.

Ouch. Maybe it had nothing to do with me. But still, it hurt.

"Okay, I'm going to go get some eggs and go home," Deb said.

"But West said—"

"West isn't here, is he? And besides, he doesn't really care. It's just a few eggs."

Fired. Deb was getting fired. *Fuck.* Except I wasn't ready to fire her yet. I didn't have a backup plan. If I could just tolerate her for a couple more weeks, then I could let her go.

She breezed through the lobby for the dining room, oblivious to me in the hallway.

I gave my heart a few moments to recover; then I squared my shoulders and went to the lobby. "Hey, Marie."

"Hi, Miss Keller." She smiled. It wasn't as real as it had been before. Or maybe it had never been real. Maybe I was seeing what I wanted to see and not what was actually there.

I went to the coffee station, then filled up a white ceramic mug and carried it with me to the dining room. If I was going to have a rough day, I might as well tackle all my headaches.

Time for war.

The moment I entered the kitchen through the swinging door, Deb came out of the walk-in refrigerator with a carton of eggs.

I arched an eyebrow as I sipped my coffee.

"Oh, I, was, um . . ."

"Leaving," I finished for her. Before I caved and fired her today. "For the grocery store. You're out of eggs at home."

She gulped, her eyes flaring with panic.

Reid, who stood beside the sink wearing a white chef's coat and a green bandanna over his auburn hair, chuckled as she set the eggs on the stainless steel prep table and scurried away.

"She thinks she owns the place," he said when Deb was gone.

"She doesn't. But I do." I nodded to the piece of paper on the counter at his side. "Is that my new menu?"

He plucked up the sheet and handed it over.

"Thank you." I took it from him, quickly scanning the updates. Curried cauliflower-quinoa salad. Creamy goat cheese polenta with ratatouille. Sesame-garlic ramen noodles. My stomach growled. "These sound delicious."

"Just because I don't want to cook vegetarian options doesn't mean I can't."

"I'm looking forward to trying them."

"I'll get what I need ordered this week. New menu starting the following."

"Excellent." I set the menu on the table beside the eggs and left the kitchen, drawing in the scents of bacon, hash browns, and pancakes from this morning's buffet in the dining room.

My mouth watered, but rather than snag a plate, I retreated to my office for my purse and keys.

Deb wasn't the only one who needed to hit the grocery store.

"I'll be back in a bit," I told Marie after downing my coffee and putting the cup in the bin for the dishwasher.

"Okay." She waved. "See ya."

I was digging my sunglasses from my purse as I walked outside, glancing up before I reached the stairs.

In the grass, on their way to the barn, walking side by side, were West and Vanessa.

The déjà vu hit so hard that I tripped on the top step. My hand shot out to grip the railing before I stumbled.

It was the same. It was almost exactly the same. All that was missing was my short hair and neon-green tee.

Vanessa's hair was the same strawberry blonde from her youth. It was curled in long waves that cascaded down her spine. She nudged her shoulder against West's, looking up at him with a smile.

He smiled back.

A real smile.

She said something that made him laugh. A deep, booming laugh that I hadn't heard in a long, long time. He was still laughing as he tossed an arm around her shoulders to bring her into his side.

Maybe they were just friends. Or maybe they were together—he probably shouldn't have kissed me if that was the case.

Even if they weren't a couple, there was affection there. Affection that could turn into love. My stomach dropped so fast I almost threw up my coffee.

What happened if he fell in love this year? Either with his childhood sweetheart or someone else?

I'd be here to watch. I'd be forced to watch.

It would break my heart.

As West and Vanessa walked away, talking comfortably, his arm still around her shoulders, the reality of our relationship hit me so hard I couldn't breathe.

He had a life. This was his life.

And I was not a part of it. I had *never* been a part of it.

West had always meant more to me than I did to him. The relationship between us was . . . nothing. We had no relationship.

As a kid, I'd built it up to be something more in my head. But we were nothing.

Nothing.

Why the fuck was I in Montana?

For Dad. I was here to do a job for Dad. That was the only thing keeping me going. That was the only reason to stay.

I walked to my car on wobbling legs and hopped inside, then drove off the ranch.

The minute I hit the highway, I could breathe for the first time in weeks.

Part of me wanted to just keep going. It would be so easy to just keep driving.

But I went to the grocery store. I bought food for my cabin. And when I made it back to the ranch, West and Vanessa were gone.

Maybe they'd sneaked off to kiss in the barn.

It didn't matter. I was here to do a job.

So I went inside and got to work. The sooner the Haven River Ranch was fully functioning, the sooner I could leave this place.

And never look back.

Chapter 12
WEST

With my arms folded over the top of a wooden corner post, I peered out over the land that had been our downfall.

Emerald meadows stretched to thick forests at the mountain foothills. The stream that cut through the grasses rushed with clear, cold water. Black cows grazed while calves danced at their feet.

It was breathtaking. No wonder Dad had been suckered. He'd coveted this land my whole life. It was paradise.

Indya's paradise now.

How long until she asked for a ranch tour? She was preoccupied with the resort at the moment. She was focused on working out of that office. But sooner rather than later, she'd ask me to take her around the ranch so she could familiarize herself with the property as a whole.

She'd love it here. She'd love the abundance of white wildflowers. Maybe she'd want to build a house out here.

Despite the reason we had this land, despite the taint of financial ruin, I'd build a house here too.

A rustic-style home with gleaming windows on every side to capture each facet of the view. A barn for a few horses that weren't for the guests to ride. A dog that would love to race through the fields. Children to take fishing in that stream and build forts in the trees.

A dream.

Why was I even out here? Punishment, maybe? To remind myself of everything we'd lost because I hadn't stood up to Dad years ago.

This was his ranch. My grandparents had passed it to him. I'd been trying to respect their decision and his ownership, knowing that someday, it would go to Jax and me.

Then I could do whatever the hell I wanted.

But I should have pushed harder.

It wasn't like Dad and I hadn't had our fair share of arguments about how things should have been run. We'd fought countless times. I'd just learned to pick my battles.

Clearly, I hadn't picked enough.

Would Indya give me the freedom to make the changes that needed to be made? Or would she be another micromanager?

Probably a good thing she'd slammed that door in my face last night. It was good that she'd stopped that kiss before we'd crossed a line.

Story of our lives, taking one kiss too far.

As good as it was, I probably shouldn't have been making out with the boss.

My boss.

I barked a dry laugh.

I was an employee. A temporary employee.

Not a chance I'd be able to work for Indya, work on *my* ranch as a hired hand, for the rest of my life. But I needed time to figure out where to go from here. Maybe, given some time, she'd open up to the idea of selling me our land. I didn't care what Dad said. He didn't know Indya like I did.

And if she never agreed, well . . . maybe I'd go find a different place of my own.

That was a worry for another day. Dad was the king of impulsive decisions, not me. So I'd stay for a bit and care for the land and cattle under my charge. Not forever.

For now.

Until it was time to move on.

With my eyes closed, I mentally sketched the house I would have built in this meadow. Dark wood siding. Wraparound porch with a few rocking chairs. Red tin roof. I gave it windows and doors. A chimney and two dormer windows. I drew that house with character and life.

When it was finished, I flipped my imaginary pencil around.

And I scratched its eraser over everything.

I erased the dream.

With a shove, I walked away from the fence and returned to my truck. Then I drove back to the resort to find my brother. His trail ride should be over soon, and I needed to apologize for barking at him yesterday.

And I wanted to make sure he was all right.

This sale had blindsided us both. He was probably angry and embarrassed. Hurt and disappointed. Furious with Dad. We shared that litany of emotions. As I came to terms with this, I could lean on Mom. When I was ready, she'd listen to me rant and rage. She'd be there as my confidante. She'd be there with a hug when Dad's betrayal cut deep.

Jax didn't have a mother.

And the only frustration I had with my own was that she hadn't stepped up to fill that void.

I loved Mom. But too much of her anger at Dad had leaked to my brother.

Rather than cut him some slack yesterday, I'd come down hard when he'd called Indya a bitch. Or when he'd told me Deb had called her a bitch.

Fucking Deb.

She was stirring up drama for the sake of holding the spoon.

My phone rang as I was driving, Jax's name flashing on the console.

"Hey," I answered. "I was just coming to find you."

"I'm at the barn. With Zak."

Oh, hell. "What's Zak doing here?"

"Don't know. He just pulled up."

"Be there in five." I ended the call and hit the gas, my truck bouncing hard as it flew down the rough road for the lodge.

Was it Mom? Had that asshole Jonathan Lee retaliated now that he'd gotten his ass fired? Or had something happened with Dad? Maybe he'd gone into town and tied one on at the bar since I'd taken his whiskey away.

Zak's truck was impossible to miss. **SHERIFF** was emblazoned on each side, and the light bar on top shone blue and red beneath the late-afternoon sun.

I skidded to a stop, my heart racing as I shut off the engine and hopped out. "Zak."

"West." He shook my hand. "Got some news."

"Is it Mom?"

"No, it's, uh, Courtney."

Fuck. The air rushed out of my lungs. Not that news of Courtney was good, but at least my mother was fine.

"What about Courtney?" Jax crossed his arms over his chest. He hated her for what she'd done to me. Jax didn't even hate his own mother for abandoning him, but for me, he'd hate Courtney.

"Got word she's back in town," Zak said. "I haven't run into her yet. But thought you'd want to know."

"Sunny too?" I asked.

Zak shook his head. "Heard it was just her."

Well, that was something. "Appreciate the heads-up."

"Welcome. I know I could have called, but I was out this direction today. Thought it would be better delivered in person." He opened his truck's door. "Coming to poker next week?"

"I don't know. We've got a lot happening around here." It was rare that I missed the monthly hold 'em night with Zak and my high school buddies. It was usually a way for me to make some money off my friends to pour into the Beartooth Chalet.

Except I didn't need that money now, did I?

"Heard about the changes around here," Zak said, his gaze drifting to the lodge. "You okay?"

"It's been . . . interesting."

"Sorry."

"Me too." I waited beside my brother as Zak drove off. The moment his taillights were out of sight, I pulled off my baseball hat to drag a hand through my hair. "Son of a bitch. I do not need trouble with Courtney on top of all this other shit."

"Maybe she'll go away."

That earned Jax a flat look.

"Wishful thinking," he muttered.

Courtney would find out about Indya. She'd do something to insert herself and be a pain in my ass.

"I'll deal with her later," I said, putting my hat on again. "You doing okay?"

Jax shrugged. "Spent the day on a trail ride with a rich guy from Salt Lake and his smoking-hot daughters."

I arched my eyebrows.

"Don't worry. It's against the employee code of conduct to fraternize with guests."

That wouldn't stop Jax. He was a good-looking kid and too much like me at that age, charming women and flashing that handsome smile too often. Though the only guest I'd ever slept with was Indya.

"Just . . . tread lightly," I said. "Until we figure out what is going to happen. And about yesterday. Sorry I was a prick."

"It's all good. You were right. Have you, uh, talked to Dad?"

"Stopped by yesterday after I left your place."

"Did he say anything? Explain?"

I shook my head. "Not really. He told me to trust him."

"Trust him. That's it?"

"Yep. You know Dad."

Jax's jaw ticked. "Yeah. I do."

Unless he felt he owed us, we wouldn't get much more than the flimsy explanation he'd shared the day Indya had arrived at the ranch.

"I'm not talking to him," Jax declared. "Not yet."

"That's okay."

In time, he'd go visit our father, but it had to be on his own terms. If he needed space, I wasn't going to push it.

"Heard about the Jonathan Lee situation," he said.

"From?"

"Tara."

I sighed. "Indya fired him."

"She shouldn't have hired him in the first place."

"She didn't know, Jax."

"You're defending her again."

"Hey." What the hell was his problem? "Be fair."

"Fair? It's true, then. You are screwing her already."

My brain screeched to a halt. "Say that again."

"That's the rumor going around."

What the hell? All because of last night's kiss? *For fuck's sake.*

"I'm not. And if I was, that's no one's goddamn business. Including yours." I pointed at his nose. And like yesterday, I was yelling at my brother again. "Don't forget who you're talking to, Jax. You can buy into rumors, or you can come and discuss your concerns with me, man to man."

Without another word, I brushed past him and stalked to the lodge.

"West," he called. "Shit. I'm sorry, okay?"

I slowed enough to speak over my shoulder. "Prove you're sorry. Go clean the barn."

"Damn it." A rock skipped across the lot from where he'd kicked it.

I left him to sulk while I jogged up the lodge stairs and blew into the lobby for the second time today, passing Marie with a wave on my way to Indya's dark office.

Where was she? I retreated to the front desk, stopping this time. "Hey, Marie. Is Indya here?"

"She left a while ago. She said she was coming back, but I haven't seen her."

"All right. Thanks." When I walked out of the lodge, Jax was just heading through the barn's open door.

Two days in a row I'd come down hard on him. But damn it, he knew better than to get in the middle of resort gossip. And he knew better than to listen to Deb.

Indya's car wasn't outside her cabin, but I took the path to the chalet anyway and knocked on the door. No answer.

We needed to talk. About the rumors. About my conversation with Vanessa this morning. Not wanting to drive home just to turn back, I walked to the barn, where I found Jax in a stall with a shovel.

"I can do it," he said when I grabbed my own shovel.

"Faster with two of us."

We worked in silence for a few minutes, finishing the first stall and moving to the second.

"Did you go to the campfire last night?" he asked.

"No." After that kiss with Indya, I'd gone home for a cold shower.

"Me neither."

The Saturday-night campfire behind the lodge was a tradition. One started by my grandparents years ago. For two weekends in a row, there hadn't been a Haven in attendance. That hadn't happened in decades.

"Next week," I said. "We'll go together. Maybe the property isn't ours. But the traditions are. No one can take those from us. Let's hold on to them for as long as we can."

"Okay," he said quietly. "It should be yours, West. It's not right that he sold it. What are we going to do?"

"I don't know. But we'll figure it out together."

He nodded and went back to work.

By the time we were done in the barn, we both needed a shower and fresh clothes. I needed to track down Indya.

"Want to have a beer?" I asked Jax.

"Definitely."

So my brother and I grabbed a couple of beers from the lodge; then we brought them back to the barn to drink in peace.

He told me about his latest adventures at the Big Timber bars. About the projects he wanted to tackle next at his house. About the horse that was becoming his favorite.

We talked about anything and everything that had nothing to do with the ranch sale or Indya Keller. And long after our beers were gone, when the stars had begun popping in the darkening blue sky, we left the barn to go home.

"Thanks, West."

I put my hand on Jax's shoulder, giving it a squeeze. "Heading to town? Or are you going home?"

"Tonight, I think home."

"See you tomorrow?"

"Yeah." He headed to his truck as I walked to mine.

Golden light spilled from the guest room windows at the lodge.

The Beartooth Chalet was pitch black. Indya's car was still missing.

Where was she? A knot formed in my gut. If she was in trouble, if she'd gotten a flat tire or something, she would have called me, right?

I pulled out my phone and hit her number. A number I hadn't called in years. Hopefully, it hadn't changed.

"This is Indya Keller. Please leave a message."

"It's West. Call me. I, uh . . . just call me." I ended the call and took another look at the Beartooth. The knot in my stomach doubled on the drive down the private road that led to my place.

If she wasn't here, where was she? Why wasn't she answering her phone?

Damn it. Indya could take care of herself. She was an adult who'd lived significantly more days outside Montana than in it. But she was here now.

And when she was here, we were tethered. It had been that way since I was a kid and Dad had ordered me to play with her. Since the days I'd introduced her to Chief and shown her my fort and taught her to play poker.

When Indya Keller was in Montana, she was mine.

Even when she wasn't.

Why wasn't she home tonight? It was getting darker by the minute. I rounded the bend that led to my place, and the moment I spotted a vehicle in front of my house, the air rushed from my lungs. The knot in my gut vanished.

"That fucking woman."

God, she was infuriating. She'd made me worry.

It had been a long time since I'd worried.

Four years, to be exact.

I parked beside her Defender and hopped out, slamming the door to my truck too hard. Mouth open, a lecture about to pour off my tongue, I stopped myself when I took one look at her face.

She was sitting on the top stair of my porch. Her face was splotchy. Her eyes red.

I'd had my heart stomped on a time or two. But there was nothing quite so heartbreaking as seeing Indya cry.

I walked to the steps, stopping before the bottom stair.

"Why are you crying, Indy?"

She lifted her chin. "I'm not crying."

"Of course you're not." I huffed a laugh. This woman. She never admitted to crying. Not even when we were kids. "Are you okay?"

"Great," she lied as she looked up to the overhang of the roof. "I like your house."

"My grandparents used to live here."

It was one of the original homes on the ranch. The wood siding had grayed over the years. The green roof had faded. The boards on the small porch creaked in the winter.

I'd moved in after college. It was small, but I didn't need much. This place was more than enough.

Except for the first time in my life, it looked too old and too tiny.

It wasn't enough for a woman like Indya.

"How long have you been here?" I asked.

"A while." She lifted a shoulder. "I need to talk to you, and I didn't want to do it at the lodge."

So she'd probably heard the rumors about us already too.

"All right." I kept my boots on the dirt, not trusting myself to get any closer.

She scooted to the edge of the stair, sitting tall with her hands primly resting in her lap. "I saw you with that woman earlier."

"Vanessa."

"Yes." Indya nodded. "You kissed me."

"I did."

"So?"

"So." I fought a smirk. She was worried I was with Vanessa. That's what this was about.

"West." She rolled her eyes. "You know what I'm getting after."

"What's that?"

"You're such a pain in the ass." She stood in a flash, then marched down the stairs, her eyes blazing gold.

But before she could storm past me for her vehicle, I caught her elbow. "Vanessa and I dated for about a minute in high school. It didn't go much beyond some making out in the barn. She married my best friend after graduation. They've got two kids, who call me Uncle West. And her husband happens to be your new contractor. He's starting work tomorrow."

"Oh." The tension in her arm melted away beneath my grip. "Thank you."

"Jealous?"

It took her a heartbeat to whisper, "Yes."

She could admit to the jealousy but not the tears. It shouldn't have made sense, but it did.

That was how it had always been between us. We belonged to each other.

Even when we didn't.

The kiss happened exactly the same way it had last night.

One moment we were locked in a stare. The next, we collided.

My mouth crushed hers, and she parted instantly so I could sweep inside.

Her arms looped around my shoulders as I hauled her off her feet. Then I kissed her with everything I had. Tongues tangling. Hands roaming. There was no door for her to slam in my face tonight.

As I carried her toward the house, her legs wrapped around my waist. She clung to me as I kept a fierce hold on her lithe body.

I'd learned a long time ago how quickly she could slip away.

Not tonight. Not this time.

The screen door flung on its hinges as I yanked it open, and we were halfway to the bedroom when it slammed closed.

Indya's legs squeezed around my hips, her mouth never breaking from mine as she ground against me. Shifting my grip, I palmed her ass as my arm snaked beneath her for support. Then my other hand slid up her spine and into those curls.

This hair. I'd missed her hair. I tugged at the roots, pulling hard enough that Indya's mouth broke from mine.

She hissed as her arms tightened around my shoulders. She rocked her center against my arousal as she bent to latch her lips around my pulse. Her tongue drew a long wet line against my Adam's apple as I crossed into the bedroom.

"Fuck," I groaned. With a smack on her ass, her legs unwound so I could set her down.

Her fingers immediately went to work on the buttons of my shirt as I took her lips again, plundering until my tongue had caressed every corner of her mouth.

She jerked the tails of my shirt from my jeans and fumbled with my belt buckle until it was hanging loose.

But before she could undo the zipper of my jeans, I took her shoulders and spun her around to face the bed. "Shirt off, baby."

She obeyed immediately.

It was only in these moments, when our clothes were strewed and our breaths ragged, that she ever seemed to follow orders.

While she stripped, I reached behind my head and yanked off my T-shirt. Then with a flick, the clasp of her bra broke free, the straps draping down her arms.

Her hair cascaded over her shoulders, the riot of blonde spirals wild and tousled. She glanced up and over her shoulder to meet my gaze.

This was reckless. This wasn't like a hookup on her summer vacations. This wasn't a fling with a random woman I'd picked up at the bar. But I shut those thoughts down, not giving a damn.

Indya was standing at the foot of my bed. Only a fool would send her away.

I gave myself a moment to drown in those caramel eyes, letting the blood pound in my veins.

How I wanted her. How I'd always wanted her.

Indya's hand reached back for my arm, her fingertips skimming my skin.

One touch, and my body lit up in sparks. Head to toe. One touch. And I was on fire.

I fitted my chest against her back. My hands came to her front, flicking that bra away. Then I floated my fingers across her ribs to her breasts. They filled my hands like they'd been made for my palms.

Her head lolled against my shoulder as I pinched her nipples, rolling them into pebbles between my index fingers and thumbs. "Oh, God."

"You still like your nipples pinched."

"Yes."

I thrust forward, pressing the erection behind my jeans into the crack of her ass, and earned a moan.

That sound. It filled the room for a perfect moment.

Then it was gone too soon. That just wouldn't do.

So I thrust my hips forward again, keeping a hold of her perfect breasts so she wouldn't topple forward.

Her moan was louder. Breathier. Hotter.

"The sounds you make." Abandoning one of her nipples, I pushed her hair off her shoulder and latched on to the side of her neck.

As I licked and sucked, she rocked against me. "West."

"I want inside, Indy." My cock ached behind my zipper, throbbing and desperate.

"Fuck me," she panted.

I flicked open the button on her jeans and slipped my free hand into her panties. The moment my hand cupped her mound, she bucked against my touch. "Like this?"

She shook her head, riding my fingers as I slicked through her wet center. "No."

"You want my tongue?"

"No."

"What do you want?" I whispered.

She reached backward, fitting her hand between us. And as I slipped a finger into her pussy, she dragged her hand over my cock. "West. Fuck me. Please."

"You're the boss."

That got her attention. The glare she sent me would have flayed a weaker man. I simply smirked and took a step away to toe off my boots.

She was still glaring as she shimmied out of her own jeans and panties. But the scowl on her beautiful face faded as I shoved out of my jeans and boxer briefs, my cock springing free.

I gave myself a few hard strokes as she watched, her eyes wide and unblinking. It wasn't like she hadn't seen me before, but I fucking loved the bit of apprehension in her gaze. I was big, but she could take me.

With a single step I closed the distance between us. Then I took her hand, bringing it to my shaft so she could feel how much I wanted her.

Our gazes clashed as she tightened her grip, her hand smooth but firm over my flesh. Our breaths mingled. Our chests heaved with thundering hearts.

Time vanished.

The years between us melted away. The mistakes, the regrets, turned to ash.

A century wouldn't dull this fire. Not with Indya.

My hand lifted to her temple, pushing an errant strand away from her face. She leaned into the touch, turning to kiss the inside of my wrist.

A gentle kiss.

It was too tender. It meant too much.

That was not the road we were taking tonight. I couldn't, not yet. So I slammed my mouth on hers in a punishing kiss.

Indya met my intensity with her own, nipping at my bottom lip as I tumbled us into the bed.

I fell into the cradle of her hips, lining up at her entrance, and, with a single thrust, slid deep.

"Oh, God," she cried as her body stretched around mine.

I sucked in a sharp breath, gritting my teeth as the pleasure zinged through my veins. I was deep. So, so deep.

"Move. God, West. Move."

I savored her tight, wet heat for a long moment, then eased out before another thrust, driving all the way to the root.

"Yes." Indya gripped my shoulders, holding on as I set a fast pace, fucking in and out with long, deliberate strokes.

"You feel so fucking good." I took her mouth, kissing her as I drove us higher and higher.

It wasn't enough. I moved faster, harder, memorizing the feel of her pussy and the way her inner walls fluttered around my length.

She rocked in rhythm with my strokes, exactly the way I liked. The way I'd taught her.

It was perfect. It was erotic. It was fucking bliss.

It wasn't enough. It was never enough.

"West." Her breath hitched in my ear as her nails dug deeper, leaving crescents in my skin.

"Come, Indy."

She detonated on a cry, writhing beneath me. Pulse after pulse, she shattered.

Heat swept through my veins, my limbs shaking. Fire raced down my spine, building hotter and hotter, until I couldn't hold back.

"Indya." I roared her name, pouring inside her as every one of my muscles tensed and trembled.

White spots stole my vision. My heartbeat dulled any other sound. And I let myself drown in the waves of my release, rolling and tumbling, until I finally surfaced for air.

Fuck, it was good. So damn good. It had always been good.

I collapsed on top of her, our bodies slick with sweat. It was an effort to pull away and roll onto my back. I reached for her, about to drape her across my chest and keep her there all night.

But the moment her breathing had returned to normal, Indya flew from the bed, scrambling to collect her clothes.

Well, damn. So that's how it would be, then. Casual wasn't new for us, so why did it piss me off? Did she really have to be in such a god-damn hurry to leave my room? She didn't even bother getting dressed.

Without a word, she walked for the door, still naked, shirt and jeans and shoes clutched to her heart.

"Indy." I stopped her before she could disappear. "Why were you crying?"

She swallowed hard. "I wasn't."

Of course not. Those chains she kept around her heart had to be so heavy. Didn't she get sick of carrying them all the damn time?

I stared at the ceiling as the rustle of her clothes sounded from the living room. As the screen door slammed. As the sound of her car disappeared outside.

I stared at the ceiling until long after she was gone, listening for the echoes of her moans.

But they were gone too.

Chapter 13
INDYA

Age Sixteen

"I missed this place. It's been too long." Dad sipped his coffee at the dining room table in the Beartooth Chalet. "Feels good to be back here, doesn't it?"

"Yeah, I guess." I dropped to a crouch to tie my shoes. It would have felt better on *any* other week this summer.

"I know you wanted to go with your friends. I'm sorry."

I shrugged.

My whole soccer team was at a camp this week. And instead of staying with them, I was in Montana because when Dad had called for a last-minute reservation, this was the only opening for the chalet.

Mom wanted the chalet. Dad wanted Montana. And I wanted soccer.

Two against one.

Me being here with my parents made them happy.

We were running short on happy lately, so I was missing camp with my friends.

"Grant?" Mom called from the bathroom. "Did you take your pills?"

"Not yet. I was drinking my coffee first."

"I'll bring them out."

Dad sighed. "Okay."

Mom was the ruthless dictator of his medication schedule. When she said it was time for his pills, it was time for his pills. Dad knew better than to argue.

While he filled a water glass from the kitchen tap, I finished tying my shoes and stood, tugging down the hems of my running shorts. "I'm going to go before it gets too hot."

"Want some company?" he asked.

Before I could say yes, Mom emerged from the bathroom with a palmful of pills.

"Absolutely not," she said. "You can't go running with Indya."

"The doctor said I should keep in shape."

"He said to ease into exercise. That means you're not running five miles with your sixteen-year-old daughter at Montana elevations."

Dad frowned and took the pills from her hand, then tossed them back with a gulp of water. "Yeah. You're probably right."

"I'll probably do ten miles today, anyway," I said. "Coach said that since I'm not at camp, to work on endurance instead."

"Ten miles." Dad cringed. "Yep, you're on your own."

"Be careful," Mom said. "Where are you going?"

"Just down the gravel road five miles and back."

"No detours."

"No detours. Promise." I walked over to kiss Mom's cheek, then hugged Dad before fitting my sport headphones around the shells of my ears.

With my phone in my armband, I walked out of the chalet, pulled up my running playlist, and jogged down the stairs, heading straight for the road that wound away from the ranch.

My muscles were stiff from too many hours traveling yesterday, so I started at an easy pace, getting used to the feel of gravel beneath my shoes.

The air was cool. Goose bumps coated the skin on my arms during my first mile. By the second, my body felt warm, and sweat beaded at my temples. By the third, I was running at a seven-minute-mile pace, pushing hard through the burn in my lungs. It got easier after the third mile.

Except as I finished mile four, the tang of blood in my mouth hadn't gone away. The fire in my lungs seemed only hotter. Was it the altitude? The dry air?

Or was the lump in my throat because I always felt like crying these days?

Dad told me not to cry. He told me it would just be harder if we were sad.

Except I *was* sad. I was really freaking sad.

Tears swam in my eyes, but I blinked them away. *No crying.*

I ran faster.

I ran so fast it didn't matter that I was sad. I ran so fast all I could think about was the burn in my thighs and the fire in my lungs.

I ran so fast that when a truck rolled up beside me, I yelped, nearly stumbling into the grassy ditch off the gravel road.

By some miracle, I managed to keep my balance and slowed to a stop, pulling the headphones from my ears as the cloud of dust from the tires blew past me down the lane.

"You okay?" West called from behind the wheel.

"You scared me." My chest heaved as I planted my hands on my hips.

"Sorry." A grin tugged at his mouth. "Hey, Indya."

"Hey, West."

Wow, he was hot. I was glad my cheeks were already red from running so he wouldn't notice me blushing.

He'd always been cute. But he was, like, hot. Really hot. His dark hair was messy, like he'd combed it with his fingers. His white T-shirt was tight against his biceps as he leaned forward on the wheel. And that smile.

White and easy and slightly crooked. It tipped up higher on his left side than it did on his right. My belly flipped as he smiled wider.

Maybe this trip wasn't that bad of an idea, after all.

"Long time," he said, his gaze roving down my bare stomach.

I was only in a red sports bra and matching shorts.

"I wondered if you'd come back."

"Yep. We're here for the week."

"You don't seem too excited about that."

I shrugged.

There was a lot in that shrug. Like how miserable the past few years had been. How hard it was to stay positive. How much I wanted to cry but wasn't going to let myself because if I did start crying, I wasn't sure how I'd stop.

My shrugs said everything I wasn't quite sure how to voice.

I shrugged a lot.

"Want to keep running?" West asked. "Or go for a ride?"

"Like on a horse?"

"No." He laughed. "Like in this truck."

I tore my gaze from his hazel eyes and took a long assessing look at his truck. It was dark green with rust spots around the wheel wells. It was dusty and old with only one bench seat. The back had a coffee can full of tools and a roll of barbed wire.

"Where are you going?"

"To count cattle."

"Why do you count them?"

"So we know we've got them all before we move them to a different pasture."

"Oh. That makes sense." Did he think I was stupid because I didn't know anything about ranching?

"So are you coming along or not?"

The road stretched over the miles I should run.

I climbed in his truck.

"There's no seat belt."

West just chuckled and put the truck in drive, then headed down the road.

He wasn't wearing a seat belt either.

I just wouldn't tell Mom.

The cab smelled like dust and oil and West's laundry soap. I drew it in, holding it for a heartbeat before relaxing into my seat.

The air whipped through the open window, cooling my hot face and drying the sweat on my skin. My hair was tight in a ponytail, but a few curls blew loose, flying across my forehead.

West slowed, turning off onto a side road that was more like two dirt tracks through the grass. "How's life?"

I shrugged.

"That bad?"

"My dad's cancer came back." My voice cracked.

It wasn't the first time I'd told someone. My friends and teachers all knew. But it felt harder to choke out the words today. Like Montana was our safe space, Dad's special escape, and now it was tainted with cancer too.

"Shit." West gave me a sad smile. "I'm sorry."

"Me too."

"I don't, uh . . . this is a stupid question. But what's that mean?"

"He had to have another surgery. And now he's on medication."

Medication to extend his life.

Medication to delay his death.

"The medication is good, and doctors are always making it better. Sometimes patients will be on it for decades."

Or sometimes it lasted less.

My parents had been honest with me. They'd shared the facts, some good and some bad. Cancer, I had learned, was all about statistics. I hated percentages. I hated the odds.

All we could do was wait.

And hope.

I leaned my arms on the window, letting the air rush over my face. The sting of tears was so sharp I had to breathe through my nose.

No crying.

Don't cry.

"Remember when we were kids and you fell and scraped your knee?" West asked as we bounced through a field.

"Yeah. You told me that girls cry."

"They do. It's okay. If you want to cry."

"I don't," I lied. The pressure in my chest was too tight, like my sports bra was three sizes too small.

West reached for a tin of Altoids in a compartment of the dash. He opened the lid and popped a mint into his mouth. "Want one?"

"Sure." I sucked on it until the urge to cry faded.

"I saw your dad's name on the list for tomorrow's trail ride," he said. "I'm taking people out. You're not going?"

"Nah."

"Bet I can change your mind." He flashed me a smile that made it a little easier to breathe.

I kept my head out the window as we made our way through a pasture. And when we reached the cattle, he counted the cows on his side of the truck while I counted the cows on mine.

"Now what?" I asked.

"Want me to drop you off on the road so you can keep running?"

"Not really."

He put the truck in park and shut it off, shifting so one of his arms was draped over the back of the seat. Then he just stared at me with a smile toying on his mouth.

It was unsettling. No boy had ever stared at me like that. My face felt hot. But I didn't want him to think I was a chicken or something, so I stared right back until, finally, I broke first.

"What?"

"Nothing." He flicked the end of my ponytail. "How's school?"

"Good."

"You're going to be a junior?"

"Yeah. Are you going to college?"

He nodded. "Montana State."

"I'm going to Baylor. That's where my parents went."

"You know that already?"

"Yeah. I really want to be on their soccer team, but I don't know if I'm good enough." I wasn't the worst person on our club team anymore. I wasn't the best, either, but I wasn't the worst. I'd worked really, really hard not to be the worst.

"You still play soccer? Are you still clumsy too?"

"Stop." I swatted at his arm. "I'm not that clumsy."

He smirked. "Says the girl who almost fell into the ditch earlier."

"Oh my God." I giggled. "You scared me. Anyone would trip."

"How loud was that music if you couldn't hear a truck come up behind you?"

"Not that loud." I rolled my eyes, my cheeks pinching as I fought a smile.

"What were you listening to?"

"Music."

"No shit." West laughed, and it was the best sound ever. "What music?"

"I don't know. Workout music." It was loud and sort of angry, and there were a lot of curse words. I didn't want him to hear it.

"Let me listen." He reached for my phone still in my armband.

"Not on your life." I shifted, trying to move away, but he just laughed and kept after me.

"Hand it over, Indy." He shifted closer, moving across the bench seat. But when he couldn't get my phone out of the band, he tickled my ribs until I was squirming, trapped against the truck's door.

"West!" I laughed so hard it hurt. "Stop."

"Fine." He held up his hands, and when I looked over, a huge smile stretched across his face.

It was beyond hot.

West Haven was gorgeous.

His hazel eyes sparkled as they dropped to my mouth.

Oh. My. God. Was he going to kiss me? He looked like he might kiss me. Did I want him to kiss me? *Yes.*

"Have you ever been kissed?"

I swallowed hard, sitting up straighter. "Yes."

Last year, one of the guys on the boys' soccer team had asked me on a date. Dad still didn't want me to have a boyfriend, so I'd had to say no. But after practice one day, when we were the last two on the field, he sat with me while I stretched. And before Mom came to get me, he'd kissed me.

I had kind of gotten embarrassed and run away. The week after that, he began dating one of the other girls on the team.

"Indy." West leaned in closer, his hand sliding into my ponytail. "I want to kiss you. Is that okay?"

I nodded and closed my eyes.

His other hand came to my face first, his palm warm against my jaw. Then he dropped his mouth to mine, and God, his lips were soft.

A flutter stirred in my belly. My heart felt like it was doing somersaults.

That boy from soccer hadn't given me somersaults.

This should have been my first kiss. I should have waited for West.

He moved his lips over mine, trailing them from one corner to the other. It was gentle. Thrilling. Every time I thought he'd stop, he kept going. And when his tongue darted out to lick my bottom lip, I felt every bone in my body turn to mush.

He smiled against my mouth, then leaned away.

I didn't know where to look or what to do, so I just stared at him while he stared at me. He had the prettiest eyes. The green and gold and brown were perfectly blended together, and the longer I stared, the more the colors seemed to move, like paint swirling.

"Are you going to go on the trail ride tomorrow?" he asked, twirling a finger around one of my curls.

"I guess."

He chuckled. "Told you I could change your mind."

"Maybe I'll change my mind again."

West kissed me again.

The next day, when Dad went to go on his trail ride, I went too.

And that night, while my parents were sitting around the campfire at the lodge, I sneaked off to meet West in the barn.

He kissed me twelve times over the week.

And when we left Montana, I didn't care so much that I'd missed soccer camp.

Chapter 14
INDYA

My knees bounced as I checked the time. Two o'clock.

Another hour until the meeting.

Another hour until I had to face West.

It had been six days since we'd had sex. Six days since I'd sprinted away from his bed like the room was on fire. Six days, and if I'd done two things well during that time, it had been avoiding West and thinking about West.

Except I couldn't ignore him forever. There were important things with the resort and ranch to discuss, and I'd delayed this meeting for as long as possible.

Anxiety churned my stomach, and my granola bar lunch threatened to make a reappearance.

And as every day had passed, I was being twisted tighter and tighter. I was jumpy and anxious. Whenever I heard footsteps in the hallway outside the office, I'd hold my breath, wondering if it was West.

Last night, I'd been sitting on the couch replying to some emails when a knock had come at the door. I'd jumped up so forcefully that my phone had fallen to the floor, and I'd slammed my shin into the corner of the coffee table.

Reid had brought over samples of the vegetarian dinner options to the Beartooth, and I'd been both relieved and frustrated to see him—at least the food had been delicious.

For all my efforts avoiding West, he'd put in as much to steer clear of me too.

Not today. One more hour—then whether I was ready to face him or not, I didn't have a choice.

What was wrong with me? Of all the idiotic choices to make, sex with West ranked number one. As if this situation weren't complicated enough.

What was I doing here? This entire adventure had been doomed from the start. Not the business—I'd be damned if I let this resort and ranch fail. But my heart was doomed to break.

It was inevitable.

Deep down, I'd known that from the moment my tires had crossed the Montana state line.

West and I had too much history.

No matter how many years passed between us, no matter how many times I'd told myself I'd moved on, there was no forgetting.

I'd loved West Haven for what felt like my entire life.

Even though I'd never said the words. Even though I'd never made him a promise.

Even though I'd married another man.

West was mine.

Even though he wasn't.

When I left here with that broken heart, I'd have only myself to blame.

Because six days ago, *I'd* been the one begging him to fuck me.

"Ugh." I groaned and buried my face in my hands. God, I was an idiot. "Never again."

Dropping my hands, I closed my laptop. There was no way I'd be able to sit still for another hour. It had been hard enough to make it through the morning, constantly watching the clock as time ticked away.

I'd texted West this morning and asked if he and Jax could meet me at three. He'd replied with a thumbs-up. I didn't know what a thumbs-up meant. Maybe he'd been too busy to type out a reply. Maybe he liked emojis.

It was the first time I'd ever texted West. I didn't know his texting habits.

Abandoning my desk, I headed to the lobby, then gave Deb a tight smile as I passed her at the desk.

She hadn't spoken a word to me this week, not since the egg incident last Sunday. Whatever. Deb didn't need to like me as her boss. At the moment, I just needed a warm body at the desk until I was ready to execute my backup plan.

Tara.

Tara was my contingency plan. She was hardworking. She was kind and, while guarded, respectful. We'd talked on Monday about her housekeeping team and the struggle finding employees on her existing budget.

So I'd increased her budget and given her a raise. An easy fix.

She'd had to sit down when I'd handed her the slip of paper with her updated salary.

The days of poor guest reviews and employees stretched too thin were over. No more cutting corners to trim expenses. Within the month, I expected a lot of new faces on the staff.

If Tara wanted to keep cleaning rooms, I'd make that happen. But if she wanted a change, I'd give her the front desk if—*when*—Deb was gone.

"Good afternoon." I smiled at the guest rocking in one of our new front-porch chairs. "Having a good day?"

"The best," the woman said, setting the book she was reading on her lap. "My husband is off on a hike, and I'm enjoying a day to myself."

"Oh, I finished that book a few weeks ago. It's fabulous."

"I'm really loving it."

"Enjoy." I waved, then jogged down the stairs and through the parking lot.

The sun streaked through the white clouds that dotted the blue sky. The scent of cut grass clung to the air.

Someone had cut the lawn around the lodge this morning. I'd woken to the sound of a mower, but by the time I'd showered and dressed, whoever had done the work was gone. A few days ago, the slow drip in the sink of the lodge's main-floor ladies' room had disappeared.

I suspected West was my mysterious groundskeeper and maintenance man.

I would have asked, except I'd been avoiding him all week, keeping busy and concentrating on details for the cabin remodel.

The sun's heat had soaked into my black tee as I walked to the farthest cabin. As I got close, the sounds of pounding hammers and buzzing power tools drifted from its open doorway.

"Knock, knock," I called before stepping inside.

My contractor poked his head out from a bedroom. "Hey, Indya."

"Hey, Mike. This looks . . . incredible."

"Thanks." He beamed under the praise, joining me in the kitchen. "I've got a great crew."

"I'll say. This is remarkable. I can't believe how much you've gotten done in just a week."

Light streamed through new black-paned windows. The old floors had been ripped away, and they'd started installing white oak herringbone flooring. I'd drawn inspiration from the Beartooth and asked Mike to install the same hardwoods in each cabin.

The old light fixtures would be replaced with recessed lighting. In the dining area, we'd hang a sleek, stylish chandelier with a Western vibe.

I filled my lungs with the smell of fresh paint from the bedrooms. Origami white, the same color that spotted Mike's hands and Carhartt pants.

Mike had come out on Monday to discuss the remodeling project. He'd made a few calls to find out the status of the materials Jonathan Lee had ordered—after I'd fired him, Jonathan had canceled those orders.

So Mike had hopped in his truck and hauled a trailer to Bozeman to pick up supplies himself. We'd had to stick with what the larger stores carried in stock, but everything he'd chosen was exactly what I would have picked myself.

It wasn't fancy, but it was crisp and authentic. Gone were the rugged, rough edge and outdated finishes. These cabins would be clean and wholesome, yet appealing to guests who expected a certain quality of hospitality.

"Want to check out the bathroom? We're just finishing up the tile."

"Love to." I followed him through the cabin.

Three of his men were in the bedrooms laying flooring, and I waved at each as we passed by. Outside in a dumpster were rolls of the old carpet.

No surprise, the bathroom tile was gorgeous. Another man was inside, working in the shower. The vanity's backsplash was tiled with cream marble in an intricate pattern.

"I don't know what to say," I told Mike. "This feels too good to be true."

In just days, he'd accomplished more than I'd expected to have done in months.

"You know, it's been a while since I did much work myself. These days, I mostly drive around and check on my crews. Spend too much time in the office with paperwork."

Mike's company built custom homes for wealthy people wanting a Montana escape. He had three houses in progress this summer, the smallest at seven thousand square feet.

"Vanessa and I were talking last night. I told her that I didn't realize how much I missed holding a hammer," he said. "This has been fun."

"I can't tell you how much I appreciate it."

"Happy to," he said. "West doesn't ask for much help. In fact, he never asks. I'm glad I could do this for him."

Mike wasn't here for the money I was paying him. He'd made room in his schedule for West.

"We should be able to get this cabin wrapped up by the end of next week. Then we'll dive into the others. I might not be around as much in

July, but my guys will take care of you. We'll get these cabins finished and then move on to the lodge."

The renovations at the lodge wouldn't be as extensive, but there were some cosmetic updates to be made in the dining rooms and guest rooms.

"I'll let you get back to work." I shook his hand. "Thanks again, Mike. Have a great weekend."

He dipped his chin. "You too."

As I returned to the lodge, my nerves returned with a vengeance. The brief distraction of the cabin remodel hadn't lasted long enough. It would be fine. This meeting would be great.

I'd grab a Diet Coke, give Dad a quick call, and then meet with West. It wasn't personal. This was a business meeting. I'd conducted a hundred of them in my lifetime. This one would be no different.

My mental pep talk was a waste of brainpower. When I spotted West's truck pulling into the parking lot, I tripped on a pebble, barely catching my balance.

"Shit." My face flamed as I glanced around, hoping no one had seen me.

Jax hopped out of the truck first, brushing the dirt from his jeans.

West climbed out next, adjusting the brim of his cowboy hat. The sleeves of his shirt were rolled up his forearms. A pair of leather gloves stuck out of a back pocket of his Wranglers. His boots were dusty.

No wonder I'd fallen into his bed last week. He looked sweaty and tired and utterly breathtaking.

He looked like the boy who'd kissed me in his truck when I was sixteen.

My heart squeezed, but I steeled my spine and changed paths toward his truck.

The moment West spotted me, his expression blanked. He looked through me, not at me.

It hurt. But I forced a small smile.

That blank look was my fault. For rushing out of his bedroom. For always keeping him at arm's length.

"Hi," I told him, then waved at his brother. "Hey, Jax."

"Hey."

"How did moving cows go today?"

Jax shrugged. "Good. Got it done."

We'd had to pull Jax off guiding trail rides today because West had needed his brother's help to move cows. Not that West had told me any of this. Jax had stomped into the office on Tuesday to tell me he couldn't take guests out today and to have Wyatt manage.

"So what did you need?" Jax asked, tapping his foot. He seemed as anxious to get this over with as I was.

"Let's talk in my office," I said, risking a glance at West.

He was staring down the road like he wanted to drive away and never look back. But when I walked to the lodge, he fell in step with Jax behind me.

"Hey, guys." Deb gave the Havens a beaming smile. She frowned my direction.

I just carried on to my office, then took a seat behind the desk.

Jax was the first to come inside, dropping into a folding chair—I really needed better chairs in here.

West didn't cross the threshold. He was back to hovering in the hallway, ready to bolt at any moment.

"Please?" I nodded to the chair beside Jax's.

He crossed his arms over his chest, but those feet didn't move.

"Fine." I opened my laptop and pulled up a browser. My designer had finished the rebranding late last night and launched the updates this morning. "This is the resort's new website."

Jax leaned closer as I spun the screen to face him. He blinked; then his eyes bulged.

My heart crawled into my throat, since I knew what he was reading. I stared ahead, to the horse painting, and braced for his reaction.

And West's.

"You. Renamed. Our. Ranch." Each of Jax's words was punctuated.

"Yes."

West's arms dropped to his sides, his hands fisting. "What?"

"She renamed our fucking ranch." Jax shot out of his chair. "Our family's ranch. Can she even do that?"

Would I ever stop being *she*? And yes, *she* could do that.

"To what?" West's voice was low. Dark.

I sucked in a breath. "Haven River Ranch."

West stayed silent.

Jax stood statue still, waiting for his brother's reaction.

My heart hammered in my chest. I gave West a few moments, let that name sink in, and then looked to the door. When I met his gaze, the intensity in those hazel eyes was so powerful I couldn't hold it.

"Is this meeting over?" Jax asked.

"Not quite yet." I stood and gestured to the hall. "I'd like to introduce you to a few people outside."

Jax didn't move. Not until West gave him a single nod.

Then, shoulder to shoulder, they stalked outside.

I followed a few paces back, forcing air into my lungs as my pulse raced.

Did he like the new name? Did he hate it? Did he hate me?

It was going to end that way, wasn't it? No matter what I did, his hatred was a foregone conclusion. I'd been a fool to think otherwise.

But I kept walking, one foot in front of the other, until we were outside.

Three eighteen-year-old boys were waiting.

"Hey, Luka." Jax shook one boy's hand and jerked his chin up to the other two. "Nicky. Gunner. What are you guys doing here?"

"Reporting for duty," Luka said. "Hey, Miss Keller."

"Hey. Welcome. Do I need to make introductions? Or do you all know each other?"

"We're good," Nicky said.

"Great." I faced Jax, because despite his shitty attitude, he was still the safer Haven brother. "Luka, Nicky, and Gunner will be working for us this summer. Trail rides. General help around the resort and ranch. Gunner is going to take the lead on fishing so we can offer that to guests a few days a week. Jax, would you mind spending a couple hours today giving them a quick orientation? When you guys are done, pop into the lodge, and I'll get you the rest of your employee paperwork."

"Yes, ma'am," Luka said.

Jax stared at me for a long moment, his eyebrows knit together. Then he shook it off and jerked his chin for the boys to follow him to the barn.

I waited until they were gone before I faced West.

"You hired all three of them?" he asked.

"For the summer."

Each of those boys had just graduated from high school. Luka was friends with Marie, and when I'd asked if she knew of anyone with some ranch experience wanting a job, she had given me his number. When I'd called Luka and invited him out for an interview yesterday, I'd told him to bring any friend who was looking for a job too.

He'd brought Nicky and Gunner.

All three of them were young. They'd make mistakes. But if it lightened West's load, even a little, then it was worth having them around.

"Maybe you can have them mow the lawn so you don't need to do it before dawn," I said.

He dragged a hand over his jaw, the stubble he'd grown in the past six days, then turned for his truck.

"West," I called.

He turned. "Yeah?"

"Do you like the name?" *Please, say yes.*

The name was for him.

It was all for him.

"Yeah, Indy. I like the name."

The relief was crushing. Before he could see the tears flooding my eyes, before he could turn his back on me, I walked away first.

Chapter 15
INDYA

Age Eighteen

"Are you sure you don't want to try camping?" Dad asked.

"One hundred percent sure." I nodded. "You guys have fun."

Behind him, standing beside the door with a bag slung over her shoulders, Mom mouthed, "Save me."

I pulled in my lips to keep from laughing.

Camping was at the very bottom of Mom's vacation to-do list. But Dad wanted to camp, so she would camp because it made Dad happy.

There wasn't much either of us wouldn't do to make Dad happy.

Like this trip. It was my graduation trip. He'd asked me where I wanted to go to celebrate, and I'd picked Montana.

For Dad.

He'd been super busy at work, and if this was his break for the summer, then I wanted him to love it.

Not that I didn't want to be here. This trip was a win for everyone. Well, except Mom, who had to go camping.

"Wish us luck," Dad said.

"Good luck." I giggled as Mom grimaced.

"Oh, Ellen." He chuckled. "This will be fun. It's an adventure."

"If I get eaten by a bear, I swear to God, Grant, I will haunt you for the rest of your life."

"I've got bear spray." He kissed her forehead. "And if it fails, I can deal with a few years of haunting."

My smile faded.

A few years.

He talked like that; Mom did too. They'd drop these subtle reminders that he wouldn't be around forever. Did they think it would make it easier when he was gone?

It wouldn't make it easier. Nothing would make this easier.

Besides, it wasn't like he was on death's doorstep. The medication was working, and the doctors were hopeful. There were no new tumors. The cancer hadn't spread to his other organs. Why was he so sure his time was almost up?

He had more than a few years. I felt it down to my bones.

"Have a good night, pumpkin." Dad opened the door for Mom. "Lock this."

"I will."

"Love you," Mom said.

"Love you too." I followed them out to the porch and waved as they made their way to the lodge.

This camping thing was a new activity at the resort. They'd pick up tents from the front desk, then hike out to one of the areas already prepped for an overnight stay.

Mom and Dad would have to set up their own tent and build their own fire. But the area was already staged with wood and matches. And they wouldn't be so far into the mountains that they didn't have phone service.

I went inside the chalet, shutting the door and flipping the lock. Then I flopped on the couch and picked up my phone to see a string of missed texts from my friends.

That concert was amazing!

We missed you IK!

Best. Night. Eva! How's Montana?

My fingers flew over the screen as I sent my reply.

Ugh. I wish I could be there! MT is good.

Four of my friends had gotten VIP tickets to a Florida Georgia Line concert last night. I hated missing stuff with them, especially because we were all going to different colleges. We'd totally stay friends, but it would be strange not seeing them every day at school.

Everything felt like it was changing.

Did you see Eli?

I waited, expecting a quick response to my text. But ten minutes later, no one in our group chat had responded. Which meant they'd seen Eli. And he'd probably been with another girl.

Was it Mia? Was he sleeping with her already? We'd broken up a week ago, but he'd always liked Mia. They were going to Texas A&M together too.

With every moment my phone stayed quiet, my friends likely texting on the side, my heart sank.

Eli and I had dated for a year. My parents were friends with his, and last summer, we'd all gone to Mexico for a two-week vacation. It was why we hadn't come to Montana. After that trip, we'd started dating.

But neither of us wanted to try a long-distance relationship. Our colleges were only a couple of hours away from each other, but he was playing on A&M's football team, and I'd be busy with school.

The breakup had been Eli's idea, but we both knew it would be easier to break up now than drag it out. That, or he'd just used it as an excuse to hook up with Mia all summer.

Thank God I hadn't had sex with him. We'd gotten close a couple of times, but I'd always stopped before going all the way.

"Whatever." I put my phone on the couch and left the cabin. Maybe a walk before dark would make me feel better.

I passed the lodge, smiling at a couple who must have had the same idea. They walked hand in hand down the road for an evening stroll.

Dang it. Either I'd have to run in front of them, which would be weird, or I could follow behind, which would also be weird.

My gaze drifted to the grove of trees where West had built his fort. Was it still there? Was he here this summer, home from college and working on the ranch? I hadn't seen him yet, but we'd been here for only a day.

He'd probably be annoyed with me for snooping, but I changed paths anyway, meandering past the barn. But before I veered toward the trees, raised voices stopped my feet.

"There's nothing wrong with where I put that gate, Dad."

West. My heart skipped. He was here.

"It's not where I told you to put it," Curtis barked.

"It makes sense to have it in that corner."

"When you own this ranch, you can put the gates wherever you want. But you don't own it. It's mine, and that's not where I told you to put the gate. So tomorrow, you're going to go move it."

"The hell I am," West hollered. "Move it yourself. If you want it done your way, then do it yourself."

"You're fixing it. Or you can forget about getting paid this summer."

West stayed quiet.

His silence must have irritated his dad, because Curtis huffed and stormed out of the barn.

I pressed my back against the wall, slinking around the corner until he was in his truck and driving away. Then I exhaled and came out of hiding, walking to the open barn door.

West was saddling a horse in a stall, his movements angry and rushed.

"Hey."

His glare whipped my direction, but the moment he realized it was me, his gorgeous face softened. "Hey."

His shoulders seemed broader. His frame larger. The line of his jaw was stronger and covered in dark stubble. He was twenty. He looked more like a man than the guy who'd kissed me in his truck two years ago.

I'd forgotten just how much my belly fluttered when he was around. Definitely more than it ever had with Eli.

"How much of that did you hear?" he asked, going back to the saddle.

"Enough."

He blew out a long sigh, dropping his chin. Then he turned and stared at me. He stared so long it was an effort not to shift back and forth on my feet.

"What?" I whispered when I couldn't stand it any longer.

"Nothing." He shook his head. "I'm going for a ride."

"Okay."

"Want to come?"

"Yes."

He led the horse through the barn and out the other side's wide doorway. I followed, hanging back as he walked in a few circles before stopping to tighten the saddle's cinch.

When he was ready, West jerked his chin for me to come over. Then he held out the stirrup so I could swing onto the horse's back.

I shifted as far forward as possible in the saddle, but the space behind me didn't seem like enough. Could this horse even carry both of us? "How do I—"

"You ride. I'll walk."

"Oh." I hadn't meant to hijack his ride. "I don't need—"

"Just hold on, Indy."

"Okay." I nodded and gripped the horn. Then he led us through a gate and into a field.

West didn't speak as we walked. The only sounds were the horse's breathing and its hooves digging into the dirt.

I settled into the rhythm of the horse's movements, stealing glances at West every few minutes.

He'd cut his hair. The ends at his nape didn't brush against the collar of his shirt like they had two years ago. But he still rolled up the sleeves of his button-down shirt. He still wore the same faded Wranglers and cowboy boots.

"How's college?" I asked, breaking the silence.

"Good. I like it."

"I'm starting in August."

"Baylor?"

"Yeah."

"Did you make the soccer team?"

"No, I didn't even try out."

He glanced up at me. "Why not?"

"It doesn't feel as important as it used to." I wanted to go to school and have fun. I wanted my weekends free to hang out with friends or go home to visit Mom and Dad. "That, and I'm not good enough."

"How do you know?"

"My coach told me."

"The fuck?" A frown marred his handsome face, and I laughed.

"It's true. Don't worry, it didn't hurt my feelings. It was sort of a relief."

The scowl stayed on his face.

"West?"

"Yeah?"

"I'm sorry about your dad."

He raked a hand through his hair. "He's a pain in my ass. He wants everything done his way, and he likes to remind me all the time that this is his ranch, not mine. I don't get a say."

"Then why do you come back?" Couldn't he get a job somewhere else for the summer?

He swept a hand out in front of us to the meadow. To the mountains and trees and cattle in the distance.

It was all the explanation I needed.

The sun was setting, dipping closer and closer to the mountains. The sky was a mixture of yellow and orange and blue. Behind us, the lodge windows reflected its golden light.

I couldn't see West living anywhere else. This was his home.

This was why he came back.

We walked for a while longer until finally he looped us in a circle, taking us toward the resort.

"Dad's not always bad," he said. "We just butt heads sometimes."

"Me and Mom do that a lot."

"How pissed are your parents going to be that you're out tonight?"

"They went camping."

"Ah." The corners of his mouth turned up. "That was my idea."

"Really? It's fun. Not that I want to camp, but Dad loved it."

"Yeah. Someday, I want to get nicer, bigger tents. Let people go glamping."

"Glamping?"

"Glamorous camping."

I laughed. "Sign me up for that. As long as I don't have to sleep on the ground."

"It's not so bad." He grinned up at me.

Maybe if West was taking me camping, I wouldn't mind so much.

We reached the barn before I was ready, but the light had faded, and stars glittered overhead.

He dealt with the horse and saddle, and once everything was put away, he pointed toward the lodge. "I'll walk you back."

"Thanks." My cheeks flushed as his hand settled on the small of my back. Tingles raced up my spine.

With every step, my breath quickened. Would he kiss me again? I was a better kisser now than I had been two years ago. I really wanted him to kiss me again.

I worried my bottom lip between my teeth as we reached the cabin, but as I took the first two steps, I realized West's hand was gone.

He stood on the ground, hands shoved into his jeans pockets.

"What?" I retreated a step, putting us eye to eye.

"Good night, Indy." His throat bobbed as he swallowed. He turned, but I threw out my hand, grabbing his arm.

"Wait."

He couldn't leave, not yet. I wasn't sure when I'd be in Montana again. What if I didn't see him again?

That thought had never occurred to me before. Not once. Because we always came back to Montana. Always. Maybe it took a year or two, but we always came back.

Except Dad kept talking like he had one foot in the grave. What if this was the last trip?

I wasn't ready to say goodbye, not yet.

"Would you kiss me again?"

"Indya." His voice sounded hoarse. His eyes searched mine.

"Please?" My heart was in my throat as I waited and hoped. "Please, West."

Don't go. Kiss me.

Maybe he heard my silent plea. Or maybe I was the one who closed the gap. One moment, we were staring at each other. The next, his lips were on mine, and his tongue swept past my teeth.

My fingers dived into his hair. He smiled against my mouth. Then I let him carry me inside.

And lock the door.

West was my first. He made it the best night of my life.

We woke at dawn so he could leave before my parents returned from camping. He kissed me before he sneaked out of the cabin.

And as I watched him walk away, I smiled, knowing this was exactly where I was supposed to be.

With West in Montana.

Chapter 16
WEST

I walked into the barn and froze.

It looked . . . different.

"Hey, West." Gunner walked out of the tack room and jerked up his chin. He was carrying a stack of empty five-gallon buckets.

"Hi." I planted my hands on my hips as he took the buckets to a shelf along the wall.

An empty shelf. Yesterday, there'd been splice wire on that shelf, but the barbed loops were hanging on the wall.

The saddles had been oiled and arranged neatly on their racks. The halter ropes and bridles were organized on their hooks. The lawn mower I'd been parking in the corner was gone.

I was still taking inventory of the changes when a hand smacked my shoulder.

"Hey." Jax passed me, with Luka and Nicky following on his heels. He stopped in the middle of the barn, then turned in a slow circle. "Looks good, guys. Appreciate the help."

"No problem," Luka said. "What's next?"

Jax checked his watch. "Would you guys mind hauling some firewood from the stack behind the shed to the guest firepit? Then you can take off. It's almost five."

"You got it." Nicky nodded before the three of them set off for the shed.

"How'd you make out on the swathing?" Jax asked.

The swathing? I didn't want to talk about swathing. I wanted to talk about the barn and why it looked . . . clean. "What's going on here?"

"What do you mean?"

I circled a finger in the air. "Did you do all of this?"

"No. I was out riding with guests all day. Luka came with me to train while Gunner and Nicky tackled this. I gave them that list you've been keeping on the workbench."

A workbench that wasn't nearly as chaotic as it had been yesterday when I'd come in to collect my fencing pliers.

"Huh." I rubbed a hand over my jaw. "Did they clean out the shed?"

"Think so."

The shed had been a disaster for months. It had become a dumping ground for rakes and shovels and other yard tools. The spot where we'd normally stow the mower had been overrun, hence why I'd been parking it in the barn.

I'd been meaning to organize it but hadn't had time.

"This is . . ." Damn.

"Pretty great, right?" Jax grinned.

"Yeah." It was fucking amazing.

"Grandma called and needs help fixing a leak in the roof of her chicken house tonight."

"Need a hand?" That was normally a job Dad would do, but since she clearly hadn't started speaking to him again, she'd called Jax.

"Nah. Should be easy. I'm going to head over now. She promised dinner, and I'm starving. Are you going to be around later? I could swing by for a beer."

"That sounds good." Did I have beer? There sure wasn't much for food at my house. Last night I'd made a peanut butter–and–jelly sandwich on questionable bread.

Maybe tonight I'd head into town. Trips to the grocery store were usually rushed and frantic. But everything on my own to-do list could wait until tomorrow. For once, that list was manageable.

The past two weeks had been a couple of the most productive in my life. Without being pulled to pitch in on the resort or take a trail ride, I'd been able to focus on the ranch. Last week, I'd replaced a stretch of old barbed wire fence that had been neglected for far too long. Then I'd moved some cattle between pastures. And this week, with the hot July weather and our abundance of grass, I'd started cutting hay.

Six meadows were lined with windrows. With any luck, the weather would hold, and it would dry over the next few days. Then I'd start baling.

Haying was one of the more time-consuming annual projects on the ranch. One that typically meant little sleep and long hours because I had to stop all the damn time and help with guest activities.

But for two weeks, I'd been able to focus without interruption.

Because Indya was running the resort, and she'd hired three kids who knew how to ride and work.

It was brilliant.

I wished I had done it myself. Not that Dad would ever have hired three kids.

We wouldn't have had much extra to pay the boys. Plus he'd always balked at the idea of teenagers working at the resort unless they were his own.

They'll make too many mistakes.

I don't have time to babysit.

It's risky letting young boys around our guests when they might say the wrong thing or get too friendly with daughters.

Dad wasn't wrong. Those were all valid reasons to keep a staff primarily of adults.

But adults needed babysitting too. Adults made mistakes. And Indya had set firm boundaries. Everyone on her payroll knew that affairs with guests was a line not to be crossed. She'd probably made that inescapably clear with these boys.

A weight floated off my shoulders as I took another look around. A weight I hadn't even realized was there.

The list on the workbench wouldn't haunt me every time I set foot in the barn. I didn't need to worry about mowing the lawn or stacking firewood. There were no emails to answer in the dead of night—I'd gladly relinquished control of the resort inbox to Indya.

"Well, shit." I'd have to admit she was helping, wouldn't I?

It was almost five o'clock, and if I wanted, I could just go home. Stop working.

It was unsettling to have free time.

But I wasn't just going to go home. There was a woman I needed to see first.

I hadn't seen Indya since she'd called us here to meet with the boys and tell us about the resort's new name. For the past two weeks, I'd made a point of avoiding the lodge at all costs—other than the Saturday campfires, which Indya had skipped. We hadn't crossed paths.

I'd needed that time to think. Time to work. Time to breathe.

We might not have spoken in two weeks, but she'd plagued my thoughts. Whenever she crossed my mind—more often than I wanted to admit—I'd pull up the resort's website.

I'd nearly memorized every word on every page.

Haven River Ranch.

She could have given it her name. *Keller River Ranch. Keller Mountain Resort.* Anything else.

But nowhere on that website, not even on the About Us section, was a mention of her name. Instead, she'd left the story Grandma had written thirty years ago about how the Havens had come to live on this land. She'd left pictures from decades ago to tell *my* family's story, not hers.

Maybe it was all strategic. Our history played well into the allure of ranching. It enticed people to spend thousands of dollars for a week in Montana.

Except my gut screamed there was something else. Something Indya wasn't telling me.

Why had she bought this ranch?

Shock and anger and devastation had clouded so much of the past month that I hadn't asked that question. I'd been too worried about, well . . . me.

But two weeks spent working alone had given me plenty of time to reflect.

Why was Indya here? For the money?

No. This wasn't a simple investment, not while she was busting her ass at the lodge each day. Was it for Grant? Or was it because of Blaine? Was this a postdivorce crisis? She hadn't told me she was divorced, but I knew Indya well enough to know she wouldn't climb into my bed if she were tied to another man.

Why? I was ready for answers. And there was only one place to get them.

I'd just stepped out of the barn when a truck door slammed, the sound shifting my attention to the parking lot.

Dad stood, hands on his hips, staring at the lodge.

There were rocking chairs on the porch. Flower planters overflowing with petunias. A hand-carved wooden sign at the base of the porch steps that read **WELCOME TO HAVEN RIVER RANCH**.

It was all Indya's doing.

A month ago, I would have hated it. A month ago, I would have glared at those flowers the way Dad glared at the sign.

A month ago, I had still been drowning in resentment and grief.

Acceptance wasn't so bad.

Dad and I hadn't spoken since I'd gone to his house weeks ago. He hadn't shown up to help with the ranch, and as far as I knew, he'd become a recluse. I wasn't even sure if he'd left home for food. Good thing his freezer was always stocked.

He must have also lost his razor and forgotten where to find the laundry room.

He looked like shit. The white-and-gray stubble on his face was nearly a beard. His jeans were dirty on the knees, and his shirt was rumpled.

There was a twinge in my chest, a pang of worry. No matter what, he was still my father. Even if I wasn't sure how to forgive him.

I guess Mom and I had that in common. We loved him even when we couldn't stand him.

Dad sneered at the lodge, then dug out the wad of Copenhagen in his lower lip before tossing it to the ground. When he spotted me, he stood straighter, wiping his mouth. "Oh, uh, hi."

"Dad." I stopped by the grill of his truck.

"Heard about all the changes around here. Came to see it for myself." His jaw flexed. "Haven River Ranch. Generations this has been Crazy Mountain Cattle, and she just renamed it."

He'd been stewing about that for weeks, hadn't he?

"I bet your grandparents are in a tizzy over this. They'll probably move to town over this."

I scoffed. "No, they won't."

Grandpa went to Big Timber only when Grandma needed a ride to the store. After he'd retired and passed the ranch down to Dad, he'd become a bit reclusive himself. He didn't mind people, especially when they came to visit him at his house. But he wasn't as social as he'd once been. Any amount of traffic caused him stress. Crowds made him irritable. And his favorite pastime was reminiscing about simpler times.

There was no way my grandfather would voluntarily live in town.

Even if he was angry about the changes on the ranch. Even if he was stewing over a new name. Like father, like son.

Maybe I'd done a bit of stewing myself.

"They took the news about the name in stride," I told Dad. "I delivered it myself. It was a surprise, but not as shocking as other announcements recently, don't you think?"

Dad's gaze dropped to the dirt. He couldn't put all this on Indya when he'd started it in the first place.

"I like the name," I told him. "A lot."

"She could have waited a damn year," he muttered. "Showed some respect."

"Well, it's hers, isn't it?" I didn't bother hiding the accusation in my tone. If he'd wanted the name to stay the same, he shouldn't have sold our fucking property. "She gets to do whatever the hell she wants. And personally, I think she showed a lot of respect considering she gave it our name, not her own."

Dad kicked at a rock. "There was no need to change the name at all."

"She did what she thought was best. That's what she's been doing. And maybe all these changes were what this place needed. I'm man enough to admit that. Are you?"

"You're defending her?"

"Yeah, I guess I am."

Dad's lip curled before he marched to his truck, ripped open the door, and jumped inside.

"Stubborn ass." I was nearly to the lodge when his engine roared to life and his tires peeled out of the lot.

He didn't get to be angry at me for defending Indya. He didn't get to be angry, period. This was his fucking fault.

What she was doing here was the right thing. She'd told me a month ago she wasn't the enemy. Had I listened? No.

It was time to wave the white flag. Stop avoiding her. Stop holding it against her that she'd raced out of my bedroom weeks ago without a backward glance.

The dull murmur of voices and laughter drifted from the dining room when I walked into the lobby.

"Hey, West." Tara was stationed at the desk.

It was Wednesday. Deb worked on Wednesday.

"Hey, Tara. What's going on? Where's Deb?"

"She got fired two hours ago."

My jaw hit the dirty toe of my boot. "What?"

"Yep. You missed it. Indya called Deb into her office, fired her, and escorted her off the property." A glint sparked in Tara's eyes.

Tara thought Deb was lazy and a conniving gossip. She wasn't wrong.

"Damn." I couldn't say I was upset about it. Deb was a huge pain in the ass; I just hadn't taken the time to replace her.

"I like Indya," Tara declared.

So do I.

And that was the problem.

"Is she in her office?" I asked.

"No. After the dust settled with Deb, she went home. I told her I'd cover the desk so she could take a night off."

"Wait. Indya's been covering the desk? What happened to Marie?"

Tara laughed. "You've been under a rock, West."

"I've been busy."

"Marie quit last week."

"What? Why?"

"There was some teenage drama with Marie and Gunner's new girlfriend, Hannah. Gunner told me that Hannah was looking for a job, so she came out and interviewed for a housekeeper position. I hired her, then came to find out that Marie hates Hannah. Marie went to Indya to have Hannah fired, and Indya told her no. That's when Marie quit."

"Huh," I muttered, rubbing a hand over my jaw.

So Indya had told Marie no, knowing that it meant we'd lose an evening desk clerk and that she'd have to cover it herself.

All so Tara would have a housekeeper. Gunner would be around to mow, organize the barn, help with the horses, and whatever else I needed for the ranch. And Grandma was finally enjoying retirement and not getting called in to cover the desk at random.

How the hell had I missed all this?

Because I'd been in a swather, blissfully cutting hay while Indya had been dealing with all the resort bullshit that I absolutely loathed.

Another thing I was going to have to admit.

She was better at running this place than I'd ever be.

Mostly because she had the time. But also because the resort had never been my priority. I didn't love it enough to put it first.

"You look like your head is about to explode," Tara teased.

"It might."

"A lot is changing."

I nodded. "It is."

"Not all change is bad."

No, it wasn't. "Thanks, Tara. Have a good night."

"You too."

Every time I came into the lodge these days, it felt like I left with whiplash. The same was true when I went to Beartooth. A part of me wanted to go home and relax. Take a hot shower and have that beer with Jax when he came over.

But I didn't go to my truck. I followed the path to Indya's cabin, then took the porch stairs two at a time to knock on her door.

She answered wearing a baggy T-shirt and a pair of skintight shorts that barely covered her ass. That wild mess of curls was piled on top of her head. Her phone was pressed between her shoulder and ear. In one hand she carried a glass of red wine with no more than a swallow left in the bottom.

"I'll talk to you later. Love you, too, Mom." She ended the call and took the phone from her ear. Then she downed the rest of that wine, shifting out of the way so I could step inside.

The moment I crossed the threshold, I realized my mistake.

Sweet rose perfume filled my nose. That scent was tied to countless memories. A kiss in my old truck. An evening leading a horse through a meadow before taking Indya's virginity. A night in my bed two weeks ago that I couldn't stop replaying on repeat.

"Wine?" Indya held up her empty glass.

I shook my head. "No, thanks."

"Do you like wine?"

"Sometimes. I prefer whiskey."

"We've never had a drink together," she murmured, walking to the kitchen.

No, we'd never had a drink together. She didn't know that my favorite whiskey was Pendleton. I didn't know if she drank only red wine or if she also liked white. I didn't know what she liked in her morning coffee, if she even liked coffee.

The not knowing festered. It had been festering since the night she'd answered her door wearing that blue negligee.

I opened my mouth, about to ask about the wine and the coffee and any other detail that came to mind, when she reached into a cabinet, rising up on her toes, to fetch a new bottle of wine.

The hem of her T-shirt rode up her body, showing more of those second-skin shorts.

Fuck. To hell with my questions. I needed out of this cabin.

"Guess you heard I fired Deb today." Indya uncorked the bottle, then refilled her glass. The liquid glugged, and as it sloshed toward the rim, a plop landed on the counter.

"Yeah. Tara told me."

"I'm not hiring her back."

"I didn't ask you to hire her back."

She fumbled the cork as she tried to stuff it back in the bottle.

"Are you drunk?"

"A little."

I'd never seen her drunk on anything but me.

The circles beneath her eyes seemed darker than they had weeks ago. Was she sleeping? "You okay?"

She shrugged.

I'd been getting those shrugs my whole damn life. They meant no, she wasn't okay.

Indya took her wine to the dining room table, where there were seven neat columns of cards on the surface.

Solitaire. The world's loneliest game.

She'd been here for a month, alone in this cabin. Her family and friends were on the other side of the country. But she chose to stay.

Why?

The last time Indya had left Montana, I'd been certain, down to my bones, that it was the last time I'd see her beautiful face. That night, I'd memorized every line while she'd slept. I'd traced every curve with my finger.

Yet here she was.

Why? Why had she come back?

I joined her at the table, the legs of my chair sliding across the floor as I took a seat. Only the table's corner and those cards separated us.

"I don't have the energy for a fight tonight, West." She set her glass aside and placed a two of spades beneath a three of hearts.

"I'm not here to fight."

Her golden gaze flicked to mine before returning to the cards.

I leaned back in my chair, kicking an ankle up over my knee. Then I watched her play solitaire, biting my tongue when she missed a move. "Where's your husband?"

"Not in Montana. Part of its appeal." She took a sip of wine, then set the glass down to move a stack of four cards. "And he's my ex-husband."

Thank fuck. She deserved better than Blaine.

"What happened?"

A shrug. I hated those damn shrugs.

"Why are you here, Indy? You could have hired someone to run this resort. Instead, you're doing it yourself. Why?"

Her hands stopped moving as she kept her eyes locked on the cards spread between us. "For Dad."

She'd cover the desk in the evenings. She'd oversee the cabin remodels. She'd fire shitty employees.

For Grant.

I wanted to tell her to live her own life. To stop doing everything with her father in mind. But how many years had I done the same?

She'd do anything for Grant Keller.

I couldn't fault her for that.

With a sweep of my hand, I pushed her cards into a pile and destroyed her solitaire game.

"West." She scowled. "Do you mind?"

"Still remember how to play poker?"

"Yes, but I'm not playing poker tonight."

"Afraid you'll lose?"

She rolled her eyes. "Maybe I just don't want to play."

I chuckled, taking the cards and knocking them against the table to build a stack.

"We don't have any toothpicks to use for betting," she said.

"So? We'll play one hand. Five cards each. One draw. Best hand wins a truth."

"A truth?"

"A truth." I nodded. "If I win, you have to tell me what happened with Blaine."

She took a sip of wine, studying me from over the rim. "And if I win, you have to tell me why you bought that land and expanded the ranch."

Goddamn this woman. She knew right where to shove her knives.

"Fine." I shuffled the deck, let her cut, and then dealt out five cards each.

She took three.

I swapped two.

"One pair." I laid down my aces with a grin.

She blew out a long breath and tossed her cards onto the table, face up.

A pair of queens.

And a pair of fours.

"Fuck."

"You lose." She giggled. "I'll take my truth, please."

"You'll get it. But not tonight." Not when I wasn't ready to explain.

An adorable crease formed between her eyebrows. Her pink mouth turned down in a frown.

She looked so much prettier when she was smiling.

So I leaned across the table, sending the cards scattering.

And kissed that frown off her face.

Chapter 17
INDYA

Kissing West was just asking for trouble. With everything happening at the resort, the sensible decision would be to cut this off. To pull away and point him toward the door. But as his mouth captured mine, all sensibility vanished.

The moment I parted my lips, his tongue dipped inside. Slowly. Deliberately. Lusciously.

My body went up in flames. The T-shirt I'd pulled on was too thick and hot. These shorts were too tight. I wanted nothing but West's skin bare against my own.

We moved at the same time, both standing from our chairs. And like his thoughts mirrored my own, he went for the hem of my shirt, breaking our mouths apart only to rip the cotton over my head.

His hazel eyes darkened as he took in my naked torso—I'd taken my bra off when I'd come home after a miserable day. West cupped my breasts, the rough callouses of his palms like fuel to the fire raging in my veins. As one hand rolled a nipple, his other dived into my hair, finding the tie and tugging it loose.

I arched into his touch, threading the thick strands of his hair between my knuckles as he bent to seal his mouth over my nipple. "Yes."

He hummed, the vibration shooting straight to my center.

My pulse shook my very bones, and the throbbing in my core was so powerful my knees wobbled.

"Indy," West murmured against my sternum as he moved to the other nipple, giving it the same torture. A suck. A lick. A nip with his teeth.

"Oh, God." I let go of his hair and reached between us, loosening the button on his shirt. "Off. Take this off. Now."

He hummed again and ignored me.

So I fisted the cotton and ripped with all my might.

A button pinged off the table as it broke free of its threads.

West's mouth gave a pop as he released me and stood tall. Then he arched one of those dark eyebrows before dropping his gaze to his shirt.

That arrogant, indignant smirk shouldn't have been attractive. But damn, it was sexy. So, so sexy.

"I liked this shirt," he said.

"It will look better on my floor." I unclasped a button, then another and another. My fingers moved quickly until I reached the end and had to yank the hem from his jeans.

There was a plain, white T-shirt beneath. Damn it. Layers? "When did you start wearing so many shirts?"

His deep chuckle filled the quiet spaces as he swatted my hands away and stripped off the button-down. Then he reached behind his head, and with a quick tug, his T-shirt puddled on the floor beside mine.

We collided in a frantic mess of lips and limbs. I rose up on my bare toes, my arms looping over his shoulders as he swept me against his chest. The coarse dusting of hair on his chest rubbed against my smooth skin, scraping ever so slightly.

West fluttered his tongue against mine before changing the angle of our mouths to plunder. His hands came to my ass, cupping my curves as he hoisted me up off the floor.

My legs wrapped around his waist, pulling tight as I tried to get closer. But his jeans and that belt buckle were in the way.

I stretched out an arm, waving for him to take me to the couch.

He moved to the kitchen instead, then set me on the counter as he tore his lips away. His finger hooked in the waistband of my shorts, tugging at the elastic and sending it snapping back. "Off."

I shimmied out of the shorts, keeping my perch on the counter, as he flicked open the clasp on his belt. My shorts were kicked free the moment he'd untucked himself from his jeans, his cock hard and thick.

My mouth went dry, and my head was spinning. It wasn't the wine; it was West. I was drunk on his touch, his kiss, his masculine, spicy scent. "Please."

He fitted his hips between my legs, urging my knees apart. And then without any hesitation, he lined up at my entrance and filled me with a single thrust.

"West," I cried out as my eyes slammed shut. It was too much and exactly right, all at the same time.

My body stretched and molded around his as our breaths mingled. The grip I had on his shoulders was bruising, my fingertips digging into rock-hard muscle.

"Fuck, you feel good," he murmured. His hands were splayed on my ass, and with a quick lift, he changed the angle, sending his cock impossibly deep.

I gasped, my body liquifying.

He eased out and slammed inside once more, groaning as I whimpered. Then he set a quick pace, holding me exactly where he wanted me as he brought us together, again and again.

A sheen of sweat coated my skin, and my hair draped around us, the ends tickling my ribs and spine.

There was so much to feel that I couldn't concentrate on any individual part. His hands on my curves. His mouth on my throat. The root of his cock against my clit.

West consumed it all, inside and out. His tongue trailed across the line of my jaw before he kissed me again, matching the rhythm of his tongue with the piston of his hips.

My toes curled. My legs quaked. Just a little bit more and—

West tore his lips away with an irritated growl.

"What?" My eyes fluttered open and immediately caught a sunbeam streaming inside.

Past his shoulder and across the room, the windows looked invisible in the evening light. Beyond the cabin was nothing but the breathtaking view. And anyone walking would see us fucking in this kitchen.

West drove inside, stealing my breath, then trapped me in his arms as he hauled me off the counter.

My legs wound around his waist, my ankles hooking above his ass and the draping waistband of his jeans. No underwear tonight.

How often did he go commando? If he wore underwear, was it always boxer briefs? I wanted to know anything and everything about this man. I wanted to ask the questions we hadn't had time to explore in the past.

Later. They'd wait until later. Tonight, all that mattered was the feel of him inside me. I latched on to his corded throat, dragging my tongue up and down his skin as he carried us to the bedroom.

Not the bedroom where I'd stayed as a kid. Not the bedroom where he'd been my first. The other guest bedroom. One I'd never slept in before. One my parents hadn't stayed in either.

Either West knew the other rooms were off limits, or he didn't want old ghosts as our bed partners tonight.

He pulled us apart when we reached the mattress.

A mewl came from my lips, the loss of him startling, as he put me on my feet.

"Turn around." West's hands came to my shoulders, then turned me away. Then with one hand flat against my spine, he eased me down to the bed.

He spread my legs apart before his body covered mine, his chest to my back, as he dragged his cock through my slit.

When the tip rubbed against my clit, my entire body shuddered. "I need more."

"I know what you need." His voice was sin and sex, full of promise as his lips whispered across my shoulder blades.

He teased until I was rocking against him, desperate to feel him inside. "West. Please."

"God, Indy." His tongue left a wet trail down my spine. "It's good. It's so fucking good."

Better every time. How was that possible?

I was drenched. After he lined up at my entrance, he slipped inside with one smooth slide.

"You're so wet, baby." His fingers skated over my skin.

It was that worshipping touch I remembered from years and years ago.

He rolled us slightly to the side, keeping our bodies connected. Then he pulled one of my legs over his own, changing the angle of my hips to fuck me with slow, measured strokes.

It was different, this position. It was something we hadn't tried before.

The pressure of his weight kept me pinned, and his hand on my leg moved up and down, keeping me spread wide.

And that fire between us kept building and building until I trembled, moving in time with the thrust of his hips as I chased my orgasm.

He reached around my hip, finding that bundle of nerves with a finger.

"West," I gasped as he began circling.

"Get there, Indy." His voice was gravelly in my ear. The hold on his control was slipping.

For me. I loved that he lost control for me.

So I lost control for him and shattered.

My inner walls clenched around him hard, pulsing and clenching. Stars stole my vision, separating mind and body. Every muscle seized, completely lost to the pleasure.

West came on a roar, pouring inside me. His arms held me tight, pinned against his frame as he drew out our orgasms, stroke after stroke. Until finally, we collapsed in a heap of tangled limbs.

My heart thundered. There was a lock of hair in my mouth. But I lay boneless on the bed, savoring the weight of his body keeping me pinned.

When I was a girl, all I'd ever wanted was to be kept by West.

These days, I had no delusions he'd want me to stay. But maybe I wouldn't be forgotten so quickly this time.

My focus returned slowly, like a leaf floating on the wind until it eventually reached the ground. My breathing returned to normal. My heart stopped bouncing off my sternum. The aftershocks faded, and my core quit pulsing.

The bed shifted as West sat up. Cold air rushed over my skin as the heat from his body disappeared.

I waited for him to leave the room. To do exactly what I'd done to him.

But he didn't rush to collect his clothes. He yanked back the covers, waiting for me to climb beneath the sheets. Then he collapsed on the bed, too, lying on his stomach with a pillow hugged to his chest. That tall frame stretched long, his toes dangling off the end. But he didn't seem to care. He just drew in a long breath, closed his eyes, and crashed.

We'd never spent a whole night together. Not once.

My heart started to gallop. I stiffened, scared to move and chase him away. Was he really going to just . . . stay?

Did I want him to stay? *Yes.*

It crossed every line; it shattered any illusion of boundaries. But I wanted him to stay. I wanted to wake up in the morning and not be alone. I wanted to find out how he drank his coffee.

So I leaned over and brushed my lips against his.

Kissing West was just asking for trouble.

But I did it anyway before I sank into my own pillow and fell fast asleep.

~

An owl hooted beyond my bedroom windows, waking me with a slight jerk. My head throbbed—the wine's fault. My body ached—West's fault.

West.

I shoved up on an elbow and pushed the hair out of my face as I stared at the other side of the bed.

Empty.

So much for sleeping together.

When had he sneaked out? Why had he even bothered to stay? Somehow, it hurt more than if he'd just left after sex.

I turned my back to his side of the bed and clutched the pillow to my chest. Beyond the cabin, that owl crooned into the night. *Whoo.*

"Shut up."

Whoo.

"Ugh. Stupid freaking bird." This was the third night in a row it had woken me up.

Whoo. Whoo.

"Fine." I whipped the covers off my body and stood, then went to the bathroom for a shower.

As the water warmed, I stared at myself in the mirror, taking in my wild hair and swollen lips. The circles beneath my eyes were getting so dark it was hard to hide them with concealer.

Maybe if West had stayed, I would have gone back to sleep.

But he was gone.

And I was alone. Again.

I abandoned the mirror, stepped under the shower's spray, and washed away the evidence of my complete and total lack of self-control.

So much for *never again.*

We hadn't used a condom. We hadn't used one at his place either. I was on birth control, but . . . we probably needed to have the safe sex conversation. I wanted to say this was the last time, but the last time was supposed to have been the *last* time, damn it. "What is wrong with me?"

Could I blame the wine? No. From the moment West had stepped inside the cabin, it had been a foregone conclusion that my willpower would crumble.

At least I'd beaten him at poker. Maybe one day, we'd play a poker game with a bit more skill than five-card draw. But for now, I was simply glad that Lady Luck had shone my direction.

Though he hadn't come through on his end of the bargain. He still owed me a truth.

Instead, he'd distracted me with an orgasm. And I'd let him. Oh, how I'd let him.

"Ugh." Why was I so weak when it came to West Haven?

With my hair wrapped in a towel, I pulled on a pair of sweatpants and a tee. Then I stripped the bedding before taking it to the laundry room. The sooner West's scent was gone from my room, the sooner I could put yet another mistake out of my mind.

It was silent outside as I brewed my coffee. The owl had accomplished his mission in waking me up, so he'd flown off to torment someone else.

"Hopefully West," I muttered, filling my mug.

The cards we'd played with last night were still scattered across the table. A few had fallen on the floor. I returned them to their box and put the deck away. Then I grabbed my laptop and phone to dive into the work I'd skipped while I'd been firing Deb yesterday.

Maybe I could have overlooked her shitty attitude. I had ignored the snide comments aimed at my back. But when I'd found her napping in a guest room yesterday afternoon, I'd had enough.

She'd promised to sue. She'd threatened her lawyer would be calling. They could all get in line. My attorneys were at the ready.

I kicked off a quick email, letting them know about Deb's termination and sending over the documentation I'd been compiling on her behavior and performance since day one. Then I opened the reservation inbox. Since I wanted to get a better feel for the questions guests and potential guests sent to the resort via our website, I'd taken over management of the email account. After answering three emails about pricing and availability, I refilled my coffee, about to tackle a few more emails, when my phone buzzed.

Blaine

I groaned. My coffee hadn't kicked in enough for this discussion. But I answered, hoping he couldn't hear the exhaustion in my voice. "Hi, Blaine."

"Indya. Good morning."

Was it a good morning? *No.* No, it was not. I hadn't gotten to learn how West took his coffee because the bastard had sneaked out like a coward.

"What's up?" I started typing a reply to another email.

It was from a guest who'd stayed at the resort once, seven years ago. He wanted to know if the pricing had changed since.

Um, yes. Other than for existing reservations where guests had already been quoted a price, Curtis's policy of keeping rates from years past was history.

"Indya," Blaine barked.

I blinked. "Huh?"

"Are you listening?"

"Not really."

Blaine had always been viciously frank. Since our marriage was over, I saw no reason to pander to his moods or ego. I could be brutally honest too.

"Nice," he muttered. "I sent you an email. Did you get it?"

"Yes."

"And?"

"And what? You sent it at five o'clock yesterday. I was busy. I saw it pop in but haven't had a chance to reply."

Not that I'd planned to reply.

"What's with you today?"

"It's 3:32 in the morning, Blaine, and you're hassling me about an email. Guess."

There was a tapping in the background. And then silence. He hung up on me.

"Asshole."

Why had I married him? Why? Was it because he'd charmed my friends? My father? Or both.

He'd charmed me too. And I'd fallen for it, hook, line, and sinker.

Just like I'd fallen for West last night. Was that why he'd come over? For a quick fuck? I'd assumed he'd stopped by because of Deb. But now, I wasn't so sure. And it wasn't like he was here for me to ask.

"No more sex with West," I vowed to the empty room as my fingers flew over the keyboard.

No more sex.

I'd been making that promise for far too long. Maybe it was time to stop breaking it.

Work was my welcome distraction for the next hour. And when the sun began to rise outside, trickling through the living room windows, I picked up my phone to call Dad.

Early mornings were his favorite. Or they had been before retirement, when he'd learned how to sleep in. In high school, whenever I'd woken early to go for a run, I'd found him at the dining room table, sipping coffee at his laptop.

I skimmed the edge of my computer with a fingertip. There'd be no typing during my call. He wouldn't like that I was working this early. That my personal life had fallen apart so completely that all I had was this job.

With a tap on my recent calls, I hit his name. It rang to his voice mail.

"You've reached Grant Keller. Please leave a message, and I'll return your call as soon as possible. Thank you."

Even in the message, the sound of his voice brightened my day.

"Morning, Daddy. Just wanted to say that I love you."

I ended the call and set my phone aside. Then I refilled my coffee and spent the next two hours glued to my laptop.

And while I returned emails, I did everything in my power not to think about West Haven.

Or how much I liked that his scent still lingered in the air.

Chapter 18
INDYA

Age Nineteen

The windows of West's truck were fogged white. My mouth hovered over his as I straddled his thighs, his cock buried deep inside my body.

"That's it, baby."

I loved it when he called me *baby*. Like I was more than just the woman screwing him in his old pickup.

His hands gripped the underside of my ass, his biceps straining as he helped me move up and down.

My legs were trembling. My heart raced. Every time I sank down on his lap, he'd hit that spot inside that made my breath hitch.

I closed my eyes and let the feel of West block out everything else. It hadn't been like this last year. Our night together had been sweet and gentle. This?

We were fucking.

And I *loved* it.

"West." My fingertips dug into his shoulders. The control I had over my body snapped, and I moved on instinct, rocking against him harder. Faster. I was close. So close.

"Oh, fuck, yes. Ride me, Indy. Just like that." He brought a hand between us, finding my clit with his finger.

The moment he began circling, I detonated on a cry. Tingles. Electricity. Fire. They coursed through my veins, mingling and melding, the sensation so overpowering that a string of incoherent sounds escaped my throat. Waves of pleasure slammed into me, over and over again. Blood rushed in my ears, so loud I barely registered West's groan as he gave in to his own release.

Wow. That was . . . wow.

When the fuzzy edges began to fade, when reality came creeping back in, I was slumped against West's body.

His head was against the back of the seat, his eyes closed as he breathed heavily. His Adam's apple bobbed, and the movement was so sexy I kissed his throat.

The corners of his mouth turned up as a hand dived into my hair. "Are you sure you have to leave tomorrow?"

I sighed. "Unfortunately."

His cock twitched inside me, and my inner walls clenched in response. West hissed and sat up straight. After a quick kiss, he lifted me off his lap, then spun me to sit before he popped the door and hopped out to deal with the condom.

I plucked my panties from the floor, then shimmied them on and righted the skirt of my sundress. Turned out, dresses weren't all that bad. Then I relaxed against the truck's seat, watching as he clasped his belt.

"That's a new buckle."

Yesterday, he'd been wearing one with a bucking horse. This one had the ranch's CMC brand embossed in silver and gold. The metal gleamed in the afternoon sun.

"It just got delivered last night. I ordered it a few months ago."

"It's so shiny. Maybe I should get a belt buckle."

West chuckled. "Because you're such a cowgirl."

"I could be a cowgirl."

He arched an eyebrow and pointed to my flip-flops.

I giggled. "Okay, no belt buckle."

"For the record, I like that you're not a cowgirl."

"You're not into cowgirls?"

"Not really. I'm into you."

A blush crept onto my cheeks as we stared at each other.

He looked gorgeous standing in the middle of a green meadow, the grass trampled beneath his boots. There wasn't a soul for miles. West had brought me far up into the mountains today, away from prying eyes.

Up here, it was easy to let myself forget it was our last day. To pretend that tomorrow, I wasn't leaving for Texas with my parents. That tomorrow, West wouldn't carry on with his life without me.

But tomorrow, I'd be gone.

He'd drive this dusty old truck down the gravel road of his life.

I'd be in my Mercedes, racing down the freeway of my own.

It wasn't fair that our roads crossed only once a year.

"I wish—" I stopped myself before I could finish that sentence.

"You wish what?" West walked over, then planted his hands on the seat and leaned in to brush his lips across my cheek.

"Nothing." I kissed the underside of his jaw. "We'd better go back. Before my parents finish their hike."

"Yeah." He dropped his forehead to mine but otherwise didn't move.

What if this wasn't the end? What if one of us changed paths?

He had one year left of college. What was he going to do after graduating? Would he ever want to leave Montana?

I still had three years to go, but I didn't have to stay at Baylor. What if I went to Montana State too?

What if.

There weren't any what-ifs.

West wasn't going to leave Montana. He wasn't going to move too far away from this ranch.

Just like I wasn't going to leave Texas. I wouldn't put thousands of miles between myself and my parents.

Dad was doing well. The medicine was working, and life was pretty much normal. But cancer never went away. It was that constant gray cloud above our heads, and as much as I wanted to be with West, I wanted to stay close to my father more.

So I framed West's face in my hands and kissed him one last time.

Then I let him drive me down the mountain.

Somehow, we'd managed to sneak off at least once a day to be together. Seven days of West.

This was the best vacation of my life.

"I had fun this week," I told him.

"Me too." He took my hand, lacing our fingers together and driving with one hand.

"Don't forget about me."

"Never."

Maybe he wouldn't, but I wasn't naive enough to think he stayed single, pining for me to return each summer.

But just the thought of leaving him, of losing him, made my insides churn.

He might not wait for me. But I'd waited for him.

No one but us knew we'd had sex last year. I hadn't told any of my friends. West had just been mine.

And maybe it was because I'd held him so close that there hadn't been room for anyone else. None of the boys at school compared. They measured short whenever I stacked them against West.

So I'd spent the past year focusing on school, ending both semesters with perfect grades. Some weekends I would go to a party, but mostly, I drove home. I spent my weekends with my parents.

I doubted this year would be much different.

Maybe that was pathetic. I didn't really care. All the girls in my dorm were hyperfocused on guys, and I just . . . wasn't.

Because every year, more and more of my heart seemed to linger in Montana, long after our vacations ended.

When the lodge came into view, I fought the urge to cry.

"We didn't get enough time," I whispered.

West lifted my knuckles to his mouth for a kiss, then let me go before anyone could see us. He parked outside the lodge, then twisted to face me. "Bye, Indy."

"Bye, West." I took a mental picture of him leaning against the steering wheel and added it to the collection I'd amassed this week.

West doing a double take when I'd walked into the barn on our first day here. West waiting outside my bedroom window that night with a handful of wildflowers. The smile on his face when I'd shown up for the trail ride he was leading. The way he'd looked in the meadow earlier.

God, I would miss him. Was that silly? We saw each other once a year at most. He didn't know that my favorite color was yellow. I didn't know if he ate his french fries with ketchup or with ranch or plain.

But he was my West. He might not have lived in Texas, but he'd been there with me all the same.

He lived in my heart.

The lump in my throat started to choke me, so I pushed the door open and climbed out before he could see the sheen of tears in my eyes. Then with a wave, I jogged from the truck toward the cabin.

The toe of my flip-flop caught on a rock, and I tripped, catching myself at the last second.

When I glanced back at the truck, West was shaking his head as he laughed.

I laughed too.

I laughed until I made it into the cabin.

Then I cried.

Chapter 19
WEST

The sound of laughing kids greeted me as I stepped out of my truck. The parking lot was packed. It had been a while since I'd seen so many vehicles outside the lodge.

Indya's doing, no doubt. The vacancies we'd had this season were gone. She'd booked us to capacity in only a month.

Most of the cars had Montana plates, numbers from Bozeman, Missoula, and Billings. We'd never targeted in-state residents before— our market had always been wealthy out-of-state travelers. But she'd gone after locals. She'd filled the empty rooms with people looking for a quick getaway.

It was brilliant.

I wished I had thought of it myself. But I'd never taken the time to think of how we could do things differently. Dad liked the tradition of how things had always been done, and a part of me had too. It was easier than taking a chance. Than failing.

Besides, these past few years we'd been operating with a skeleton crew. It was better for everyone if the guest count was low, even if that meant we sacrificed cash flow.

We weren't short staffed any longer. Indya had doubled the employee count. In just one month, so much had changed it was hard to believe.

It was hard to resent too.

On my way to the lodge, I'd stopped by a cabin to say hi to Mike. He'd been wrapping up for the day, cleaning the last of the construction mess inside the first cabin. His crew had already moved on to the next.

The work he'd accomplished in such a short time was amazing. The cabin had been transformed. It was clean. Bright. Airy.

The floors matched the herringbone white oak I'd put in Beartooth. The same flooring I'd padded across barefoot at midnight when I'd sneaked out of Indya's bed like a damn coward.

She terrified me.

Indya Keller absolutely fucking terrified me.

Part of me wanted to hide out in my house and avoid her for a good long while. But she'd had the lucky cards last night, and I'd promised her an explanation.

Besides, I'd tried avoiding her. It wasn't working. It just made me . . . miss her.

It felt like I'd been missing Indya my whole life.

Following the sound of laughter, I made my way to the lodge just as a couple of kids came racing out from the backyard, kicking a soccer ball on the lawn. I grinned, about to head inside, when a wild mess of blonde curls came next.

The smile on Indya's face flatlined my heart.

She chased the ball, stealing it from one of the kids and passing it to the other. Then that kid kicked it past what must have been their invisible goalpost, because Indya's arms shot in the air as she cheered.

She looked . . . happy.

She looked like the woman I'd known years and years ago. Her smile was one I hadn't seen enough in the past month.

My doing, at least in part.

I changed paths, walking across the grass toward the group.

Indya had the ball, dribbling it as she moved, but when she spotted me, she passed it to a kid and left them to play their game.

The light in her eyes dimmed.

My doing. Not in part.

"How can a woman who trips over everything in sight kick a ball like that and keep her feet?"

She laughed. "One of life's greatest mysteries."

I hadn't heard that laugh enough this past month either. "Got a minute?"

"Sure." Indya tucked a lock of hair behind her ear.

"How about a walk?"

"All right." She nodded and fell in step at my side.

We walked away from the lodge and past the barn, far from any guests who might overhear. Then I led her through the gate that opened into the pasture where we normally turned out the horses.

It was the same pasture that I'd walked her through years ago when she'd ridden my horse and I'd led it by the reins.

"Feels like a lifetime ago that we were out here together," I said.

"It was a different life."

"I guess so." Gone were the teenagers desperate for a moment alone.

"Nice night," she said.

"Yeah." The days had been hot lately, summer coming on strong in early July. But it cooled in the evenings, and out here in the meadow, it smelled like home. Grass and dirt and rose perfume.

Indya was in a simple black tank and a pair of fitted jeans. She had on a pair of Air Jordan high-tops. It should have been ridiculous, a woman who owned a ranch wearing expensive Nike shoes. But not a damn thing about Indya was ridiculous.

She looked beautiful. Sexy.

"Thank you," I said.

"For?"

I glanced back to the lodge. "We needed you."

"Oh." She ducked her chin, but not before I caught the slight smile on her pink lips.

"You won the poker hand last night."

"I did."

"Then I owe you answers." I took a few more steps, mentally tracing back and back, to the beginning. "Do you remember when we were kids and you caught my parents arguing in the lodge?"

"I remember."

"Mom left Dad after that. She moved to town. They got divorced."

"I'm sorry."

"It was the right decision. They were miserable. He cheated on her. Did I ever tell you that?"

"No." Her mouth parted. "I had no idea."

"It was just once. He went to the National Finals Rodeo in Vegas with some friends. Got hammered one night and had sex with a woman he met at a bar."

Indya's face soured. "Oh."

"Yeah. He fucked up. When he came home, he owned it. He confessed it all to Mom and begged for a second chance. She loves him, so she stuck around. Tried to move past it. And I think maybe they would have made it, but a year later, the woman from Vegas showed up at the ranch. With Jax."

I'd never forget that day. When the bus had dropped me off at the stop, it wasn't Mom waiting to get me like usual. It was Grandma. She had driven me home, and when I'd walked through the door, I had been greeted with a baby's cry.

Dad had been walking Jax around the living room.

Mom had locked herself in their bedroom, but I'd heard her crying too.

"Jax's mother left him here. As far as I know, she's never been back or tried to contact Dad again."

"Oh my God." Indya's eyes widened. "I had no idea. So Jax is your—"

"Brother. There's no *half* about it. But we have different mothers."

Jax didn't resemble a Haven. He had blue eyes instead of hazel. Blond hair in place of brown. I'd never met the woman, but I could only guess that Jax looked like his mother. The woman who'd destroyed my family.

And crushed Mom's heart.

"Do me a favor? Keep that between us."

"Of course," Indya said.

There were people who had no idea Mom wasn't Jax's mother. I preferred it that way. I never wanted Jax to be treated differently just because he wasn't Lily Haven's flesh and blood. And it was one of those sordid stories that we kept fairly quiet. As quiet as possible in our small town.

The gossip was inevitable. It was something Mom had dealt with mostly. But living on the ranch had helped. She'd been able to stay secluded, especially in the beginning, when the rumor mill would have been churning full speed.

"Mom stepped up," I told Indya. "She didn't leave Dad. She took care of Jax. Fed him. Changed diapers. Rocked him in the middle of the night. Taught him to tie his shoes. She acted like his mother. The only thing she never let him do was call her Mom."

"Why?"

"No idea. Anytime I'd ask, she'd change the subject. All I know is that she taught him early on that her name was Lily. If he called her Mommy, she'd correct him."

Indya stayed quiet, probably because there wasn't much to say. It had been strange for me as a kid. To hear her correct Jax. To reserve *Mom* for me and me alone.

But that choice of hers had been a crack that had kept widening and breaking my parents apart.

"Mom and Dad started fighting all the time. I'd wake up in the middle of the night to hear them arguing. She just couldn't get over the fact that he'd cheated. She'd wanted more kids, but there'd been some complications when I was born. Dad having a baby with another woman broke something inside her. It got worse and worse until one day, Mom called it quits."

"The day I overheard them."

"Yeah." The day I'd overheard them too. "The divorce was fast. But it cost Dad. Mom had spent decades working on this ranch, but she didn't want to stay. This was her home, and it wasn't like they could sell the house and split the money. Dad owed her for what she'd done here, so he paid through their settlement. She bought a place in town and started working as a nurse."

"And you stayed on the ranch?"

"I was back and forth. During football season, I stayed in town with her so I didn't have to drive. In the summers, I lived with Dad because I was working out here. They never forced me into a custody situation; they let me choose."

"And Jax?"

"He stayed with Dad. Mom would come out and visit him, especially during those early years. But over time, they saw each other less and less. Before Jax left for college, they had a big fight."

"Over?"

"Him having to call her Lily."

"Ah." Indya nodded.

I loved my mother. But by making that choice so long ago, when her feelings had been raw and ruined, she'd hurt Jax too.

"It's a mess." I sighed. "Has been for decades. The divorce was expensive for Dad. Add to that, he had to hire managers for the resort. Before then, Mom was running the show. No one ever worked as hard as she did. No one ever cared the way she did. It was hers. Until she left, and then it was just someone else's job. Dad had to get more and more involved to compensate."

Looking back, I saw the slow deterioration. I saw the decisions Dad had made that I would have made different. But for the majority of those years after Mom had left, I'd been a kid. I hadn't realized the financial balance between the resort and ranch.

And even when I'd finished college, when I'd come back to work, I'd taken Dad's advice. I'd followed his orders.

He was my father. He'd been running this place for years.

Why wouldn't he know what he was doing?

Anytime I challenged him, he challenged back. He made sure I knew my place. If it had been any other person, any other employer, I would have quit. But he was my father. I'd given him the benefit of the doubt, for far too long.

"Mom was owed every dime. I'll never be bitter about that. She poured her blood, sweat, and tears into this place. But that was the first chink in the armor. Another crack that grew over time."

Indya hummed. "Then the land purchase."

"That fucking land," I grumbled.

"Melvin. That was the neighbor, right?"

"Right." Not a surprise that Indya had done her research and knew the previous owner's name. "They'd lived out here for nearly as long as my grandparents. I went to school with Sunny Melvin."

"Did something happen to them? Is that why they sold it?"

"Sunny's parents were divorced, like mine. It was his mom's family's ranch. She didn't want to live out here, deal with brutal winters, so she moved away after he graduated. To Florida, I think. And handed everything over to Sunny."

That arrogant shit.

"We didn't have much to do with him. Every now and then his cattle or ours would get out and cross a fence. But otherwise, Sunny and I were never friends. He wasn't the kind of man we'd invite to poker club or out for drinks."

"Why not?"

"He's a liar and a cheat." He had been that way in high school and had never grown out of it. "But Sunny wasn't really the problem. It was Courtney."

Indya's shoulders stiffened as we walked. She knew the name.

"Courtney was working here as the manager. She took over all the tasks that Mom used to tackle. She loved the resort. She loved guests. And the longer she was here, the more we just let her run the show."

I'd stopped asking questions. I'd stopped engaging in resort business. I'd let Dad and Courtney have their morning meetings over coffee. And while the two of them were talking about whatever it was they'd talk about, I'd be outside working.

"She pitched the land purchase to Dad. Said she'd heard it in town that Sunny was considering selling. Dad always wanted the Melvin land. He always talked about how it would complement the Haven ranch so well. How we could use it for more guest cabins. How they had better hay ground and a center pivot, so we could get more than one cutting a year."

"Did Courtney know he wanted that land?"

"Absolutely."

"So she dangled the bait."

"And he took it. Without hesitation. Never told me he was going to buy the land until he'd already gone to the bank and taken out the loan."

"Curtis." Indya cringed.

"Courtney never mentioned it either. They both knew I would ask questions, so they kept me in the dark."

Indya's jaw dropped. "Seriously?"

"Seriously." The sting from Courtney's betrayal had faded in time. But damn if my pride wasn't still tender even years later. "She was sleeping with Sunny. After the purchase cleared, they left Montana together."

"What?" Indya's jaw dropped. "That's why she wanted it to sell. So they'd have money."

"Yep."

She cringed again. "I'm sorry."

I shrugged. "It's done."

Except Courtney was back. Without Sunny. Why?

I hadn't cared enough to ask around since Zak had told me she'd come back. With any luck, she'd disappear before summer turned to fall.

"That land purchase stretched us," I said. "You know that already. Dad didn't negotiate on price because he was afraid he'd miss out. We're in a dip in the cattle-market cycle. When Courtney left, Dad took it hard. He was angry and refused to hire another manager. Things were fine for a while, until they weren't. Until the resort kept bleeding money. Until the ranch couldn't cover the losses. Until it snowballed. Until . . ."

"Until," she whispered.

Until we went broke.

Until Indya.

"Thank you for telling me," she said.

"Welcome."

"I'm sorry, West. For everything."

"No more apologies." I let my hand brush hers. "You're not to blame."

That was on Dad.

And it was on me.

I could have pushed. I *should* have fought harder.

We walked in silence for a few more minutes until we moved in tandem, turning back for the lodge.

"It bothers me that I didn't know you wear nightgowns. It bothers me that I don't know if you like red wine or white. Waffles or pancakes. Summer or winter."

If tonight was the night for confessions, I might as well lay it all out there.

I knew her heart. I knew her laugh. I knew her shrugs and the way she looked every time she was fighting tears. But that wasn't enough. Not anymore.

"It bothers me that I know you, Indy. And I don't."

She stopped walking, waiting until I faced her. The unguarded look in those caramel eyes, the vulnerability, nearly sent me to my knees. "Red wine. Pancakes. Winter. Normally I wear an oversized T-shirt to bed. My mom got me that nightgown for my birthday, and I was trying it out. I don't like how the straps move when I sleep, so I haven't worn it again."

The air rushed from my lungs.

Indy reached for my hand, then slipped her fingers into mine. "It bothers me too."

Fuck, this woman. She had no idea what she did to me, did she? "Then we'll fix it."

"All right." A smile ghosted her lips. "We'll fix it."

I kept her hand in mine as we continued walking. By the time we reached the lodge, day was giving way to night. The sky was tinged in pink tones, casting the world a rose-colored tint.

We stayed in lockstep to the Beartooth, and before I could let go of her hand, she clamped her own around my wrist, tugging me forward.

Up the steps. Through the door. Into her room.

And this time, instead of sneaking out, I stayed naked in Indya's bed until dawn.

Asking her questions, giving her answers, all through the night.

Chapter 20
INDYA

Age Twenty-One

West and I lay on a plaid wool blanket in the middle of a mountain meadow. There was an empty bowl between us stained with the strawberries he'd picked me from his grandmother's garden. Above us, clouds drifted through the blue sky.

He'd brought me to this meadow before, two years ago. This was where we'd come on the final day of that family vacation.

Today was another last day.

There was a rock digging into my spine. The blanket was scratchy beneath the bare skin of my arms and legs. But I refused to move. Not until the very last second.

When my parents and I had arrived in Montana earlier this week, West hadn't been here. A friend of his had gotten married in Hawaii, and as a groomsman, he'd left for the celebration.

He'd returned to the ranch just last night.

I was leaving tomorrow at dawn.

So while Mom and Dad had taken a day trip into Big Timber for the Sweet Grass Fest parade and street fair, I'd stayed at the resort for this.

For one day with West.

He was supposed to go to the rodeo tonight. Could I convince him to stay with me instead?

Sex on this blanket hadn't exactly been comfortable. Not that I was complaining. West had given me two orgasms already, one with his tongue and another with his cock.

I wanted more. I wanted him in my bed.

West checked the time on his phone.

I wasn't going to get what I wanted, was I?

"Where were you last summer?" He almost sounded mad.

I liked that he was mad. I'd been mad too.

"I had an internship with an advertising company. They only hire two interns each year from the entire country, and they don't give vacation time. So Mom and Dad came up here without me."

"I remember. Your dad beat me at a game of horseshoes."

Dad had beat West? Doubtful. Dad played horseshoes exactly once a year. In Montana. West probably played constantly with guests. "Did you let him win?"

"Yes."

"Thanks." I smiled, tearing my eyes from the sky to face him.

West's hazel eyes were waiting. "It's good to see you, Indy."

"It's good to see you too."

After we'd had sex, both of us had redressed. My dress was rumpled from being balled up on the grass.

He was wearing a pair of faded Wranglers and the CMC belt buckle I remembered from two years ago. His navy T-shirt strained at his biceps.

West had always been muscular and fit, but his body had changed from two years ago. He was broader. Stronger.

Gone was the boy who'd introduced me to his horse. He was twenty-three now. And in my whole life, not once had I laid eyes on a man more handsome than West Haven.

Even though he'd changed some, added more stubble to that chiseled jaw, it still felt like just yesterday we'd been together in his old truck. Time was always strange when it came to West and me.

It existed. And it didn't.

He'd gotten a new truck at some point. His sleek gray Chevy Silverado was parked beside us, the paint gleaming in the afternoon sun. Not a patch of rust in sight.

I missed his old, dusty green pickup.

"How's work going?" I asked.

It was a question I'd ask on a date. This wasn't a date. This was a hookup. My brain knew the distinction. My heart was struggling with the difference.

This wasn't a date.

But I wanted it to be a date.

He looked to the sky again. "Work is okay."

"Just okay?"

"Just okay."

I twisted onto my side, propping up on an elbow. "If you could do anything in the world, what would you do?"

"This."

"Have sex with me on a scratchy wool blanket?"

He laughed, and it transformed his face. West, the broody, serious cowboy, was gorgeous. But this West, carefree and smiling, was breathtaking.

I traced a finger down the line of his nose, then dropped to his mouth, memorizing that smile with my touch.

He grabbed my wrist in a flash, trapping my hand to his lips. Then he nipped at the pad of my finger before letting me go. "Yes, I'd have sex with you on this scratchy wool blanket every day if I could. But otherwise, I want to work on this ranch. It's what I know. It's where I want to be."

"Even though it's just okay?"

"Yeah. It's not the ranching that's tough. It's Dad. He's not the easiest man to work for. He's got his ideas, and I've got mine. If they aren't in line, we butt heads. It's been like that my whole life. Mom says it's because we're both stubborn."

"Sorry."

"Meh. Don't be. He's my dad. I love him. And we get along most of the time. You're catching me at a bad time. We got into it before I left for Hawaii."

"About?"

"Junk. He's got a pile of it growing in a corner of the ranch. Old, broken-down equipment that's nothing more than scrap metal. I told him we should get rid of it. Clean it up. He acted like I was asking him to cut off an arm."

I giggled.

The corners of West's mouth turned up. "If he wants to keep that shit, fine. It's not worth fighting over. Someday, he'll take a step back and retire. If I have to wait until then to make some changes, then so be it."

"Besides the junk pile, what changes?"

"I don't know." He shifted, mirroring my position to face me. "We could run more cattle. I'd like to focus my time more on the ranch and less on the resort."

"You don't like the resort?" My eyebrows furrowed.

West pressed a finger to the crease, rubbing it away. "I like the resort. But you asked if I could do anything in the world. That would be running this ranch. I'd hire someone else to handle the resort."

"You want more cows and less hassles with guests. Got it. What else?"

"Maybe more land too. I might rename the place someday."

"Really? What would you call it?"

"Haven Ranch. Haven River. I don't know. Something along those lines."

Something with his family's name. That fit. Crazy Mountain Cattle Resort was fine, but this place should be named after the Havens. "I like it."

"Dad would throw a fucking fit." West rolled his eyes. "So I doubt it would ever happen. But . . . if we're talking dreams."

I liked talking about West's dreams.

"What about you?" He ran his thumb across my chin. "You've got one more year of college. What's next?"

"Work." I sighed. "The advertising company offered me a job after graduation, but I think I might go to work for Dad's company instead."

"Real estate, right?"

"Yes."

"Do you like real estate?"

"It's okay."

"Just okay?"

I nodded. "Just okay."

Dad loved it. And he loved the idea of me coming to work as his protégé. For now, that was enough for me. We'd likely get into disagreements, too, but mostly, I was excited to work with him every day.

He'd been pushing too hard. He was tired more often than not. When I'd call to check in between classes, there was a strain in his voice that made my insides twist. The liveliest I'd seen him had been this week. He'd told me this morning he'd felt rejuvenated by the Montana air.

But our lives weren't in Montana. So tomorrow, we'd return to Texas. I'd finish college, then go to work for Keller Enterprises. Maybe I could ease Dad's burdens until he was ready to retire.

West's phone rang on the blanket between us. He picked it up, silencing it before I could see the name on the screen. Then he tossed it behind him before he rolled me onto my back. "Wish we had more time."

"Me too." I pushed a lock of dark hair off his forehead. "How important is this rodeo?"

He leaned in, brushing his lips across mine as his hand snaked beneath the skirt of my dress. "Not that important."

Chapter 21
INDYA

My gaze drifted from my laptop to the painting hung on the office's wall.

The watercolor horse stared right back.

I'd assumed it had been West's artwork. It looked like something he'd choose for an office.

But maybe Courtney had used this space when she'd worked here. Had this been her office? Had she spent hours behind this desk? Had she loved that chair I'd tossed weeks ago?

Maybe the reason West rarely came through the door wasn't because of me.

But Courtney.

Her name was now linked in my brain to this office. To this ranch. To its downfall.

I had a name to blame. *Courtney.*

And *Curtis.*

West had struggled with his father for years, but I'd always thought their arguments were over minor disagreements, like the location of a fence's gate. Or a junk pile of equipment.

How could Curtis have gone behind West's back and made that land purchase? Had he known it was foolish? Had he assumed West would disagree?

Whatever Curtis's reasoning, it was wrong. Just like it had been wrong for him to sell this ranch to me without involving West either.

I'd assumed that West had known. That while I'd been scrambling to pull this off, Curtis had kept West in the loop. The few conversations I'd had with Curtis during the negotiations had been brief.

But he'd really just dismissed West entirely. Was that how Curtis's father had treated him? Was that just the Haven way?

It was such a betrayal. How was West so calm about it? It had been over a month, and every time I thought about it, I got angry.

Yet West had seemed so steady during our walk last night. Or maybe he was numb.

Well, I had enough rage for us both. And Curtis wasn't even my father.

Dad had always said such wonderful things about Curtis. He'd called him *good people*.

Had I put too much stock in my father's opinion? Had his high regard clouded my own judgment?

Dad had gotten it wrong with Curtis. He'd gotten it wrong with Blaine too.

Just the thought of Blaine's name made my lip curl. His latest email was at the top of my inbox, marked unread. I didn't need to open the message to know what was inside.

A demand.

Blaine was always making demands. But we weren't married anymore. I owed him nothing. So he could take my silence as an answer.

No.

It was the same answer I'd emailed him after his early-morning call.

With a quick tap on the delete key, his email whooshed into the digital trash. I opened up Google, about to check our recent reviews, when a knock came at the door.

"Hey, Indya," Tara said as she walked inside. "Do you have a minute?"

"Of course."

She frowned at a folding chair before taking a seat.

"I know I need better chairs. It just hasn't been a priority." And I didn't get many visitors in here. The staff, even the new employees, seemed to avoid my office. Anytime I had an interview, I conducted it in the dining room, where it was light and spacious.

"I have a—" She stopped herself, her eyes narrowing on my face. "You look exhausted."

"I am exhausted." I wasn't even offended at the comment. It was the truth. "I haven't been sleeping well. There's an owl outside the cabin that has made it his or her personal mission in life to ensure I get no more than four hours of rest per night."

Though the owl had been noticeably absent last night. That, or I just hadn't heard it with West in my bed.

"An owl. You know, one of the boys could take care of that problem for you."

I yawned, covering it with my hand. "Boys?"

"West or Jax. I'll never not think of them as boys. Lily is my best friend in the world, and they're the closest thing I have to sons of my own."

"Ah." That was sweet. "I'm sure the owl will go away soon."

"I'm surprised West didn't chase it off." There was a glint in Tara's eyes.

Damn it. If Tara knew West had been in my bed, it was only a matter of time before the rest of the resort did too. If they didn't already.

I hadn't seen him since he'd slipped out of the Beartooth at dawn. But obviously someone had been paying attention.

We couldn't keep doing this, could we? We couldn't keep pretending like we were the same people we had been before. This wasn't a weeklong tryst. I wasn't here on vacation.

For the first time in my life, I could have West for more than seven days. Except we were still sneaking around like teenagers. There were no promises. No commitments.

And I *was* leaving. Maybe not in a week, but I was leaving.

I was going to have to give him up again, wasn't I?

Forever this time.

The ache in my chest was so powerful it made it hard to breathe. I reached for my water bottle, then took a long drink to clear the lump in my throat. Then I forced a smile for Tara.

"What's up?" I asked, refusing to even acknowledge her comment about West.

"The county grader is here for the road."

"Finally." I sighed. "It only took me eleven phone calls." And each of them worth my time and persistence if the washboard and potholes would be a thing of the past.

"Pays to be the squeaky wheel."

"I am not afraid to pester."

"Good." She laughed. "We need more pester around this place. Which leads me to my next topic."

"Okay," I drawled.

"I think we need to hire a float position. Someone who can cover the desk or pitch in with housekeeping, depending on occupancy."

"Good idea. I'll get a position listed."

She blinked. "R-really? I had a whole speech prepared to convince you."

"Would you like to give it?"

"Not really." She laughed. "Thank you."

"Absolutely."

I'd already put together financial projections with added staff members. My spreadsheets had been keeping me company in the early-morning hours after Mr. Owl had woken me from a dead sleep.

The cost of another staff member would not significantly impact our returns as long as we maintained a 70 percent occupancy rate in the lodge during the summer season. We needed only 30 percent occupancy in the fall and spring. And I'd been conservative with my estimations and planned zero for the winter.

Now that the resort had no debt and I'd given it a healthy influx of capital, it would be a profitable business. If things kept going well, by next year, some of the cash flow could be channeled into improvements.

We were 94 percent occupied for the rest of the summer season. There were a few rooms on a few odd days still vacant, but otherwise, we were booked to capacity. I'd asked my marketing company to give me an ads liaison, and the campaign we'd launched on Facebook and Instagram, targeting Montana residents, had worked.

"How are the guests?" I asked Tara. "Everyone happy?"

"No complaints. The wine selection has been a huge hit. And Reid's new menu is the talk of the town. We're getting calls from people asking if the dining room is open to the public."

"Really?" *Huh.* "I'll be damned."

Forcing Reid to add vegetarian options to the menu had inspired him to get creative with our food offerings. He'd pitched the new menu to me two weeks ago, and when I'd given him the go-ahead, he'd ordered supplies immediately.

All I'd asked was that we keep the traditional Saturday campfire cookout and that he pair dinner meals with our new wine selection.

Mom's personal sommelier had sent me his latest recommendations. The two massive wine coolers I'd bought for the kitchen were now fully stocked. Those coolers were the reason Lisa, our bartender, now smiled whenever we crossed paths.

It had taken me weeks, but I'd finally gotten the financials in order.

The ranch had been the easy part. West had begrudgingly sent me his spreadsheets last week. Curtis might not have let him in on the land purchase, but otherwise, West ran the cattle operation with precision and efficiency.

He kept detailed income and expense records. He had spreadsheets for pasture rotations and cow tags. He used hedging to offset market risks, and while some years were better than others, the ranch made good money.

Compared to the ranch's data, the resort's accounting had been a hot mess.

Curtis had lumped all the departments together, and getting an accurate idea of which areas made money and their respective margins was impossible.

Not anymore.

Cabin reservations turned the highest profit, or would once the remodels were complete. Rooms at the lodge were a close second. Excursions were also quite profitable, though the total revenue amount was low because there was only so much we could charge to stick a person on a horse. Still, it was in the black.

Dining and alcohol? Bright red. My price increases for our all-inclusive packages would help, but if we could pull in locals for date nights or special celebrations, that might chip away at the losses too.

"We should open the restaurant to the public. I'll talk to Reid about what that would entail. We'll need a reservation system and to decide how many additional patrons we could accommodate on top of guests. We'll probably want a dedicated page on the website. Maybe the occasional ad in the local paper."

"Your brain moves a mile a minute, doesn't it?" Tara asked.

I smiled. "Most days."

There wasn't another option. If I was going to turn this resort into a successful business in less than a year, there was no time to dawdle with these changes. Before I left Montana, Haven River Ranch needed to work like a well-oiled machine.

"I'll let you work." Tara stood. "I'd better get back to the desk anyway. Finish up a few things before I head home."

"Thanks. For everything."

"Right back atcha. I doubt Curtis will ever admit it, but you're doing incredible things here, Indya. We needed you."

That lump returned to my throat, double the size, but I managed to choke out a garbled "Thank you."

She'd used West's exact words.

We needed you.

It had been a long time since I'd felt needed. Wanted. I'd missed being wanted. Probably because the man who'd always made me feel desired was West, and we'd spent too many years apart.

But maybe this year in Montana wouldn't be so rough, after all. Maybe West and I could fall into a friendship of sorts. Go back to where we'd started.

Get to know each other, like we had last night.

We'd talked for hours about nothing. About everything. We'd asked each other endless questions while we'd been curled together in my bed.

His favorite food was cheeseburgers. He couldn't remember the last physical book he'd read, but he listened to audiobooks—thrillers were his favorite. If he were stranded on a deserted island and he could take only three things, he'd choose an axe, a lighter, and me.

He'd choose me for his island.

Every time I thought about it, I smiled.

My phone vibrated on my desk, and the name on the screen not only erased my smile, but triggered an eye twitch. *Blaine.* It was like he could sense I was in a good mood. That, or I'd deleted his email. If I sent him to voice mail, he'd just call again and again and again.

"Hello," I answered.

"You're ignoring me."

I pinched the bridge of my nose. "I answered your call, didn't I?"

"And my email?"

This man could annihilate a nice day faster than a lightning bolt could split a tree. "The answer is no. It will continue to be no, regardless of how many times you ask the same question."

"Indya."

"Blaine." I mimicked his warning tone. "Send the papers. There is no reason for me to come to Texas to sign them. I'm busy working. So unless there's something else, please hear me."

That was all I'd ever asked of Blaine. Not just to listen. But to *hear me*. I wasn't sure he was even capable. I'd spent our marriage screaming into a void.

Blaine stayed silent on the other end of the line. A silence I'd received far too many times.

It meant he wasn't done arguing. It meant he'd keep pushing and pushing and pushing until I caved.

Not this time. I wasn't giving in. He'd already gotten everything he wanted. This last concession, this distance, was mine to keep.

I ended the call, not caring that it would only antagonize my ex-husband. It wasn't the first time I'd hung up on Blaine. It wouldn't be the last.

The horse in the painting was staring at me when I glanced across the desk. Was he frowning? It looked like he was frowning.

He was probably Courtney's horse. A grumpy horse.

I didn't feel like suffering through his attitude for the rest of the afternoon, so I closed down my laptop, stowed it in my tote, and left the office for the kitchen.

Reid was dressed in his usual chef's coat and baggy pants. Tonight's bandanna was orange. Rather than tennis shoes, today he was sporting red Crocs with yellow socks.

"Howdy," he said from the prep table, where he was mixing an orzo pasta salad.

My mouth watered at the sight of crisp cucumbers and plump tomatoes.

"Hungry?" he asked.

"Starving." I hadn't eaten since breakfast.

Reid grinned and went to fetch a plate. And after I ate some of the pasta salad, we talked for nearly two hours about opening the restaurant to the public.

He had his concerns. I was learning that Reid's first reaction to new ideas was an automatic no. But the longer we talked, and the more time I gave him to ponder, the more he considered the possibility. By the time the waitstaff was prepped for the dinner rush, Reid was penciling out additions for his budget.

A budget he'd bitched and moaned about when I'd presented it to him weeks ago.

A budget he had quickly embraced and was now ruling with an iron fist. Apparently, he didn't like being dead last in the profit margin race.

"I want this to be reservation only," he said. "People need to think ahead to eat here."

This wasn't an exclusive restaurant in New York City. If this was going to work, we weren't going to turn customers away. He'd probably come to that conclusion himself. Eventually. If not, I'd set the parameters myself.

"Let's both mull this over for a bit," I said. "We can firm up details in a few days."

He nodded. "All right."

"I'll let you get back to work. Thanks for your time."

"Do you want dinner?"

Yes. I was starving, and that pasta salad hadn't been enough. "Would you mind?"

"What do you feel like? The special tonight is a barbecue burger."

"That sounds great. Would you mind making two?"

"No problem. Give me a few. We'll wrap them up and bring them out."

"Thanks." I waved and left him to work, wandering through the dining room to visit with guests while I waited.

I'd just finished a conversation with a newlywed couple from Utah when one of the waitresses appeared with a plastic to-go sack with two containers inside.

"Here you go, Miss Keller."

"Thank you." With my food in hand, I left the dining room.

Tara's new clerk was at the desk. She was one of Hannah's friends from high school, and though incredibly shy, she was sweet. I smiled at her, then hurried out of the lodge and to my car parked outside the Beartooth.

My nerves spiraled as I made my way to West's house. This was okay, right? Me showing up with dinner? He wouldn't think this was clingy or needy, would he?

It had been a long time since I'd worried about this stuff. The last guy I'd dated was Blaine. And even then, I couldn't remember being this anxious or excited to just . . . see him.

West had always given me butterflies.

My heart was racing by the time I parked outside his house. The moment I stepped outside and slammed my car door, he walked out his door.

His stride was easy. Confident. A swagger of sorts, but not forced or cocky. It was confident. That was West. He stood at the top of his porch stairs with a crooked grin toying at his lips. "Hey."

"Hi." Someday, I wouldn't sound like a breathless teenager when I saw him. Not today, but someday.

He was dressed in jeans and a faded navy Montana State University T-shirt that strained around his biceps and stretched over that broad chest. His hair was damp, his feet bare. He'd probably worked all day outside and come home for a shower.

"What's in the bag?" he asked.

"Dinner."

"Dinner. That's a new concept for us."

"What do you mean? We've had dinner together before. What about all those hot dogs we cooked over the campfire?"

"Woman." He rubbed a hand over his jaw, covering a smile. "Sometimes I wonder if you were born to argue with me."

"I like arguing with you."

"I like it too."

God, it was fun, flirting with West. We hadn't flirted enough. "The dinner is a bribe."

"Oh, this should be good." Humor danced in his vibrant hazel eyes. "What are the terms of this bribe, Miss Keller?"

"There's an owl outside the cabin. He keeps waking me up."

"An owl?" West quirked an eyebrow.

"I'm not making it up. He wasn't there last night. But there's an owl, and he hoots, and it wakes me up. So I'm bribing you with dinner. Burgers and pasta salad in exchange for eight hours of undisturbed sleep."

He walked down the stairs, taking each step deliberately. His movements were timed with the thuds of my heart. And even though his feet were bare, he stepped onto the gravel, closing the distance between us until his chest brushed mine.

West's gaze roved my face, probably seeing the exhaustion that Tara had so bluntly called out earlier. He twirled a lock of my hair around his index finger. "You know I can't promise eight hours of undisturbed sleep."

I was counting on it. "Seven."

His eyes narrowed. "Six."

"Deal." I lifted up on my toes, searching for his mouth, when the sound of a car made me pause.

West's eyes darted over my head to the road. His entire frame went rigid.

"What?" I turned, seeing a shiny red Honda.

"Fuck," he clipped.

The car turned, then parked at a different angle than I'd pulled in the Defender. Parallel to the house, not perpendicular, like the driver expected to be kicked off the property.

"Who—"

Before I could finish my question, the door opened, and a woman stepped out. She glanced around before shoving her sunglasses into her sleek, dark hair.

Her brown eyes landed on West, and she stood taller, shutting the car's door and rounding the hood. She moved with grace, practically floating over the coarse gravel of his driveway.

All my life I'd been jealous of women who didn't trip over their own feet.

She smiled, and it was stunning. Without a doubt, she was the most beautiful woman I'd ever seen.

I'd had that same thought when I'd met her, years ago.

"Hey, West."

He stared at her for a long moment; then the tension in his frame seemed to melt away. "Hi, Courtney."

Chapter 22
INDYA

Age Twenty-Three

"Why are you nervous?" Dad asked.

"I'm not nervous."

"Indya." He frowned whenever I lied.

"What's going on?" Mom asked from the back seat.

"Nothing," I said, then tucked my hands under my thighs to keep from fidgeting as we pulled into the resort.

It looked the same as it had two years ago. Well, not exactly the same. The barn looked weathered, the wood siding grayer than the brown I remembered from past visits. There used to be two whiskey-barrel planters beside the lodge's stairs, but they were gone, and instead, four baskets of flowers hung from the porch posts. But otherwise, the lodge and cabins appeared largely unchanged.

It looked the same.

But it felt different.

This trip felt different.

And I was freaking nervous.

I searched the grounds for a dark-haired cowboy. West was nowhere in sight. And as we parked, no one came out of the lodge to welcome us to Montana. Not that we needed to be greeted. We knew our way around.

Except I couldn't remember a trip when Curtis or a desk clerk hadn't met us in the parking lot and helped carry our bags to the Beartooth Chalet.

Dad must have noticed the absence, too, because his forehead furrowed as he climbed out. "I'll go check us in."

Mom and I joined him on the gravel. She waited until he was inside before she dropped her smile. "He's not feeling well. Maybe we should have skipped this trip."

"But he loves it here."

She swallowed hard and blinked a few too many times, vanishing tears. If Mom wasn't smiling too brightly around Dad, she was hiding tears around me.

We wore faces for my father. She hid the sadness, and I hid the worry.

At least she could be real around me.

I kept the facade in place for them both.

"This will be good for him," I said. "We'll have a nice, relaxing week. No camping this time."

"Absolutely not." Mom laughed, following me to the back to open the hatch of the Escalade we'd rented at the airport in Bozeman. In the past, we'd had our pilot bring us to the Big Timber airport, but they'd been doing maintenance on the runway, so we'd had to drive over from Bozeman.

Was that why Curtis wasn't here? Maybe in the past, he'd get a call from the airfield's shuttle service when we arrived.

Dad emerged from the lodge just as I pulled our last suitcase out of the car.

Still no Curtis.

Or West.

I tried not to let the disappointment show. It wasn't like West could come running over and sweep me into his arms anyway. No one, especially my parents, knew about our relationship. But I'd been waiting two long years to see his face.

God, I'd missed him. More than was rational.

It wasn't like I hadn't dated in the past two years. There had been a few boyfriends, but no one had made me want . . . more.

None of those men had tempted me to upend my life. But for West, maybe it was time to try. To make a few big changes.

What if I moved to Montana? What if West and I had more time than a week?

Just the thought of asking, of putting myself out there, made my insides twist. But no matter how nervous I was, no matter how hard it would be to put myself out there, this was the trip when I'd finally ask.

What if I stayed?

"I'll handle the luggage," I told my parents. "You guys go in and relax. I took a nap on the plane. Neither of you slept."

"We can help," Dad said.

"Shoo." I waved him away.

It was only because of Mom that he actually left. She looped her arm with his, letting out an exaggerated yawn, and all but dragged him inside.

I took one last look around the resort, paying special attention to the barn and corrals. There was no shiny gray truck. No rusty old green one either. No West.

After slinging my Chanel over a shoulder, I picked up both of Mom's suitcases and hauled them inside. Then I came back and retrieved Dad's and my own so we could unpack.

When my clothes were folded and stowed in the same dresser of the guest bedroom I'd been using for ages, I found Dad in the living room.

He stood at the window that overlooked the field beyond the cabin.

I took the spot beside him. "You okay?"

"Are you?"

"It's just been a long day." A long year.

The week after I'd graduated from Baylor, I'd started working for Dad's company. To say the past twelve months had been a crash course in large-scale real estate was an understatement.

It was like Dad was attempting to purge the knowledge from his brain and drill it into mine.

I was running out of room in my head. My skull ached constantly. So did my heart.

Did I want to work in real estate?

No. Not even a little bit. But I would for Dad.

"Is this about Harry Mitchell?" he asked. "I heard you talking to him."

"Trying to talk to him," I muttered.

Dad sighed. "I know he's been hard on you. But if you can survive having him as a client, you can survive anyone."

"I'll be okay." It wasn't a matter of surviving Harry Mitchell. It was a matter of not slapping the pig in the face.

Just because he was a billionaire oil tycoon did not give him the right to treat me like I was incompetent. It also didn't give him the right to stare at my chest or pinch my ass.

Dad didn't know that Harry had crossed the line on more than one occasion. I'd kept that to myself. But I had complained that Harry treated me like a child with his condescending tone. He also referred to me as *little girl*.

I fucking hated Harry Mitchell.

But soon, he wouldn't be my problem. The commercial development we were brokering for him was nearly complete. Then he'd be a distant, unpleasant memory.

"I'm glad we took this trip," Dad said.

"Me too." I leaned my head on his shoulder. A shoulder that seemed harder, bonier, than normal.

He'd lost too much weight this winter. If there was a cold or flu virus in Texas, he'd caught it. Illness after illness had kept him out of the office. His immune system just wasn't strong enough. So I'd stepped up to do anything in my power to help.

I was living at home again, and even though it felt pathetic to be back in my childhood bedroom at twenty-three, it was easier on Dad. I went to the office and met with his clients. We leveraged as much technology as possible, but some days, he wasn't up for videoconferencing. So I'd bring the work home, running everything past him in the evenings while he reclined in his chair. Then hit the ground running with his instructions each morning.

Tired didn't even begin to cover it. I was mentally and emotionally strung out. And all I wanted to do was quit.

Could I quit? A year ago, it wouldn't have even crossed my mind as an option. But now? Maybe.

Maybe we all needed to quit.

It was on the tip of my tongue to mention it to Dad. To ask him if we could just . . . stop.

If he could stop.

But I held it back. Before I mentioned a word to my father, I needed to see West.

If he still wanted me, maybe this wouldn't be my only trip to Montana this year. Maybe it would be easier to convince Dad to retire.

If West didn't want to give a relationship with me a try, well . . . I'd be devastated. But I'd still talk to Dad—only it would be a different conversation.

"We needed this trip." Dad shifted, wrapping an arm around my shoulders and pulling me into his side. "We've been working too hard."

"Agreed. Especially you."

"Nah. I'm good. Still alive."

Still alive.

It never stopped being strange that we talked about his death so often.

"Grant?" Mom called from their bedroom, where she was probably unpacking his clothes. "Did you take your pills?"

"Yes, dear."

"Just checking."

I giggled. "How many times is that so far today?"

"Twelve," he whispered. "Bet she makes it to twenty."

"Totally."

He'd started counting how often she asked about his pills. Thirty-one was the record.

We'd joke about it together, but he never gave Mom a hard time. He just said "Yes, dear" ten or twenty or thirty-one times a day.

Still alive. The medication was hard on his body, but he was still alive. And cancer was the fourth member of our family.

Mom and Dad seemed to have found peace with it, but as far as I was concerned, cancer could fuck right off.

"What's next?" Dad dropped a kiss to my hair, then let me go, clapping his hands. "Should we go for a walk before dinner? Explore?"

"Explore a place we've been countless times?" Mom asked as she came out of the bedroom carrying her Kindle. "Can't we just relax and read until dinner?"

"I did want to start that mystery you bought me." Dad joined her on the sofa, letting her snuggle into his side. "Where did you put it?"

"In your backpack."

"Where's my backpack?"

"Oh, shoot." I gave him an exaggerated frown. "I didn't grab it from the back seat."

"I'll get it." Dad made a move to stand, but I waved him off.

"No, I'll go." It would give me another chance to search for West.

I snagged the keys from the table, about to head outside, when a knock came at the door.

My heart skipped. *West?*

It was an effort to walk to answer it instead of run. When I turned the knob, I saw it wasn't West on our porch.

It was a woman with black hair that fell in sleek panels over her shoulders. She looked to be about my age. Her smile was as bright as the light twinkling in her wide brown eyes.

"Hi. Welcome." She lifted the gift basket looped over her forearm. "I meant to have this waiting for you when you arrived, but I'm a bit behind schedule today."

"Thank you." I took the basket, glanced at its contents. Dried fruit. Huckleberry jam. A bottle of red wine.

"Everything is made in Montana."

"This is lovely."

"Is this your first time staying with us?"

"Um, no. My parents and I have been here before." Quite a few times.

"Oh, goodness." Her eyes widened as she pressed a hand to her forehead. "Have we met before, and I've forgotten?"

"No."

Hers was a face I wouldn't have forgotten. She was the most beautiful woman I'd ever seen.

There was a sinking feeling in my stomach. A feeling that had been there all day.

This trip was different than any of the others, wasn't it? Not a good different.

"Phew." She let her hand fall. "Too many names and faces lately. Where are you from?"

"Texas."

"Ah. When was the last time you visited?"

"Two years ago." My head began spinning as my stomach fell farther and farther and farther down. "We've been coming here since I was a kid."

"Oh, that's cool. I grew up in Big Timber and always knew about the resort but didn't really start hanging out here until West and I got together." She lifted her left hand and flashed her solitaire diamond ring. "I took over as manager about the same time we got engaged."

The floor disappeared beneath my feet.

Down. Down. Down.

"I'm Courtney." She extended her hand.

It was an effort to keep my smile in place. To keep my chin up. But I managed.

I had Harry Mitchell to thank for that. Having suffered through his presence for months, I'd learned to school my features. To fake it. If not for Harry, having to shake Courtney's hand might have sent me to my knees.

"It's nice to meet you, Courtney." I slipped my hand into hers. "I'm Indya Keller."

Chapter 23
WEST

"I should go." Indya took a step toward her Defender, but I caught her elbow before she could escape.

"Head inside. I'll be right behind you."

"But—"

"We have an owl to discuss. And I'm hungry."

"I don't—"

"Inside, Indya."

She frowned and grumbled something under her breath. It sounded a lot like *stubborn ass*. But when she brushed past me, she walked toward the house, not her car.

I twisted to watch her disappear inside, the screen door slamming shut, then faced Courtney and arched an eyebrow. "Court."

"West." Her smile wobbled, revealing her nerves. "So . . . I'm back."

"I heard." I crossed my arms over my chest.

"How, um, are you?"

"Not interested in small talk. What do you want?"

She scrunched her nose, something I'd learned in our time together meant she was losing her patience. The yelling would come next. Followed by tears.

When Courtney wasn't getting her way, she threw a tantrum.

There'd never been any point in arguing with her. She didn't know how to argue or debate. It was just . . . drama.

Always fucking drama.

Well, Sunny could deal with her drama. I wanted to go inside and have dinner with Indya, then make sure she got some sleep. I was sick of seeing those circles under her eyes.

Courtney looked past me to the house and did another nose scrunch.

She had to know that Indya had bought the ranch. And knowing Courtney and how much she thrived on gossip, she'd probably heard that Indya was the most beautiful woman to grace this ranch in decades. And that I'd been spending plenty of time at her side.

Hence this visit.

I'd never really thought about seeing Courtney again. About how it would feel. Maybe it should have bothered me. Maybe I should have been angry or hurt. The day she'd moved out of the house, I'd been both.

But as I reflected on it now, that short pain had been more about the cheating and Dad's loyalty to her over me. It was my pride that had been wounded, not really my heart.

I'd convinced myself it was love.

It wasn't.

The resentment was gone. So was the sting of betrayal from her affair with Sunny.

Now I was just annoyed. I was standing in my bare feet and giving my attention to the wrong woman.

Courtney had always been the wrong woman.

Deep down, I think she knew it too.

I'd never told a soul about Indya. I'd kept her to myself all those years. But Courtney wasn't stupid. Manipulative, but intelligent. She'd known that my heart wasn't entirely hers.

Was that why she'd cheated? Did I even care?

No. Not a bit. This visit of hers had already lasted too long.

"Courtney," I barked. "What?"

Her eyes snapped to mine, narrowing into a glare. "You're fucking the new owner already. I heard she's a real b—"

"*Do not* finish that sentence."

She was smart enough to shut her mouth.

It would chap Courtney's ass if she knew I'd been fucking Indya on and off for years. But that was none of her goddamn business. "If you're not here for a reason, I'm done."

"I just wanted to check on you." Courtney's chin began to quiver. "See if you're okay."

"I'm good." Surprisingly good considering all that had happened in the past month.

Courtney sniffled and crossed her arms over her chest. "We never really got closure."

"We did. The day you left."

"I'm—"

Sorry. The word she never could bring herself to say was *sorry.*

"I'm not staying," she said, straightening her shoulders. "In case you were worried."

"I wasn't."

"I'm moving."

"Congratulations."

"Are you going to ask where I'm moving?"

"No."

"Sunny and I broke up."

There it was. The reason for this visit. Attention. Maybe she thought I'd spent years pining for her. Well, she could get attention from anyone else.

This was a waste of my time.

I'd spent too many years catering to other people. Dad. Courtney. Even Mom to the extent that I played the go-between for Dad.

I'd picked my battles. I'd bitten my tongue.

No more.

It was time to do what I wanted. And right now, that was eat a meal with Indya, then take her to bed.

Without another word, I turned and stalked away.

Courtney let out a huff when I reached the porch, but I didn't bother turning back as I walked through the door.

Indya was in the kitchen, staring out the window over the sink to the field beyond the house.

The sack with dinner was on the counter, the handles still tied. I loosened the knot, the plastic rustling as I fished out our containers. Then I carried them to the table off the kitchen.

"What do you want to drink?"

"Water," she murmured, not moving.

I pulled two glasses from the cabinet and took up the space behind her, my chest pressed firmly against her back as I trapped her in place. Then I reached past her to turn on the faucet, letting it run cold before I filled the glasses with clean mountain water.

No filter needed.

"I could have left," she said. "Let you talk."

"I don't need to talk to Courtney. Everything has already been said." I kept the glasses in both hands but tightened my arms, like a hug, and pulled her away from the sink.

She stiffened, not wanting to move her feet.

"Work with me, Keller. Shuffle."

Indya relaxed and let me pull her away. But even when we weren't against the counter, I didn't let her go. "West."

"Keep shuffling."

"You're going to spill that water."

"Not if you shuffle your damn feet."

She laughed and shuffled, trapped against me as we made our way toward the table. Only when we reached her chair did I let her go to sit.

I set down our glasses, grabbed napkins and forks, and then joined her, taking the chair across from hers so I could look at her as we talked.

We both popped the lids on our containers, the scent of the meal making my stomach growl. And without any fanfare, we tore into our burgers, eating them while they were still warm. Until Indya broke the silence.

"My office. Was it hers?"

I swallowed the food in my mouth and shook my head. "It was mine. She took the one Mom used years ago. Then after Courtney left, Tara took it for storage."

Indya poked at her orzo pasta salad with a tine of her fork. "Oh."

"That chair you tossed? Courtney gave it to me as a Christmas present."

Her eyes widened.

"I hated that fucking chair." I chuckled. "But I do like the horse painting. Don't throw that one out."

"Your grumpy horse."

"He's not grumpy." I scoffed. "You just don't recognize him. That's Chief. I introduced you to him when we were kids."

Recognition dawned, and a smile ghosted her lips. "Chief."

"Mom had a local artist paint that for me after he died."

"I'm sorry."

"It's okay. Just don't toss my painting."

"You should have it. I'll bring it out."

"Nah. Keep it in the office. I like that you can keep Chief company every day." And that he could be there for her too.

I went back to my burger, taking two bites for her every one. Either she didn't like Reid's food—doubtful, because it was delicious—or Courtney's visit had stolen her appetite.

There were questions bouncing in that gorgeous head of hers. They were written on her mesmerizing face. So I ate, knowing she'd ask when she was ready.

And we could have the conversation we should have had years ago.

"Why did you keep working for me?" she asked. "You could have quit like your dad."

Not the topic I'd expected, but a fair question. "No matter who owns this ranch, it's still mine. This is all I know. It's all I've ever wanted. I couldn't just walk away. I don't know how Dad did. Still don't. I just . . . couldn't let it go."

The ranch.

Maybe Indya too.

"Do you ever wonder—" She stopped herself with a shake of her head. Then she took a bite of burger that was so large her cheeks bulged. Like if her mouth was full, it would keep that question inside.

Did I ever wonder what we could have been?

Yeah. I'd wondered. So many times I'd lost count.

She swallowed, then chased her food with a gulp of water. "Did you ever look me up on Instagram or Facebook? Before?"

"No."

During the spans in between the Keller family vacations, I hadn't let myself search for Indya. No social media. No calls or texts. Indya had always been mine, but only while she was in Montana.

"Why not?"

She was afraid I didn't want her, wasn't she? "Self-preservation." At its finest.

"What do you mean?"

"I never let myself hope that you'd come back." Or that she'd stay. Until now.

Maybe I was safe to finally hope.

"Did you ever look me up?" I asked.

"No." She shook her head.

"Why not?"

She gave me a sad smile. "I think I was afraid of what I'd find."

Other women. Another love.

A fiancée.

"Courtney and I went to school together," I said after taking my last bite and wiping my hands on a napkin. "Since kindergarten."

Indya stiffened. "We don't have to talk about her if you don't want to. You don't owe me an explanation."

"Maybe not. But I'll give you one anyway."

We'd never made promises. We'd always known what we had was limited to a week, sometimes less. That didn't mean what we'd had wasn't important.

"Remember that trip when we only had a day? After I came back from Hawaii?"

"Yes. I remember all the trips."

"So do I." I gave her a sad smile, then leaned deep into my chair. "I almost asked if you wanted to try sticking it out. Do the long-distance thing. But every time I played the logistics out in my head, I saw it ending in a wreck."

"Me too." There was sadness in those caramel eyes. "But if you would have asked, I would have done it anyway."

Damn. She'd never hinted at wanting to try. Never mentioned staying together.

It didn't change anything, knowing she'd wanted that too. But it was another regret.

"That day felt like a goodbye," I said. "Something about it was different. You left, and I was sure I'd never see you again. Figured you'd graduate, take that job with your dad's company, and get on with your life. Actually sort of pissed me off."

"That I had to finish college?"

"Yeah. How dare you?" I teased.

She smiled a little. If we could end this night with that tiny smile, I'd call it a win.

"That winter, I was at a bar in town. It was cold and snowy. I was bored and got drunk, so I didn't drive home. Courtney was there, and she let me crash on her couch that night. We started dating on and off for about six months after that. It wasn't serious. That spring, I got busy with work and stopped seeing her altogether. Summer came. You didn't. The next time Courtney called and asked me out for dinner, I said yes."

We'd dated seriously that time. She was always around. For a while, Courtney made her whole world about me, and it was easy to get wrapped up in that feeling.

She moved to the ranch. Started working at the lodge. It reminded me of my parents, and the nostalgia in that was more powerful than I'd realized at the time. I got wrapped up in that too.

When Courtney started dropping hints about getting married, I picked them up and bought her a ring.

She didn't even give me the chance to propose. I stashed that ring in my dresser drawer. She snooped and found it. Put it on and started telling the world we were engaged.

We would have gotten engaged, so I went along with it. Then Dad gave her the job as resort manager, and we settled into this life.

I'd gotten swept up in the idea of sharing this ranch with a woman who loved it.

A woman who didn't live in Texas.

Indya dropped her eyes to her lap. "We came back."

She came back.

"I know."

When I'd learned that the Kellers had returned for a vacation, my whole world had tipped upside down.

Courtney had come home after work. We'd traded tales about our days. And she'd prattled on and on about the guests. She loved gossiping about them, usually to run them down because she was jealous.

She told me she'd met a woman with blonde curly hair from Texas.

I'd been sitting on the couch. If not, that news would have knocked me on my ass.

Courtney had gone on and on about how the Beartooth Chalet was a magnet for snobby rich girls.

Indya Keller didn't have a snobby bone in her body. Not that I'd said that to Courtney. I had just sat there, stunned, and when I'd finally mustered the courage to speak, I had taken the coward's way out.

I had left for the week, camping out in the mountains alone.

Until Indya was gone.

Would things have been different if I could have faced her that year? Would I have called it off with Courtney before she'd started sleeping with Sunny? Would Dad have bought that Melvin land?

"Where were you that week?" she asked.

"Camping."

"Avoiding me."

I locked eyes with her. "Yes."

"I stayed in the cabin most of the week, faking migraines." She let out a humorless laugh. "I had these plans that trip. I was determined to get Dad to retire and slow down. I was going to ask if you wanted to date or . . . I don't know. Stop hiding from everyone. I was even considering moving to Montana."

My heart stopped.

Fuck.

It was a good thing I'd gone camping. I might not have been head over heels in love with Courtney, but I'd cared for her. Especially then. We'd been sharing a house. Building a life. I'd planned to make her my wife.

It was easier now to say I would have broken it off with Courtney. After she'd betrayed me, cheated on me.

But then? I don't know what I would have done if Indya had conveyed her interest in moving to Montana. Probably broken hearts.

Hers. Mine.

I almost felt bad for Courtney. She'd never stood a chance, had she? Not against Indy.

Maybe that was why I'd always been angrier at Dad. When Courtney had left, I had just gotten on with my life. I hadn't missed her. Yeah, my pride had taken a hit with the cheating, but that had healed quickly enough.

"Do you still love her?" Her voice was no more than a whisper. "Courtney."

"No."

She stared at me for a long moment.

I stared back.

"I wish . . ." Her voice cracked before she stood, then moved in a flurry to sweep away the remnants of our meal and toss the trash in the garbage.

Fuck. I raked a hand through my hair, wanting to start this night over. To take her inside the minute she'd mentioned that damn owl so we would have been halfway to my bedroom before Courtney had ever shown up. Wanting to have skipped this whole heavy conversation.

But it was one we couldn't keep avoiding.

And it wasn't over yet.

I leaned my elbows on my knees, waiting until she stopped moving. Indya was at the sink again, eyes fixed out the window.

"What are we doing, Indy?"

She shrugged.

That damn shrug. "That's not an answer."

"I don't have an answer. What are we doing, West?"

"I don't have a fucking clue." I stood and crossed the room, then wrapped her in my arms. I buried my nose in her hair to breathe in the rose scent of her perfume.

Her hands came to my forearms, holding tight as she leaned her head against my shoulder. She was dead on her feet. The longer we stood there, the more her body sagged into mine. After her second yawn, I swept her into my arms and carried her through the house.

When we reached my bedroom, I set her on her feet and went to my closet for a plain white tee. Then I traded her shirt for mine.

The hem hit her midthigh. She kicked off her jeans and unclasped her bra, then dragged it out of a sleeve and tossed it to the floor. Her hair was a mess, always bigger at the end of the day than the start.

Never in my life had I been awestruck by a woman like I was with Indya. Something expanded in my chest, making it hard to breathe. Maybe it was seeing her in my shirt. Maybe it was just having her here.

Mine. She was mine.

I framed her face in my hands, dropping a kiss to her forehead. Then I placed my hands on her shoulders and steered her to the bed, where I yanked down the covers. "Sleep."

She opened her mouth, probably to argue, but I pressed a finger to her lips before she could speak.

"In you go."

"Okay," she murmured, nearly collapsing on the mattress.

While she snuggled into a pillow, I went to the living room and kitchen to shut off the lights. Then I returned to the bedroom, stripped down to my boxer briefs, and climbed into bed.

The minute my weight hit the mattress, she burrowed into my chest, her nose to my heart.

My hands dived into her hair, threading a curl around each finger. Then I twined my legs with hers as I wrapped her up tight.

"What are we doing, West?" she whispered against my skin.

Were we picking up where we'd left off? Or was this a long good-bye? I wasn't sure I'd survive another goodbye with Indya.

"Starting over. You good with that?"

Her entire body relaxed. "Yeah. I'm good."

"Thank fuck," I breathed.

She curled in deeper, like she was trying to crawl inside my body and stay awhile. "I wish."

There was no trailing end to her sentence this time. There were no words she'd left unsaid.

I wish.

"I wish too, baby." I breathed in her sweet scent, holding her tight until her breaths evened out and her body went limp with sleep.

I wish.

I wished I had kept her. I wished our timing had worked years ago. I wished I had waited.

I wished she had waited too.

Chapter 24
INDYA

Age Twenty-Four

"This is it?"

If Blaine asked me that question one more time, I was going to yank my hair out.

"Yes." I ripped the zipper closed on my now-empty suitcase. My clothes were stowed in the dresser's drawers. My shoes were in the closet. And my patience was hanging on by a thread. "This is it."

He pursed his lips into a flat line as he hummed.

"Stop." I pinched the bridge of my nose. "Just. Stop."

"Stop what, Indya? I asked a simple question."

Snap. That frayed thread disintegrated. "Look, I know you don't want to be here." Blaine preferred luxury resorts on tropical beaches. A rugged Montana adventure was not his style. "I know this isn't your type of vacation. But we're here because it makes Dad happy. So can you lose the snobby attitude and chill the fuck out?"

His expression hardened as his lip curled. "I'll lose my attitude when my wife loses hers."

"Why do you always do that? Say it that way?"

"What?" he snapped.

"My wife." I let the air quotes fly. Had I known he would use those words with such disdain and contempt, I might not have taken the title.

Blaine planted his hands on his hips. "Are you on your period?"

My jaw dropped, and I saw red. "Are you on yours?"

Without another word, I stormed to the bedroom door, then ripped open the door and slammed it on my way out.

The Beartooth Chalet's living room and kitchen were empty. Thank God, Mom and Dad had gone for a walk. They didn't need to hear us arguing.

Mom said the first year of marriage was an adjustment.

It was only the first month. Weren't we supposed to be in the blissful newlywed stage? How many more *adjustments* did Blaine and I need to make so we wouldn't fight daily?

It hadn't been like this before the wedding. We'd been . . . happy. Busy, but happy.

Blaine had taken over the bulk of running Keller Enterprises after Dad had retired the past winter. And while I'd stayed working, too, I'd also been swamped planning the wedding.

We'd had a few squabbles in the past year, but none of those arguments had amounted to much. Until my first day as Mrs. Hamilton. We'd fought ever since, over and over and over.

On our honeymoon, we'd gotten into a huge argument over a bellhop. The poor kid had lost one of Blaine's suitcases. Instead of being patient and letting the hotel locate it for us, Blaine had demanded to speak to the manager and ordered the kid be fired.

I'd lost my damn mind and refused to speak to him for five days. It was only after he'd apologized and assured me the kid still had a job that I'd finally ended my silence.

The day after we'd made up from that argument, we'd flown home. And then started fighting over everything else.

I wanted to go out for drinks with a friend from work. Blaine was pissed because said friend was a single guy from Human Resources.

I cooked us a romantic dinner one evening. He never bothered to call and say he'd be three hours late coming home.

I wanted to go on a quiet summer trip with my parents because Dad hadn't been feeling well lately. Blaine loathed the idea of Montana.

Fight. Fight. Fight. I was so damn tired of fighting. Most days I wanted to scream.

Most days, I cried instead.

The lump in the back of my throat felt permanent, but I swallowed past it as I flew out of the cabin, needing some air.

Blaine had been griping about this trip for weeks. I never should have brought him along.

It was hard enough being here. It was hard enough knowing eventually I'd have to face West. It was hard enough thinking this could be Dad's last trip to Montana.

Was it too much to ask that my husband give it a chance?

Whatever. He could fight with me behind closed doors. As long as that attitude didn't show to Dad, I'd deal with Blaine myself.

Not that he'd ever dream of offending my father.

My parents adored Blaine.

Dad had hired Blaine a year ago, after our last trip to Montana, and it was because of Blaine that Dad felt like he could retire.

Blaine was young, only five years older than me, but he'd started at Keller Enterprises with experience and ambition.

He had charm and a sharp wit. He was polished. Poised. He came from money—not as much as me, but money. His taste was expensive, and it showed in his designer clothes and watches.

There'd been a hole in my heart after our last trip to Montana. Blaine had filled it.

When he'd asked me out to dinner a few weeks after he'd started working at Keller, it had just made sense. We made sense.

Blaine's life mirrored my own. There'd never been an obstacle between us. Everything had just moved naturally. We'd dated for six months. We'd moved in together the week after he'd proposed. We'd gotten married in a lovely spring ceremony at my family's country club.

When had we stopped making sense? Maybe we'd just spent too much time together lately. Maybe when we got home and he got back to work, we'd both relax.

Blaine worked all the time—the only thing we didn't seem to fight about. Mostly because his hard work meant a successful Keller Enterprises. A successful Keller Enterprises meant Dad didn't have to worry.

About my future. About Mom's.

Yesterday, he'd told me he could die in peace knowing that Blaine was around to provide for his girls.

Goddamn it. Tears flooded fast. Too fast to blink them away. So I wiped at them instead, furiously catching them at the corners of my eyes before they could leave tracks down my cheeks.

Was it so much to ask that we stop talking about Dad's death? He was fine. He was alive. The doctors hadn't given him any indication that he was nearing the end of his life. So couldn't we just *fucking* drop it?

I was walking so quickly it was nearly a jog, but my flimsy sandals kept me from running. So I walked and walked. Until the tears were gone. Until the sting in my nose had faded. Until I wandered off the shoulder of the gravel road, lured by a patch of small white and purple wildflowers.

I stopped to pluck one of the blooms and touched a petal with my fingertip.

They were the same flowers I'd picked here as a girl. God, that seemed like a lifetime ago.

What was I doing here?

As much as I wanted to blame today's fight on Blaine, maybe it was me. Maybe he'd been right and we should have stayed home.

Maybe he could sense my anxiety about coming to Montana.

About seeing West.

Not that Blaine had a clue about West. No one did.

I hadn't seen him when we'd checked in. I hadn't seen Courtney either. Did they still live on the ranch? Were they married now? Was she pregnant already?

Did they fight all the time too?

I picked another flower, then another. I'd made myself a small bouquet when the rumble of an engine sounded, causing me to stand tall and turn.

An old green truck, spotted with rust—a truck I hadn't seen in ages—rolled down the gravel road.

My heart leaped and squeezed and pinched all at the same time. It was the strangest mix of hope and joy and despair and sadness I'd ever felt in my life.

I'd missed that truck.

I'd missed the man behind the wheel.

West eased his pickup to the side of the road, coming to a stop.

The sense of déjà vu was so strong it locked me frozen in place as he climbed out and rounded the hood.

A cowboy hat shaded his face. The sleeves of his button-down were rolled up his forearms. His faded jeans draped to boots as dusty as his truck. The sun bounced off his belt buckle.

He was perfect.

And he was no longer mine.

"Hey, Indya."

I forced air into my lungs. "Hi, West."

The corners of his mouth turned up as he joined me in the grass. "Heard you were here for the week."

"Yeah."

Had his wife told him that? My gaze shifted to his left hand. There was no ring on his finger, but that didn't mean anything. West wasn't exactly the jewelry type.

"How's your dad doing?"

I nodded, breathing through the surge of emotion.

No crying.

Don't cry.

Tears flooded again. Damn it. I was going to cry. All because West asked about Dad.

He wouldn't ask if I was okay. Not yet. Not until he asked about Dad. Because he knew that if Dad was okay, then I'd be okay too.

I bent to snag a flower, using the movement to blink the tears from my eyes and hide my gaze. "He's all right. Very excited to be here, as usual."

"Good. And you?"

I shrugged and picked another flower, this one purple.

"Heard you got married."

"Yeah. About a month ago." The ring on my finger had never felt heavier. The same was true of the weight on my heart.

West let me keep picking until my bouquet was double in size. "Why are you crying, Indy?"

Damn him. Damn him for knowing me too well.

I stood tall, lifting my chin. It quivered. "I'm not crying."

"Indy." His beautiful hazel eyes softened. His arms lifted, like he was about to wrap them around me.

But I doubted his wife would appreciate that.

Nor would my husband.

I took a step away.

His arms dropped to his sides.

"How's Courtney?"

A frown hardened his face. "That, uh, didn't work out."

For the second year in a row, the ground disappeared beneath my feet.

He wasn't married.

He'd never gotten married.

Oh, God. It hurt. Fuck, it hurt. I wanted to scream again.

This trip was such a mistake.

"I—" There was nothing to say, so I shut my mouth. Then I stared at West as he stared back. A thousand words hung in the air between us, words we'd never say. Words we should have said years ago.

"Indya."

My name cut through the air, breaking my eyes away from West.

Blaine walked our way. His stride was easy. He didn't look like he was hurrying, but those long strides betrayed him.

His jeans were dark and stiff. His boots were shining and new. His shirt was starched. He looked entirely out of place on a gravel road.

West bent, the movement stealing my focus. He plucked a white flower, then handed it over as he stood. "Good to see you, Indy."

"You too, West." I took the flower and added it to my bouquet.

Later that night, I slipped away from the Beartooth and left that bouquet in West's childhood fort.

Chapter 25
WEST

Giggles welcomed me into the lodge.

Two women—twentysomething girls—stood beneath the chandelier, talking to Jax.

He had his cowboy hat in hand. His jeans were dusty, and he was still wearing his chaps. He'd probably just finished up the last guided trail ride of the day.

When he flashed them a grin, the giggles grew louder.

Behind them, at the front desk, Tara rolled her eyes.

I cleared my throat, walking to my brother's side and clapping him on the shoulder. "Jax. Ladies."

One of the girls blushed so red that her cheeks matched the hot pink of her tank top.

"Got a minute?" I asked Jax, jerking my chin toward the opposite end of the lobby.

"Sure." He waved at the girls. "See ya."

As they raced up the stairs, whispering to each other, I smacked my brother on the arm.

"Hey." He rubbed the spot. "What was that for?"

"Jax." I gave him a flat look.

"We were just talking," he said, feigning innocence.

Tara scoffed. "And I'm seven feet tall."

"Just watch the flirting with guests," I said.

"Do what you say, not what you do?"

"Huh?"

Jax's gaze shifted toward the open dining room doors, where Indya stood with a couple of guests at the bar, smiling as they talked.

The tables were clothed but empty. Dinner wouldn't start for another hour, and tonight was the campfire, so most people would eat outside. But the bar was open to serve drinks, and Reid had set up a small table with appetizers.

"Indya's not a guest," I said.

"But she was. And you broke all the rules."

Yeah. I'd broken the rules. Without remorse.

It had been a week since Indya had come to my place with dinner. A week of her sleeping in my bed.

A week of us starting over.

It wasn't really starting over. There was no forgetting our history. And even if that were possible, I wouldn't want to erase our past.

But there was no denying that everything was different this time around.

Indya was here.

And I wasn't letting her go.

She smiled at the guests as they talked. She pushed a curl out of her face. Whatever she was telling them, they hung on her every word.

Indya was entirely in her element, like she'd been born for this. My heart swelled too big in my chest.

I loved her.

I fucking loved that woman.

I'd loved her my whole damn life.

"Damn, she's pretty." Jax's statement stole my focus. "Think she'd go for a younger man?"

I smacked his arm again.

"Kidding." He chuckled. "Have you tried some of the new food?"

"Indya brought some over the other night. It's good."

"Really good. And Reid is making up a staff menu too. Stuff that we can grab and eat on the run."

Indya had mentioned it last night. She didn't want the staff worrying about meals while they were working. It was her idea, not Reid's—though Reid would definitely take credit. Not that Indya was the type who needed credit.

"Heard Courtney was out the other night," Jax said, lowering his voice.

"Yeah," I muttered.

"What did she want?"

I shrugged. "Attention. Closure. I don't know."

"Think she'll be back?" Jax asked.

"No."

There was nothing for Courtney on the ranch. She had to know that now.

"I'd better get home and shower," Jax said, lifting his arm to take a whiff. "I'm heading into town later. Want to come?"

"Nope." My plans for tonight involved the beauty in the dining room.

"Figured." Jax smirked. "See ya."

"Don't drink and drive."

"I'll probably just stay in town tonight." Either at a friend's house or in some woman's bed.

"Bye." I lifted a hand to wave but kept my focus aimed on Indya as she finished up her conversation.

As the guests took their cocktails toward the hors d'oeuvre station, she strolled through the room, skimming the table linens with her fingertips.

When she spotted me, a smile lit up her face.

A smile that reminded me of white wildflowers and green fields. Of my old green truck in a mountain meadow. Of summer weeks with Indya Keller.

"Hi." She stopped three feet away, a polite distance.

There was nothing polite about what I'd do to her later.

"Come here." I crooked a finger.

She took half a step.

"Indya."

She nodded to Tara.

"Ah." If she thought we were keeping our relationship a secret, she was dreaming.

In a fast sweep, I hauled her over my shoulder.

"West!" she yelped. "Put me down."

"Bye, Tara," I called. "We'll be back for the campfire in a bit."

"Bye, West. Bye, Indya."

"Oh my God." Indya's voice was muffled, like she'd dropped her face into her hands.

I grinned and carted her out the door.

"You made your point." She wiggled once we were down the porch stairs. "Are you going to put me down?"

"Nope." I smacked her butt, tightening my hold on her legs, and headed for the Beartooth.

"I can walk."

"We both know that's an exaggeration of the truth."

"West Haven, you put me down right now."

That earned her another swat on the ass.

"You're such a caveman. Everyone is going to be talking about this."

"Exactly." I slowed, setting her on her feet but keeping hold of her elbow until she had her balance. "I want everyone to know you're mine. Employees. Guests. Anyone who sets foot on this ranch. We were a secret for too long, baby. I'm not hiding this anymore."

A blinding smile transformed her face. Beautiful. She'd stolen my heart. I was so busy memorizing that smile that I rocked on my heels when she pounced, leaping into my arms.

The moment her legs circled my waist, her mouth was on mine, her tongue sliding past my lips. The moan that sank from her body into mine was part passion, part relief. That sound went straight to my cock.

I carried her inside the Beartooth, then kicked the door closed. As it slammed shut, I spun us around, then pressed her against the hard wooden surface.

"West." Her legs fell from my waist to straddle my thigh. "I need you inside."

My mouth locked on her throat. "You want my fingers, my mouth, or my cock?"

"All of it," she panted, grinding against me, seeking that friction for release. "I want all of it."

"That's my girl." I nipped at her earlobe, then flicked open the button on her jeans.

She whimpered as I took my leg away to spin her around.

I wrapped an arm around her shoulders, holding her back against my chest. Then I thrust my arousal against her perfect ass. "Spread your legs wider."

She obeyed instantly, making space so I could slip my hand down her belly, down into the waistband of her jeans. As my fingertips moved beneath her lace panties, her head lolled against my shoulder.

"Are you wet for me?"

"Mm-hmm." Her hum was heady with desire.

My finger slipped through her center. She was soaked. Fucking soaked. My cock throbbed against my zipper.

"Oh, God." She began that rocking motion of her hips again, this time against my hand. "I changed my mind. I need you inside. Now."

"Patience."

She shook her head. "Fuck me, West. Please. I need to feel you."

"Not yet." I curled a finger inside.

"West, please." Her breath hitched.

"Not yet, baby." I pressed the heel of my palm against her clit. "This first. Then I'll fuck you."

She let out a frustrated growl, but her hips rocked faster against my hand, her limbs beginning to tremble as she chased her own release. "More."

I dragged my mouth across her neck, trailing kisses along the line of her jaw. My cock ached for her. My heart pounded as her moans filled the cabin. "You feel so good, Indy."

She kept rolling those hips, fucking herself on my fingers. "More."

I brought my finger to her clit, drawing circles over the bundle of nerves. That was all it took for her to tumble over the edge.

"Yes." She exploded, her body trembling and shaking as she cried out.

My name on her lips was magic.

It was my future. I wanted this every night. This woman in my arms. Her pleasure at my fingertips.

When she came down from her orgasm, sagging against me as she worked to regain her breath, I picked her up and carried her to the bedroom.

We stripped each other out of our clothes, leaving them puddled on her bedroom floor. Then I covered her body with mine and sank inside that tight, wet heat.

"West." She wrapped her legs around my back, her heels digging into the base of my spine to pull me deeper.

"Fuck, baby." I pushed the hair away from her face and drowned in her caramel eyes.

We started slow, savoring every second until her legs and arms began to tremble again. Then I pistoned faster and harder, her breasts bouncing with every stroke.

I bent and took a nipple in my mouth, sucking hard on one and then the other. "You're perfect, Indy. You're so fucking perfect."

"Harder, West. Please." She clawed at my shoulders and writhed beneath me.

"That's it, baby." I moved faster. "Come for me."

Her back arched just as my name left her lips, and she shattered. Pulse after pulse, she came apart.

That clench of her pussy was my undoing. I gritted my teeth, fighting the shaking in my limbs. But as she squeezed harder, her orgasm drawing out longer and longer, it triggered my own.

I came on a roar, spilling inside her. I lost myself in Indya's body until we were spent, and I collapsed, boneless, and wrapped her in my arms. My fingers dived into her hair. Any excuse to touch it, I was taking it.

She clung to me as our hearts thundered, our skin slick with sweat. Then she buried her face in my neck and giggled.

It was almost as sweet as the sound of her coming on my name.

"What?" I shoved up to an elbow, pushing her hair away from her forehead.

She returned the gesture, shoving her fingers into the hair at my temple. "It hits me now and again that we have time. That we don't have to rush every minute together. It's surreal. I'm just . . . happy."

"Me too."

Nothing else mattered. Nothing but Indy.

"I'm hungry." I eased our bodies apart and kissed the corner of her mouth. Then I climbed out of bed, taking her hand to help her up too.

She pulled on her panties and retrieved a pair of cutoff denim shorts from a drawer. She fished her phone from the jeans she'd been in earlier. She pulled on her bra and my shirt, then buttoned it just over her heart. The sleeves draped past her fingertips, so she rolled them up as she sauntered out of the bedroom.

I pulled on my jeans and a T-shirt she'd stolen earlier this week that was folded on top of her dresser. Then I found her in the kitchen, standing in the open refrigerator.

"You don't want to go to the campfire?"

She shrugged. "I kind of like it just us."

"I kind of like it too." I wrapped her up, kissing her temple as we both stared at the empty fridge shelves.

Just us. It was a luxury that wouldn't last.

What would Dad say when he learned Indy and I were together? He and I had a long road to walk to rebuild our relationship, if that was even possible. If he had a problem with Indya, it might ruin us for good.

Mom would want to meet her sooner rather than later. Tara had probably shared a lot, and before long, I expected another visit from my mother to learn about the woman who'd captured my heart.

Then there were the logistics of work and the ranch. I still wasn't sure how to wrap my head around the future and what that looked like. But none of it mattered, not tonight.

Tonight was just for us.

"I need to go to the store," she said. "There's not much to work with here. But I could make breakfast for dinner."

"Sounds good. What can I do?"

"Pour me a glass of wine." She stood on her toes to kiss the underside of my jaw, then started hauling ingredients onto the counter. She'd just cracked an egg into a bowl when a knock came at the door.

"Expecting anyone?" I asked.

"No. It's probably someone from the lodge. Would you get it?" She glanced to her fingers, covered in egg whites and holding a broken shell.

"Sure, baby." I fastened the last button on my jeans as I crossed the room, then opened the door.

It wasn't an employee on the porch.

It was Indya's ex-husband.

Fucking *Blaine*.

Chapter 26
INDYA

It was Blaine's blond hair that made me do a double take as I glanced from the sink to the door.

West's frame blocked most of the threshold, but as he crossed his arms over his chest, his body shifted, and I caught sight of Blaine's hair.

I'd know that hair anywhere.

Blaine wore it short and flawlessly styled. Whenever I'd muss it with my fingertips, he'd fix it immediately, making sure every strand was in the right place. It was always combed and gelled, even on the weekends when we were home together. It didn't matter that there wasn't anyone in the world to see him disheveled; he had to be perfect. His morning routine included thirty minutes at the bathroom mirror working on that damn hair.

It was a stark contrast to West's dark strands, especially tonight. West's hair was sticking up at odd angles thanks to my fingers tousling it in the bedroom.

Oh, God. What the hell was Blaine doing here? If he was here to back out of our deal . . .

No. He wouldn't back out. Not now. We'd come too far. Besides, Blaine hated Montana.

I refused to let him ruin this for me. Refused. So I washed my hands, squared my shoulders, and crossed the room on bare feet, keeping quiet.

"Where is Indya?" There was venom in Blaine's question.

"Right here," I said, coming to a stop beside West.

Blaine looked me up and down, taking in West's shirt that was too big on my frame. I'd tucked it into the front of my shorts, but the tail tipped so low it hung to the hem of my shorts, only their frayed edges hanging longer.

He kept his gaze locked on mine as he spoke to West. "I'd like a minute alone with my wife."

"Ex-wife," I corrected.

Blaine's expression turned murderous. "Indya, you have made me travel all the way to Montana for this."

"I didn't make you do anything."

"Didn't you?" He arched an eyebrow. "You had a choice."

Had I known he'd come here, maybe I would have gone to Texas after all. Except for too long, I'd changed my plans to accommodate Blaine's. I'd bent to his will. His demands.

Maybe I should have bent one more time.

Then this would be over.

He didn't need to explain why he was here. I knew why.

"Your office, Indya. Let's go."

Fuck you, Blaine. It took every shred of my control to keep those words inside.

I was about to take a step, to swallow my pride so this would just be over, when West's hand found the small of my back.

He gripped my shirt, not hard, but enough that there was no way I was leaving this house. Then he offered his free hand to Blaine.

"West Haven."

"Blaine Hamilton." Blaine looked like he'd rather touch a rattlesnake, but he shook West's hand. And winced.

West squeezed so hard that one of Blaine's knuckles cracked.

I pulled in my lips to hide a smile. For me, those hands meant pleasure and worship. For Blaine, well . . . maybe he'd think twice before barking orders in my face.

"I don't believe we've actually met," West said, releasing Blaine.

No, they hadn't met. The one and only time I'd brought Blaine to Montana, I'd never tried to make introductions. Not that West had been around much that trip.

Just that day he'd found me in a meadow along the road, picking flowers.

The day he'd told me that his engagement had fallen apart.

The day I'd cried in the shower until the water had run cold, devastated that he hadn't gotten married.

But I had.

We were so close this time. Finally. After all these years, we might actually get it right.

Unless Blaine fucked it up.

"West." I looked up to him, my eyes pleading. "Can we have a minute?"

It didn't surprise me in the slightest when West shook his head. Maybe if Blaine had been polite, West would have left us alone. But Blaine was being Blaine. So whatever he'd come here to say, West would hear too.

My heart sank. This wasn't how I wanted him to find out the truth.

I just hoped, when it was done, he'd understand. So I sighed and stepped back, waving Blaine inside. "Come in."

"Your office." He pointed to the lodge.

"Is in here tonight." West's jaw clenched, and only a fool would argue with his tone.

Blaine was an asshole. But he wasn't a fool. "Fine."

He bent to pick up the briefcase at his feet, then stepped past West. His glare stayed locked on me as I led him to the dining room table. The moment he was in a seat, he pulled his phone from his pocket, then sent his fingers flying over the screen. "My assistant is in the lodge. Waiting to join us in your office."

I sank into the seat opposite his, Blaine's presence zapping any energy I'd had from earlier.

West came to stand behind me, his hands going to the back of my chair.

"Why did you bring your assistant?" I asked.

"He's a notary." He unfastened his case and pulled out a manila folder.

The paperwork.

He was here to see our deal through.

"What happened to Monday?"

"The attorneys finalized the contract this morning," he said. "I want this finished and see no reason to wait."

So he'd flown all the way to Montana on a Saturday, dragging his poor assistant along, when he could have waited. It couldn't be finalized until Monday anyway. Why come here on a weekend?

Blaine was a pain in my ass, but he wasn't impulsive. He was strategic in everything he did. Unless . . .

Unless he was scared.

He met my gaze and, for a split second, let me see a hint of insecurity. Fear. A weakness he would never admit.

His future was in my hands.

Until I signed his papers.

"You think I'll change my mind," I said.

"Yes. And I'm not taking that risk." He turned the papers to face me and slid them across the table.

His desperation was showing.

I almost laughed. Maybe I would have if it weren't so sad.

Was that why he'd been so insistent in emails? Was that the reason for the calls? If he knew me, he'd know there was nothing to worry about.

I wouldn't waver from my decision. Not in the slightest. I'd given him my word. I didn't break promises.

But Blaine didn't know me. Not even a bit. How was it possible that I'd been married to this man for years and we were practically strangers?

West and I had been together only during stolen weeks. Fleeting summer vacations. Yet he knew me. Maybe not the little details, but we were fixing that. Together.

Maybe if Blaine had bothered to put in a fraction of the effort West had shown me, maybe if he had dropped his guard when we were married, we would have ended our marriage as friends.

It still would have ended. That was inevitable.

Blaine had never been in love with me. I'd never been in love with Blaine.

But we might have at least parted ways on good terms.

Not for each other's sake. But for Dad's.

My father had loved Blaine. And in his own way, I think Blaine had cared for Dad too.

A knock came at the door.

I shifted to stand, but West moved across the room first, then opened the door to a Black man dressed similarly to Blaine in a pair of starched jeans and a solid polo shirt.

He must be new to Blaine's staff, because I didn't recognize him.

The assistant carried his own briefcase. He set it on the table before taking a seat in the chair beside Blaine. Then he wordlessly opened the case to retrieve a pen and his notary materials.

I looked between the two of them, waiting for an introduction that never came.

"I'm Indya." I stretched my arm across the table. "Nice to meet you."

The assistant froze, only his eyes moving to Blaine.

"Sam," Blaine said.

"Samuel, actually. I go by Samuel." He took my hand, offering a kind smile. "Pleasure, Miss Keller."

"Welcome to Haven River Ranch, Samuel. You can call me Indya. This is West."

He stood behind me again, arms crossed and legs planted wide. His gaze was locked on the papers Blaine had shoved my direction.

Papers I would have to explain. Later.

"I'd arranged for a notary on Monday," I told Blaine. "There was no reason for you to travel out here."

"Well, I'm here. This won't take long. Then you can go flit around with your cowboy."

West was my cowboy.

He'd always been my cowboy. Blaine might have seen West only once, but there was no doubt in my mind that he knew West was mine.

And had been long before Blaine had entered my life.

"Shall we?" I pulled the papers closer and began flipping through the contract.

It was the same version I'd already read. My attorneys had also been through it in great detail and had sent me their approval. But I quickly checked the high points to ensure everything was solid.

"May I borrow your pen, Samuel?" I asked.

"Of course." He handed it over.

Maybe my hand should have been shaky. Maybe I should have had those second thoughts Blaine feared enough to fly to Montana today. But I was steady and solid as I initialed every page and signed my name on the last.

Samuel needed my driver's license, so I stood and retrieved it from my purse as Blaine signed the contracts himself.

One copy for him. Another for me.

Once they were notarized and finished, both he and Samuel packed up their briefcases.

"Thank you, Miss Keller." Samuel offered a kind smile.

"Come back and stay with us sometime," I said.

"I might just do that."

Blaine scowled.

Samuel ignored it.

I liked Samuel already. I'd wager that within months, he'd find a better boss.

He left first, nodding to West as he passed.

Blaine stood, and for a moment, I thought he'd disappear without a word.

I should have known better. Blaine always had to have the last word. After the divorce, he'd told me that we'd lasted longer than he'd expected.

"Was that so hard?" He smirked.

"Hard? No. Unnecessary? Yes. I would have sent these to you Monday."

"You don't close a seventy-five-million-dollar deal through FedEx, Indya."

The number was intentionally dropped as a slap in the face. Not mine.

West's.

"Get out, Blaine." The glare I sent him was lethal.

His smirk only widened as he sauntered out, slamming the door behind him. He'd fly back to Texas tonight, probably on the Keller Enterprises jet.

Would it even be Keller Enterprises by morning? Knowing Blaine, he had new signage ordered and at the ready.

The company, Dad's company, was gone.

Something broke in my chest.

Not my heart.

My hope.

There was a reason Blaine and I had stayed married. Not by any effort on his part whatsoever. Not for love or affection. But because of my iron will to make it work with a man whom my father had adored.

Dad loved Blaine. So I'd kept Blaine.

"What was that?" West asked.

The lump in my throat was so big it was hard to speak. "I—I sold him Dad's company."

It was real now. It was done.

This was how it had to end. I'd been preparing myself for months. But that didn't make it hurt any less.

Tears flooded my eyes, and no matter how fast I blinked, I couldn't chase them away. The contract on the table was too white. Too loud. So I stood and moved the hell away from those papers.

My head was swimming. My limbs were sluggish, and I swayed on a step.

"Whoa." West caught my arm before I could fall. "Indy."

"I'm okay. I just need a minute." I forced air into my lungs and wiggled free, then walked to the door. As I stepped onto the porch, the hot summer air seemed to only make it worse.

My heart pounded so loudly I couldn't hear anything else. My throat was on fire. My nose burned. And those fucking tears wouldn't stop.

One fell down my cheek as I reached the first step.

This time when my knees buckled, I caught myself, grabbing the railing as I sat with a thud on the top stair.

It was gone. Keller Enterprises was gone.

Dad had spent his entire life building that business. He'd gifted it to me.

And now it was gone.

A choked, hoarse sound escaped my throat. I swallowed hard and shifted to dig my phone from my shorts pocket. My hand was shaking as I pulled up Dad's name.

This was the one thing in the world I didn't want to tell him, but he deserved to know. He deserved to hear it from me.

He'd understand. Dad always understood. He'd tell me it was okay. That I'd done the right thing. That I'd made the choice he would have made too.

Except he wouldn't have let it go this far. He would have made better choices. Fewer mistakes.

Dad should have been here to make these decisions, not me.

I hit his name, then held my breath as I pressed the phone to my ear.

"We're sorry. You have reached a number that has been disconnected or is no longer in service. Please check the number dialed and try again."

Wait. What? I pulled the phone away, checking the screen. It was Dad's contact. It was his number.

I called it again.

"We're sorry . . ."

"No." My whole body flinched. "No, no, no."

My fingers flew over the screen, and this time, the person I called answered.

"Hi. Good timing. I was just thinking about you."

"Mom." My voice was raw. "I just called Dad, and it said his number was disconnected."

The line went silent.

"Mom. Why is his phone disconnected?"

A hard body pressed against my side. West's strong arm wrapped around my shoulders.

If I looked at him, I'd break. So I kept my eyes trained forward, my phone hard against my ear as I waited for my mother.

"My new assistant got me a new phone." Her former assistant had retired, and Mom had recently hired a twentysomething woman to help around the house and with technology. "She switched providers so I'd have better service in the house. She asked me if I should cancel his line and—"

"Get it back."

"It's been years, honey," Mom whispered.

No. I needed that phone line. I needed that voice mail. Somehow, in all these years, I hadn't filled up his inbox. Either because someone deleted them from time to time—maybe Mom's old assistant, who'd also worked with Dad for a time—or there was a glitch or the universe knew I needed Dad's voice.

"Get it back."

"Indya."

"Get it back, Mom," I yelled. "Please. You should have checked with me. That's all I have left. I need it back."

"I'm sorry." Mom's voice wobbled. "I'm so sorry."

Tears streamed down my face as I let the phone drop. It clattered on the wooden step, slipping past the railing and landing with a thud on the ground.

I hauled myself to my feet, then managed to make it down the stairs without falling and walked across the lawn.

There were noises coming from the lodge. The scent of campfire smoke drifted in the air. There'd been enough rain this summer that we could still have a Saturday-night fire. What happened when it was too dry? Too dangerous?

I'd never been to Montana in August. Dad always preferred June, when it was lush and green. When the grass was covered in dew each morning and you'd need a sweatshirt to ward off the evening chill.

He'd loved Montana in June.

He'd loved Montana.

The tears continued to fall as I walked. Step after step, I followed the one path I hadn't taken since I'd moved here.

Through the field behind the lodge and along a beaten path that wrapped around a grove of quaking aspen. Past the trees was an incline that took me up and over a small hill and into a quiet mountain-valley meadow.

Mom and Dad's camping spot.

It was arguably the most beautiful place on the ranch. The mountains framed the scene in the background. The trees that circled the area stood tall and proud, their tops waving in the breeze.

I stopped walking.

And collapsed to my knees.

West knelt behind me and wrapped me in his arms. "Let it go, Indy."

"It hurts." I sobbed.

"I know, baby." He held me tighter. "Let it out."

So I did.

For the first time in my life, I let West see me cry.

Chapter 27
INDYA

Age Twenty-Five

There were ashes on the wind. They blew across the field in a gray cloud that thinned to white, then . . . nothing. Gone.

Mom let out a shaky breath and dropped her chin.

I held her hand tighter.

Don't cry.

No crying.

Today, I couldn't cry. I had to be strong for my mother so she could finally stop holding it together for my father.

I bit the inside of my cheek so hard the metallic tang of blood coated my tongue, but my eyes stayed dry.

"He'll be happy here." Mom sniffled. "He always loved Montana. And I think he knew last year it would be his final trip. We walked out here together, and he told me this was where he wanted to stay."

Mom began to weep, gentle sobs no louder than that whispering wind.

I shut off my ears. Today, if I listened, I would cry.

I couldn't cry.

If I cried, I'd scream. If I screamed, I'd rage. I'd fill this meadow with so much pain that the grasses would wither. The flowers would rot. The trees would break.

I'd ruin Dad's resting place.

So I tuned out the sound of my mother's broken heart and stared blankly into the distance.

Should it hurt this much? We'd had years preparing for Dad's death. Years of him reminding us that he was *still alive*, just not for long.

I'd give anything to hear him say those two words again.

Still alive.

Fuck you, cancer. Fuck you.

Tears flooded my eyes. Mom was still crying. I held my breath and counted my heartbeats. *One. Two. Three.* The pain was bearable by the time I made it to twenty.

Mom wiped her eyes and rested her temple on my shoulder. "I'm glad it was just us today."

"Me too." I squeezed her hand.

We stood together in silence. I wasn't sure for how long, but it was easier in the quiet. I could still hear Dad's voice. If I closed my eyes, I could pretend he was beside me, face tipped to the blue Montana sky to let the sun warm his skin.

What if I stayed here forever? What if I just stood here until I was nothing but ashes in the wind too?

Mom was the one to break the silence. She bent to pick up the box we'd carried out here and tuck it under her arm; then she turned and walked away.

What if I stayed?

"Indya?"

I cleared the emotion clogging my throat. "Coming."

The moment I turned my back on the field, turned my back on my father, grief and loss ripped through my heart so violently I stopped, pressing my hand against my sternum until it subsided and I could move again.

Every step was harder than the last, but I forced myself to walk, lengthening my strides until I was at Mom's side. Then the two of us returned to the lodge.

"I think I'll rest for a bit," she said as we walked into the lobby. "Do you want to meet for dinner?"

"I'm not all that hungry. You go without me."

"All right." I followed her upstairs to the second floor, waiting until she was in her room before continuing to mine three doors down.

The Beartooth Chalet was booked this week. Mom thought it was a blessing. She wasn't sure she could have stayed in the cabin without Dad.

But as I closed the door to my room, it felt . . . wrong.

We should be in the cabin tonight. We should be sitting on the couch, remembering all the naps Dad had taken in that exact place.

I couldn't stay here. I couldn't sit on the bed in this small room. So I escaped to the hallway, then rushed outside, where it was easier to breathe.

My feet carried me out of the lodge and past the barn, toward the fenced corrals where once upon a time, West had introduced me to his horse.

What was that horse's name? Clyde? Chance? Why couldn't I remember?

My phone vibrated in my pocket, and I pulled it out to a text from Blaine.

Go okay?

Two words. Was that really all Blaine could spare for me today? Was making a fucking phone call to his wife on the day she'd scattered her father's ashes too much to ask for?

Apparently.

I cleared the notification, not bothering with a reply.

Blaine was working. That was the reason he hadn't come along. Not that I'd invited him in the first place.

He'd been the dutiful husband this past weekend at the memorial service, shaking hands and accepting condolences. He hadn't missed the public gathering.

But he had missed the moment that actually mattered.

Mom was right. It was better this way, just the two of us.

And now, just me.

I rested my arms on the corral's top rail and breathed. I stood alone for hours, just staring into the distance.

The sun was beginning to set when I felt him.

I didn't turn as West took the space beside me, propping his forearms on the rail.

He stood with me, both of us watching the sunset in quiet. Every few minutes, I blinked away the threat of tears. I bit my bottom lip when I felt my chin quiver.

I fought and fought and fought, holding back that grief.

"You can cry, Indy."

"No, I can't." I shook my head. "Not out here. I feel like I could fill every empty space with how much it hurts. It's too big. It feels too big."

"Okay." He took my hand, pulling it off the fence. Then he led me from the corrals, past the barn, and into the lodge.

He wordlessly pulled me to the second floor, down the hallway, and to my room. West held out his palm for the key.

I dug it from my pocket, not sure what he wanted in my room but trusting him anyway.

He knew I was married. He felt the ring on my hand. This wasn't about sex.

When the door clicked, he led me inside. "Take off your shoes."

I obeyed, toeing them off as he did the same for his boots.

His hat was tossed on the dresser; then he pulled me onto the bed.

And into his arms.

He held me so tight my nose was pressed against his throat. My hair was tangled in his hand.

He brought me to a space that wasn't so big.

So I could cry.

This was my chance to give in. To let go of the body-racking, soul-splitting, life-changing cries.

But I hadn't once let West see me cry.

I wasn't starting today.

So I inched deeper into his chest, drawing from his strength as he held me for hours. Until the stars sparkled in the midnight sky beyond my room.

It took every bit of my willpower to keep it all inside, but not a single tear soaked his shirt. And though it took hours, finally, I fell into an exhausted sleep.

~

I feigned sleep as West tiptoed out of my room. I'd woken when he'd shifted off the bed in the early light of dawn.

Only when he was gone and the door was shut did I open my eyes.

Then I stretched a hand to his side of the bed, still warm from where he'd slept last night. I hauled his pillow into my face, drawing in his scent. Leather and soap and wind.

I'd miss that smell. For the rest of my life.

After one last inhale, I forced myself out of bed, then straightened yesterday's rumpled clothes as I padded to the window.

West crossed the parking lot with that confident, easy stride of a good man.

Besides my father, West Haven was the best man I'd ever known.

He reached a silver truck and opened the door, but before he climbed inside, he turned and found me at the window.

We stared at each other. Memorized each other.

This was the last time I'd see West, wasn't it? This was finally our goodbye.

I pressed my hand to the glass.

He dipped his chin. Then he got in that truck, one I didn't recognize, and drove away.

As his taillights disappeared down the gravel road, I pulled my phone from my pocket and opened my recent calls.

Nothing from Blaine. One from my mother.

And eleven days ago, a call from Dad.

Eleven days. We'd talked about the weather. He'd asked me what Blaine and I were doing for dinner that night.

It had been only eleven days, but it might as well have been a lifetime.

I touched his name. The call went straight to his voice mail.

"You've reached Grant Keller. Please leave a message, and I'll return your call as soon as possible. Thank you."

His voice.

God, I missed his voice.

I missed his hugs and his laugh and his smile.

I missed him so much I couldn't breathe. But I sucked in a short inhale and forced myself to speak.

"Hi, Daddy. I was just calling to say hello. I miss—" A sob broke free. I squeezed my eyes shut. "I miss you. I love you. I'll call you tomorrow, okay? I'll call you every day."

An hour later, after my suitcase was packed and loaded in the back of our rental car, my mother and I drove away from the Crazy Mountain Cattle Resort.

"I don't think I'll come back here," she murmured.

I glanced in the rearview mirror, taking one last look at the lodge. Then I locked my gaze on the road, refusing to turn back. "Neither do I."

Chapter 28
INDYA

"It's getting dark," West murmured against my temple. "We should go back."

We were still sitting in the meadow where I'd scattered Dad's ashes. The ground was hard. A lump of dirt was digging into my rear, and the grass poked at the bare skin of my legs.

We should go back. We should move.

But I couldn't summon the strength to stand.

There were things to say. West deserved an explanation after Blaine's visit. Instead, I'd cried for what felt like hours.

How long had we been out here? The air was growing cold, the evening temperature dropping as the sun dipped lower and lower in the sky.

"Come on." West shifted first, his arms loosening.

When he helped me to my feet, my eyes locked on his T-shirt. His shoulder was soaked from my tears. Another day, another time, I'd feel embarrassed. But I was too numb to care at the moment.

"Sorry." My voice was ragged from the sobs.

"No apologies." He pushed a lock of hair away from my face. Then he clasped my hand and led me along the path, toward the Beartooth. To home.

A temporary home.

This had always been fleeting.

And it was time to explain why.

Darkness was nearly upon us by the time we made it back to the lodge. The campfire was burning bright, its embers floating into the night sky. People were talking and laughing. Someone was playing a guitar.

It was a happy tune. Familiar.

"Wait." I stopped, tugging on West's hand until he stopped too. "What's that song?"

He listened for a moment. "Sounds like 'Here Comes the Sun.'"

He was right. That was it.

"Dad loved the Beatles." My eyes flooded. There shouldn't be tears left in my body. Not after I'd cried so hard. But that music drew them up from the well, bringing a new wave of grief.

I swiped at my cheeks, wiping them dry. "I have to stop crying."

West stepped closer, his hand cupping my jaw. "Why?"

Yeah. Why?

I'd held them back when Dad was around. I'd pretended they didn't exist for Mom. I had never once cried in front of Blaine, because he would have seen it as an annoyance.

He hadn't been here to hold me on my worst day.

But West had been. He'd always been there.

Yet even then, I hadn't been able to cry.

"Girls cry. That's what you told me once. I didn't want to cry when we were kids because I wanted you to like me. And as I got older, the tears scared me. I was always worried that once I started crying, I wouldn't be able to stop."

They were endless. Or maybe they simply felt endless because I'd been hoarding them for way too long.

But I had stopped. Tonight, I'd stopped. And I felt . . . better. Lighter.

"Will you still want me if I'm a crying girl?" I sniffled.

West ran his thumb across my bottom lip. "My girl can cry whenever the fuck she wants."

I laughed. Or maybe it was a sob. Whatever the noise, it was muffled as West hauled me into his chest.

My arms snaked around his waist, holding tight. I pressed my ear against his heart, listening to its beat as the musician at the campfire changed tunes.

Metallica. That was better.

"We should go inside and talk," I said, but I didn't so much as shift my weight. I didn't let him go.

I liked it out here, beneath the emerging stars.

West must have liked it, too, because he rested his chin on my head. "So . . . your dad's company."

"It's Blaine's now." A sour taste spread across my tongue. I'd have to learn to live with that. There was no going back.

Blaine was likely halfway to Texas, and I doubted I'd ever hear from him again. Mom would keep me apprised of any changes she noticed. If Blaine did change the company name, she'd hear about it and convey the news. But otherwise, it was over.

"I think we should sit," I said. The picnic table outside the lodge was empty. It was far enough away from the guests that no one would overhear, but there was enough light coming off the lodge that I'd be able to see West's face.

He'd be able to see mine.

We walked to the table; then he took one side while I sat on the opposite. The bench seat was rough, the wood prickly on my thighs. The boards of the table itself were raised at the seams, with tiny splinters ready to poke.

This table needed to be chopped up for firewood, but I couldn't bring myself to have it destroyed.

Not when it was the table of toothpick poker and paper airplanes.

We'd just get a new table. Maybe I'd move this one closer to the Beartooth, and it could be my personal picnic table.

"As you know, Blaine only came here once. The year before Dad . . ." *Died.* Four years, and I still couldn't say it.

"I remember," West said.

"He hated it." I should have divorced him for that alone. "Not that he admitted it. This was not Blaine's type of vacation. But he mentioned a few times how much he liked the property. If I would have paid closer attention, I probably would have noticed the dollar signs in his eyes."

Across the table, West stiffened.

"He met your dad on that trip. And Blaine must have done what Blaine does. He charms the people who have something he wants. He charmed your dad."

Part of me wanted to blame Curtis. To call him a fool for believing Blaine's facade.

But I wasn't all that different. Neither was Dad.

"He's very good at winning people over," I said.

For a time, I'd fallen for Blaine's charm. My father had died absolutely adoring his son-in-law. And Curtis had been a victim too.

West sat perfectly still, waiting for me to continue.

"I didn't know it until recently, but Blaine kept in touch with your dad. Apparently, they'd talk every few months. Knowing Blaine, it probably started as him asking your dad for advice. He might have pretended to be planning a trip or wanting to know about Montana ranching. I have no idea. But it would have been a topic that made Curtis feel important."

After all, that was what Blaine had done with *my* father. They'd bonded over interesting real estate deals and love for me.

Except Blaine hadn't loved me. Yet he'd made damn sure that my dad thought we were soulmates. From the outside looking in, Blaine worshipped the ground beneath my feet.

West's jaw flexed. "Dad used to mention Blaine. I knew they talked from time to time."

"You did?"

He nodded. "It wasn't frequent, but Dad made a comment a few years ago about wanting to run an idea past Blaine. It was like getting whiplash. Dad acted like Blaine was a friend. Someone to call for advice."

Another mark against Curtis's favor. He'd gone to Blaine when he should have talked to West.

"Earlier this year, your dad told Blaine he was struggling and that finances were tight," I said.

West's lip curled. "For fuck's sake. So much for keeping that private. What the hell was Dad thinking?"

"I don't know." I shrugged. "Maybe he was hoping to get input. Whatever that discussion entailed, it ended with Blaine offering to come in as a silent partner. To buy into the ranch and float him some money as a capital investment."

"Fuck." West pounded a fist on the table, then dragged a hand through his hair. "Damn him."

Blaine? Or Curtis? I didn't ask. "Your dad declined."

"Are you sure?"

"Yes. He told Blaine no."

Some of the tension crept from West's shoulders. "Well, that's . . . something."

"It was never about getting your dad's business." I gave West a sad smile. "It was about getting mine."

Blaine's ultimate goal had always been Keller Enterprises.

"Your dad gave Blaine an opening. We separated about a year ago. I filed for divorce. He contested. He wanted Dad's company, and I told him he could go to hell."

But Blaine was smart. Too smart. He'd been playing us all, especially me, maybe from the start.

Blaine and I had fought and argued nearly the entirety of our marriage. It never had gotten easier. There were times when we had gotten along, usually when he was working long hours and rarely at home, but I couldn't remember us ever being happy.

While we'd dated, during our engagement, we'd been happy. In the beginning, we'd been happy.

Until I had become his wife.

And he didn't need to charm me anymore. He'd already won.

"We didn't have a good marriage," I told West. "We used each other. He wanted Dad's real estate company."

"And you? What did you want?"

"To stop missing you."

"Indy." West swallowed hard. His eyes, as dark as the sky, were full of pain and regret.

"I wish," I whispered.

West stretched a hand over the table, covering mine.

After the trip when I'd met Courtney, when I'd thought West had moved on with his fiancée, I would have done anything to forget that pain. To stop thinking about him. Missing him.

Loving him.

Blaine had been a wonderful distraction.

But that was where it had ended. A distraction. Had Blaine known I was just using him to forget?

Yes. Maybe not in the beginning, but definitely after our vacation. Somehow, after his one and only trip to Montana, he'd known I'd loved this ranch. And maybe he'd known how I felt about West.

Was that when he'd realized he could use both against me? Was that why our marriage had been so contentious?

Blaine had never stood a chance at winning my heart. It had always belonged to West. From the day we'd met when I was eight years old.

And Blaine had used that knowledge to get exactly what he'd wanted.

"This ranch was Blaine's bargaining chip. He came to me and told me that the resort was failing. That Curtis had admitted buying that land had been a mistake, and making the bank payments was getting tough."

West's nostrils flared as he listened. That was not business Curtis should have shared, especially with Blaine, but it was done now, and in a way, I was grateful.

It had brought me back to Montana when I'd vowed never to return.

"Blaine is a shark. He circled the waters for years, waiting and biding his time. He told me he was going to offer thirty million dollars to Curtis for this ranch."

West's jaw slackened. "What the fuck?"

Thirty million dollars. Enough money for the Havens to buy a ranch twice the size of this one.

"That's far more than it's worth." West's forehead furrowed. "Why would he do that?"

"He wanted to make an offer your dad couldn't refuse."

"What if Dad had said no?"

"Blaine would have waited it out, hoping the bank would foreclose and he could sweep in for a steal."

West shook his head. "I don't understand. How did you fit into this?"

"Blaine never made that offer to your dad. Obviously. It was a threat to me instead. He told me that he was coming after your property, ruthlessly and by any means necessary. And I had the power to stop it. All I had to do was sell him Keller Enterprises for seventy-five million dollars."

"Okay," West drawled. "Still not seeing how the ranch plays into this."

"Keller was worth one hundred and twenty-five million. Blaine knew he couldn't get financing for that amount, so we made a bargain. He had enough capital to fund half of the purchase. I sold him that half plus signed over control as CEO. In exchange, he knew the ranch was off limits. Then I called your father. The ranch and resort were vulnerable, something I made clear. If it wasn't Blaine waiting for the bank to foreclose, it was going to be someone else."

West dropped his chin, staring at the table. "So *you* made Dad the offer he couldn't refuse."

"Yes."

"And the paperwork tonight?"

"The last half of Keller."

"You could have kept it. After you bought the ranch, you could have kept that other half of Keller."

"I didn't want it." It was the confession I'd held in for as long as those tears. "That was Dad's dream—his path, not mine. And despite our problems as husband and wife, Blaine was always dedicated to Keller. He'll do right by Dad's business."

He was the right person to be in charge.

Just like West was the right person to run this ranch.

Financially, this entire thing had been a train wreck. I'd walked away from millions. Maybe there was another way for me to have done this. But I'd made the decisions that had felt right.

I'd followed my heart.

"Blaine, or someone like him, would have taken this place and broken it into pieces," I told West. "He would have brought in a developer and leveled the resort. He would have sold the cattle and carved out hundred-acre plots to sell to his rich friends who wanted to say they owned a ranch in Montana. Everything that Dad had loved, Blaine would have destroyed."

"So you bought it so that he wouldn't break it apart and destroy your father's vacation spot."

That's what he thought? "No."

"Then why'd you do it?" West met my gaze. "You could have kept Keller, sold it at full price, and let him take this place. It cost you millions to cut that deal with him and discount Keller. That's more money than I'll see in my lifetime. Why?"

Why? Wasn't it obvious?

"I bought it for you. I came for you. I have loved you since I was eight years old." I steeled my spine, swallowing past the lump in my throat. "Your father and I have an agreement. I came here for exactly one year. That was how long I estimated I'd need to turn the resort around. At the end of that year, I will resell the ranch to him for five million dollars, with the understanding that he will sign it over to you immediately. All I asked was that he keep it between us while I was here."

Curtis could pay off his debts and make millions.

All he had to do was take orders from me for a year.

And West . . .

West could have his ranch. Free and clear. He could have his dream.

Yes, I could have just bought the place and immediately signed it over to West. But I'd wanted to fix it first. For Dad. For West.

For myself.

I didn't want to work in real estate. That was something I'd never admitted to Dad. In truth, I wasn't sure exactly what I wanted to do with my life.

But a year in Montana had seemed like a good place to start.

And whether West wanted to admit it or not, his hands would have always been tied with his family dynamics at play.

He might have wanted to rename the ranch, but would he have gone through with it? Would he have spent the money necessary to make improvements to satisfy a wealthy traveler? He knew about the clientele we were attracting here. But I *was* the clientele.

Besides that, I'd been worried he wouldn't accept. That he wouldn't let me sell it back. West's pride would probably have kept him from making a deal.

I hadn't wanted to risk that he'd walk away.

And now that we were together, part of me needed to know that he was in it for me, not because I'd given him this ranch.

So that was the deal I'd made. Those were the terms I'd set.

One year in Montana.

Then this ranch was West's.

His expression turned to granite as he stared across the table. His hands balled into fists. A growl escaped his throat as he spoke through gritted teeth. "How could you do this?"

I had thought he'd be glad. Relieved, at least. But I'd never seen him so cold, like there wasn't a single emotion behind those hazel eyes.

"I'm—" I stopped myself before I could say *sorry*. I wasn't sorry. Not a bit.

I loved him. I loved him enough to sacrifice a year and give up fifty million dollars.

He stared at me as tears, more fucking tears, started anew.

God, I was tired of crying.

I stood in a flurry, scraping my legs on the rough bench as I climbed free. Then I walked to the Beartooth.

There was a bottle of wine with my name on it.

After all, tonight I should celebrate, right? I might not have sold Dad's business for the market value, but I was a very rich woman. Millions of dollars would join the other millions of dollars to my name.

And each was pointless. Insignificant.

I'd give every cent to my name for another day with Dad.

I'd give it all for West.

The toe of my sandal caught the edge of a flagstone rock. I pitched forward, about to crash to my knees, when two strong arms banded around me, keeping me on my feet.

"Never again. I never want to see you walk away from me again."

I sagged into his hold. "You're mad."

"Yeah, I am fucking mad. You should have told me from the start. Dad too."

"I'm sorry." For the secrecy, I'd apologize.

"This is too much, baby." He sighed. "I can't take it."

"You have to. It's why I did it in the first place. I knew you'd say no. That you'd be too proud to take it from me. And I wanted . . . I wanted to try. To do something here that made a difference. I wanted to stay. For once, I just wanted to stay."

West buried his face in my hair. "You are staying. For good. I'm not watching you leave this ranch again."

I wiggled, twisting in his arms to see his face.

He framed my face in his hands. "I have loved you since I was ten. Since you left a paper airplane and flowers in my fort. I love you. I have always loved you."

"Say it again."

He dropped his mouth to mine, his words a whisper against my lips. "I love you."

"I love you too."

His mouth slammed down on mine, his arms hauling me off my feet.

I clung to him as a smile stretched across my mouth. Oh, God. A laugh bubbled from my chest. Was this happening?

West pulled away, his forehead dropping to mine.

"Is this real?"

"We've always been real, Indy." He leaned back, taking my face in his hands. "I'll prove it to you tonight. And every night, for the rest of your life."

"What about the ranch?"

"I don't know. This is a lot to take in."

"What if we did it together?" *Say yes. Please, say yes.*

"Together." He spoke the word like he was trying it on for size. It must have fit, because a smile tugged at his mouth. "Okay, together. We'll do it together. All you have to do is stay."

That sounded like a good idea.

So I stayed in Montana.

For the rest of my life.

Epilogue
WEST

Seven years later . . .

"Kade! Kohen!" My voice echoed through the halls. I held my breath, waiting to hear their giggles or whispers, but the house was silent.

Where'd they run off to this time?

"Boys! If you're hiding, you've got three seconds to get down here. It's time to go to the campfire."

Nothing.

They had to be outside. My boots pounded on the herringbone hardwood floors as I walked through the entryway and out the front door. I checked both sides of the wraparound porch, scanning for my sons. But wherever they'd run off to, they weren't by the house.

I zipped up my Carhartt coat and jogged down the porch stairs, scanning the snow for footprints.

Two pairs of tracks trailed off the side of the house, leading to the grove of trees behind our home.

The fort.

I was an idiot for not checking there first.

With my fingers to my lips, I let out a piercing whistle that ricocheted in every direction. This time, my call was answered with laughter.

Kade emerged from the trees first, followed closely by Kohen. Their cheeks were rosy. Their smiles bright. As my five-year-old sons raced across the field of snow between us, their blond, curly hair bounced and flopped.

"Daddy!" Kohen pumped his legs faster, passing his twin brother as their boots crunched in the snow.

I bent as they ran straight for me, then swept them both into my arms.

"Guess what we found?" Kohen asked.

"A bird!" Kade answered for him. "It hurt its wing, and we rescued it."

"You rescued a bird." Well, at least it wasn't a baby skunk, like the one they'd "rescued" this summer.

As they told me all about the bird and their makeshift cage, I carted them to the truck, then deposited them both in the back seat while they kept talking.

Then I climbed behind the wheel, making a mental note to go and set the bird free later—if it hadn't escaped already.

"Daddy, do you think we can watch any airplanes tonight?" Kohen asked as we headed down the road for the lodge.

"I don't think there are any planes flying in tonight, bud."

"What about tomorrow?" Kade asked.

"Maybe. You'll have to ask Mommy."

"If there are, can we watch them?"

"I thought you wanted to go riding tomorrow."

"Oh." He tapped his finger on his chin, then leaned toward Kohen's seat to consult with his brother.

I chuckled as they whispered, finally coming to a consensus.

"Riding. *And* watching the airplanes." Kohen had a smug grin as he made their announcement.

"Okay. You can ask Mommy if any planes are coming in tomorrow. We'll watch them and go riding." We'd put in a runway on the ranch last year for private planes and jets. The boys loved to watch them fly in.

"I hope so." Kohen crossed his fingers on both hands. "I love the planes."

"Me too," Kade and I said in unison.

It was impossible not to smile around these kids. And in just a few weeks, we'd have another.

Indya was eight months pregnant with our baby girl, Grace. We were naming her after my grandmother.

My grandparents had both fallen in love with Indya since she'd moved here seven years ago, but Grandma absolutely adored her. They got weekly pedicures together at the resort spa. Mom would occasionally drive out to join them.

And just last week, Grandma had hosted Indya's baby shower.

Our whole family was excited about the baby, but especially the boys. This morning, we'd found them sleeping on the nursery floor in their sleeping bags. They'd sneaked in there last night for a campout.

It would be nice to have a nursery this time around. When the boys were newborns, their bassinets had been crammed into our bedroom. We'd still been living in my old place, waiting for Mike to finish construction on our house.

We'd moved in four years ago, and as far as I was concerned, it would be my home for the rest of my days. It was the home where we'd make our family. The home where we'd make memories. The home where Indya and I would turn old and gray together.

The house wasn't flashy. It wasn't massive. But it was our sanctuary. It was our dream house, built in a beautiful meadow, a place Indy and I had picked out together.

We were far enough away from the resort to have our privacy, but the trip from our front door to the lodge was five minutes.

"Daddy, I'm hungry. Can I have a snack?" Kade asked.

"Me too." Kohen gripped his stomach, like if he didn't eat something immediately, he'd starve.

"Yes, you can have a snack," I told them as I pulled up to the lodge, parking beside Indya's SUV in the lot we'd made for employees.

The resort had been in a constant state of change for the past seven years. There were times when I couldn't remember what it had been like before Indya.

The lodge itself had been remodeled and expanded. Indya had wanted to offer suites to guests, not just single, hotel-style rooms. She'd nearly tripled the building's footprint, stretching it all the way to where the old barn used to be.

Though, technically, it was still there. The architect had incorporated it into the design, and the space was now a ballroom, where we hosted weddings and events.

There were new stables set away from the lodge and cabins. Beside that building was a shop for the ranch equipment. Every structure, including the cabins, had the same wooden siding and a red tin roof.

We had five additional cabins, plus the spa. The airstrip and hangar were the most recent additions. Indya was currently planning a small stretch of employee apartments for the seasonal staff who came to work at the resort each summer.

It was amazing what millions could accomplish.

But even more, it was amazing what my wife could accomplish.

She had a vision. She had her goals.

For seven years, I'd been the lucky man who got to hear her ideas first.

The lucky man who could call her his wife.

We'd gotten married the fall after Indy had moved to Montana. She hadn't wanted a lavish ceremony or reception, not without Grant here to celebrate and walk her down the aisle. So we'd gotten married in the meadow where they'd scattered his ashes, surrounded by our closest friends and family.

Indya had tripped on a lump in the grass as she'd walked down the short aisle.

I'd caught her.

The boys took off running for the porch, their boots pounding on the steps as I jogged to keep pace.

Dad was in the lobby, talking to a guest. The minute the boys spotted him, they took off running.

"Papa!" The twins giggled as they crashed into his legs.

"There are my boys." He bent to hug them both, waving as the guest said goodbye. "What are you guys doing?"

Kade launched into the bird-rescue saga as Kohen told him everything they wanted to eat for a snack. Crackers. String cheese. Cookies.

"Well, okay." Dad nodded. "You've had a busy day. No wonder you're hungry for . . ."

"Crackers. String cheese. And cookies," Kohen repeated.

"That's quite a list. Should we go see if Reid has anything special in the kitchen?"

"Yes!" They each grabbed one of his hands and dragged him toward the dining room.

"I'll bring them to the office when we're done," he told me.

"Thanks."

Dad gave me a small smile as they walked away.

I gave him a small smile back.

Things with my father were . . . okay. Not good. Not bad. Just okay.

He was a wonderful grandfather to my children. He was kind and gracious to my wife. But I harbored a lot of hard feelings for Dad. Seven years, and it was still hard to move past his betrayal.

That wound just hadn't healed.

So we were okay. We talked. We had him over for dinner once or twice a month. But there was always a strain.

It was the same between Jax and Dad. I hoped, someday, it would get easier. For all of us.

I nodded to the front-desk clerk as I made my way toward Indya's office. Like the rest of the building, it had undergone its fair share of changes too.

She sat behind her desk, her phone pressed to her ear. The room itself was three times the size it had once been.

In front of a row of floor-to-ceiling bookshelves, there was a sitting area, where she could visit with employees or guests. Along the wall was a cabinet that hid a TV for the boys to watch whenever they were here.

Behind her chair, through the wall of windows, was the large patio. The original firepit she'd left in place, but now there was a plethora of benches and tables and chairs. This time of year, the staff would turn on propane heaters every afternoon for the guests who wanted to sit outside with a cocktail before dinner.

"I promise, Mom," Indya said, her eyes sparkling as I walked into the office. "I've had zero signs of contractions or labor. You won't miss it."

Ellen had planned to be here when the twins were born, but Indy had gone into labor two weeks early. This time around, Ellen was coming a month before the due date, just to be safe.

She'd spend that month in the Beartooth.

"We'll see you Monday. Love you." She let out a sigh as she set her phone down. "Hi."

"Hi." I sat on the edge of her desk, bending low for a kiss. "You okay?"

"It's been an afternoon."

"What happened to spending a few quiet hours in the office to catch up before the barbecue?"

The Saturday campfire tradition was one of the few things unchanged. Tonight, the boys would roast hot dogs over the fire. Reid would set up a burger bar inside. After dark, we'd bring out the fixings for s'mores.

And my family would spend an evening with the guests who'd come to stay on our property.

Indya had insisted it be our place. Together, as equals. She'd changed the entire structure so we each had equal shares. And she'd carved off a significant portion for Jax too.

"My plan to tackle my inbox got derailed." She sagged in her chair.

"What happened?"

Indya glanced to the painting of Chief hanging on the wall across from her desk. "I'm pretty sure Sasha is going to quit."

"What? Why?"

Sasha had been a godsend this fall. She was our new resort manager and treated this place like it was her own. She was young but smart and hardworking. Guests adored her. The staff respected her. Because of Sasha, Indya had been able to spend more time at home over the past three months, while I kept my focus on the ranch.

Sasha absolutely could not quit.

"She hates Montana," Indya said. "She hates the winter. She hates the outdoors. And she hates Jax."

"Jax? Why does she hate Jax?"

"I don't know. But I asked her to coordinate with him on the guest excursions, and you should have seen the look on her face. It was like I'd asked her to have a meeting with Satan. I'm pretty sure the only thing keeping her here is the paycheck."

"Okay. Not ideal. But it's a nice paycheck. Maybe she'll hate it here a little less once the snow melts."

Indya rubbed at her temples. "I don't want her to quit."

"Neither do I." We at least needed her to stick it out through the spring and summer.

"What if she leaves? How am I going to run this place with a baby? We tried that once, remember?"

I remembered. Indy had practically run herself into the ground.

"Hey." I splayed my hand on her belly. "We'll figure it out. If Sasha quits, then we'll take Mom up on her offer."

Mom was contemplating retirement from the hospital in Big Timber, but she wasn't ready to quit working quite yet. Whenever Tara needed an extra hand or was short staffed, Mom would pitch in. Spending more time out here—being closer to Indya, me, and the boys—must have made her nostalgic.

She'd offered to help out during Indya's maternity leave.

The only reason we hadn't jumped on that offer was Dad. Well, and Jax. There were still hard feelings there, even if Jax swore it was fine.

Plus Mom still hadn't spoken to Dad. Not a word, to my knowledge, in over a decade. If she came to work here full time, she couldn't ignore him any longer.

Dad came to the lodge every day, mostly to drink the coffee and bullshit with guests. But also because he was trying to make amends.

To Indya.

To Jax.

To me.

If Mom worked here, either he'd avoid the lodge altogether—which would be uncomfortable as fuck if she gave him the silent treatment—or their standoff would end and the rest of us would get caught in the cross fire.

"I'm going to figure this out." Indya raised her chin. "She can't quit."

"Okay."

Sasha probably didn't realize she was working for the most determined woman on earth.

Laughter in the hallway made me twist toward the door as Jax strode inside, Kade carried under one arm, and Kohen under the other.

"Thieves in the kitchen." He took the boys to the couch in the sitting area and dropped them with a plop. "How should we punish them?"

"We're not thieves, Uncle Jax." Kade jumped up on the couch, poking at Jax's chest.

"Yeah." Kohen popped up beside his brother. "Papa was getting us a snack."

Jax narrowed his eyes, bending to their level. "What kind of snack?"

"Cookies."

"Did you steal one for me?"

Kohen glanced over his shoulder, sneakily trying to hide it as he slid what looked to be a chocolate chip cookie out of his pocket and into Jax's hand.

"Where's mine?" Indya held out her hand. "Mommy's hungry."

Kade leaped over the back of the couch, then produced two cookies from his pocket for his mother.

"Thanks, baby." She smiled and kissed his cheek before taking a bite. "Jax, I need to talk to you."

"About what?" he asked as he chewed and joined me beside her desk.

Indya pointed at his face as her nostrils flared. "You have to be nice to Sasha."

"What? I am nice to Sasha."

"Then why does she hate you?"

"Did she actually use the word *hate*?"

"No. But she's not your biggest fan." Indya clasped her hands together. "I'm begging you. Be nice. I need her to stay until after my maternity leave."

"I am nice."

"Then be *nicer*," I said.

He pursed his lips but nodded. "Fine. Did you have to hire someone so . . . uptight?"

A soft growl came from the doorway.

I whirled, just in time to see Sasha's straight brown hair stream behind her as she stormed toward her office across the hall.

Indya's hand shot out like a viper as she smacked Jax in the gut. "You. Are. *Killing*. Me."

"Well, she is uptight," he whisper yelled.

"Jax." I rubbed my mouth, hiding a laugh.

Sasha was uptight.

And Jax took next to nothing seriously.

"Mommy, can we watch the planes?" The boys both hopped up on the desk beside me.

"I don't think we have any planes coming in this weekend."

Kade and Kohen groaned in tandem.

"But Nana is flying in on Monday. On a jet."

"Yes." Kohen fist pumped. "I love jets."

"Me too." Kade nodded. "Can I have my hot dog now?"

"You just ate a cookie," I said.

"But I'm soooo hungry."

Indya laughed, holding out a hand so I could help her to her feet. Then she put her hands on her belly, rubbing at the sides that had been aching this week. "I'm soooo hungry too."

"Then let's get you something to eat." Not a hot dog. She wouldn't eat one while she was pregnant. But since Reid had fully embraced Indya as his boss, he always made sure to have something special for her on Saturday nights.

We bundled up in coats and hats and gloves and spent our evening on the patio. The boys chased each other around until well past their bedtime, and when both started yawning every minute, I loaded my family into the truck, leaving Indya's car behind for tomorrow.

"I love you," Indya said as we drove toward home.

I brought her hand to my knuckles for a kiss. "I love you."

"Do you think Dad would like this?" Indya asked, eyes trained on the lodge. It glowed golden against the night, the snow a perfect blanket at its feet. "Maybe I changed too much."

"No, baby. He would have loved it. He'd be proud."

Grant would have wanted her to live a life of her own making.

She stared at the Beartooth. Like the lodge, its lights shone bright. Inside, a new family was making memories in that little chalet. Then she glanced to the boys in the back seat.

"My wishes came true," she whispered.

"So did mine."

We were living a dream together.

On the Haven River Ranch.

Acknowledgments

Thank you for reading *Crossroads*! Writing this book was pure joy, start to finish. Once upon a time, I thought working at a Montana guest ranch would be my dream job. Turns out, writing is my dream job. But this book gave me the chance to escape into a different reality every day, and I loved every second.

Thanks to Maria Gomez and the team at Montlake! Working with you has been another dream.

Thanks to Elizabeth Nover for your invaluable advice. To Georgana Grinstead for being the best of the best of the best. I could not do any of this without you. Thanks to Nicole Resciniti. To Vicki Valente and Logan Chisholm. And to my friends and family. I am so grateful for you all and unbelievably blessed to have you at my side.

About the Author

Photo © 2019 Lauren Perry

Devney Perry is a #1 Amazon, *Wall Street Journal*, and *USA Today* bestselling author of over forty romance novels. After working in the technology industry for a decade, she abandoned conference calls and project schedules to pursue her passion for writing. She was born and raised in Montana and now lives in Washington with her husband and two sons.

Don't miss out on Perry's latest book news: subscribe to her newsletter at www.devneyperry.com.